ALIAS THE DEAD

Persons this *Mystery* is about—

TONY KENYON,

lean and muscular, seems fit in spite of his rumpled clothes and temporarily beaten look. Disillusioned by both the world and himself, he is, at 28, alone and out of a job—unless he takes the one just offered to him—that of impersonating a dead man.

LEON MORLEY,

a private detective with a blocky figure, and a keen mind and manner that command respect, has had his heart and pocketbook set upon finding the long-lost son of a millionaire.

JOE COMSTOCK, SR.,

a wealthy newspaper publisher, is a slightly stooped, pasty-skinned old man, pathetically eager to believe that the son he hasn't seen in sixteen years has finally come home.

SALLY HAYDEN,

Comstock's secretary, is a slim, dark-haired, and lovely girl who finds her heart strangely at odds with her head where Kenyon is concerned. Tenderhearted, sensitive, Sally adores her employer and hates to see him frightened and unhappy.

NORA COMSTOCK,

Comstock's daughter-in-law, is a sleek, curvesome, and self-reliant redhead who is prepared to be the perfect picture of a deserted wife throwing herself upon the family's mercy—or, if it seems better, a widow.

PAUL SHERMAN,

Comstock's stepson, and managing editor of his paper, has a colorful background about which he doesn't talk much. Tall and thin, he has a worried, over-worked expression on his face.

MARION SHERMAN,

Paul's wife, tall, thin, and cold, has a long angular face and a constant air of boredom. She is a little too poised and superior for Kenyon's taste.

(Continued on next page)

ALIAS THE DEAD

Persons this *Mystery* is about—

(Continued from preceding page)

CARL SHERMAN,
Paul's younger brother, short, plump, sleek-haired, runs an insurance office and is the complete extrovert. Carl is Nora's idea of the end of the rainbow.

SPENCE ARDEN,
a local radio commentator, is a good-looking blond with a tweedy, pipe-smoking air about him. He has a bland, unruffled manner, a cosmopolitan air, and probably nobody fools him more than once.

LIEUTENANT NASH,
a chunky, sandy-haired, and red-faced police officer, has a slow, deliberate way of speaking. Outwardly polite, he is inwardly frustrated, admittedly thwarted in this case from the beginning by the personalities involved.

SERGEANT BAUER,
Nash's heavy-set, gray-haired assistant, becomes, at times, just a bit too confident for his own good.

MR. FLEMING,
an FBI agent, is neat and efficient-looking. He likes to bring his criminals in alive.

RUDY,
a gunman with a missing finger, has a broad, thick torso topped by a round, close-crowned head. Although he doesn't look very bright, he looks exceedingly powerful, and he is very clever with a rope.

CLARENCE,
Rudy's sidekick, proves to be a big help in an unsavory sort of way.

HILTON,
the Comstock's butler, opens the door to more than one overpowering surprise for the family.

ALIAS THE DEAD

What this *Mystery* is about—

• • • Double MYSTERY and triple MURDER involving something bigger than money, deadlier than passion or ambition . . . A relatively innocent IMPERSONATION that explodes into danger and violence . . . A BIRTH CERTIFICATE, a 4-year-old LETTER, and a GOLD LOCKET quietly filched from a dead man . . . Five $100 BILLS which eventually turn up in an unlikely pocket . . . A shadowy, gun-toting PROWLER who seems to have desperate need for something in the house—but what? . . . A great deal of BLOOD in a room containing a body and a severely wounded man . . . Hocus-pocus concerning a red-stained LETTER OPENER . . . A savage FIGHT beside the body of a once-pretty girl . . . A girl's YELLOW PAJAMAS which fool the police . . . A CRACK IN A CLOSET which seems, at first, to be a fine vantage point from which to watch an apparent murderer . . . Several tiny NOTES desperately scribbled in the dark . . . A SHACK on a river which is the scene of a chain-lightning series of startling crises . . . A PAYOFF that is a bolt right out of the blue for all concerned, including the murderer and the reader.

Wouldn't You Like to Know—

• What happens when an innocent young man steps into a dead man's shoes?
• Why the nice old man wanted so desperately to believe that the impersonator was his son? And why the pretty young woman didn't?
• The proper etiquette concerning a wife you didn't know you had?

(Continued on next page)

ALIAS THE DEAD

What this *Mystery* is about—

(Continued from preceding page)

- And her reaction concerning a husband ditto?
- Why the real son refused to inherit half the estate?
- What colorful Nora hoped to get out of the danger-packed setup? And what she did get?
- Why Sally couldn't make up her mind whether to love or hate Kenyon?
- How a decent young man happens to be found sitting on a corpse?

———————

YOU will learn the answers in this ingenious, jolt-laden murder mystery in which a slick and brilliant plan of gentle fraud is upset by a couple of corpses—and the innocent impersonator finds he must break the case or hang.

DOUBLE MYSTERY AND TRIPLE MURDER

....

ALIAS
THE
DEAD

By GEORGE HARMON COXE
Author of "Murder for Two,"
"Assignment in Guiana,"
"Silent Are the Dead," etc.

Author's Dedication—
For JANET

WILDSIDE PRESS

www.wildsidepress.com

ALIAS THE DEAD

List of *Exciting* Chapters—

Alias the Dead

Chapter One

OFF-COLOR ASSIGNMENT

WHEN THE CITY EDITOR LOOKED up and saw Tony, he leaned
back in his chair and drummed his copy pencil on the edge
of the desk. Tony stood there and felt his stomach dissolve
into emptiness.

"No go, huh?" he said.

The city editor was apologetic. "I'm sorry, Kenyon. Last
week when I told you to stop by I thought there'd be a
spot. It just didn't work out. You know how it is."

Tony gave him a twisted grin. He said he knew how it
was.

"I should have phoned you and saved you a trip."

"It's all right," Tony said. "It's a nice morning. I
didn't have anything else to do. Well"—he took a paper
from a stack on the adjoining desk and turned away—
"thanks anyway."

Out on Hill Street the morning was bright and warm,
with the smell of more heat in the air. Traffic noises rico-
cheted about him and a high red streetcar of the Venice
Short Line rocked past, its bell clanging at some indiscreet
motorist. At the corner the semaphore arm of the traffic
signal waved him on and he walked along, head down
and unmindful of his surroundings until he came to Pershing Square. Here he found a place on a bench with three
other men and sat down to brood.

As always, the benches were well filled. With men
mostly, though here and there were women shoppers, their
laps filled with bundles and their feet dangling or thrust
straight out, to rest them. Farther along, near the foun-
tain, two groups of men had gathered to listen to some

soapbox orator and argue—about the war, probably, or some new crackpot scheme to give everyone a hundred dollars a week pension. It had all become familiar to Tony Kenyon these past months, the orators, the pigeons, the men and women who were going some place and used the walks for that purpose, the sitters. Most of them were old, and glancing about him now he saw the vacant stares, the shabby clothes, the mantle of futility each had fashioned for himself. He glanced down at his unpressed suit and the worn cuffs of his topcoat. Without his realizing it his hand strayed to his face and was feeling the stubble which should have been removed before he left his room.

With hardly a glance at the front page of his paper, he turned to the help-wanted section. At least he wouldn't starve. The war had made any such possibility exceedingly remote. If a man wanted to work he could find something. The West Coast Manufacturing Company wanted laborers. Argonaut Aircraft wanted men from eighteen to fifty, experience unnecessary; sixty cents an hour—increasing to seventy-five in six weeks—a forty hour week. He paused to do some mental arithmetic. With ten hours overtime the seventy-five cent rate would make him better than forty dollars a week; as much as he'd ever made on the Gainsburg, Indiana, *Star*. Only he didn't want that kind of job. His eyes skimmed the columns, flicked over to the personals, and stopped. The advertisement seemed to stand out on the page.

WANTED: Young man, 26-28, with a taste for adventure. Must be blond, blue-eyed, and free to travel. Unusual and profitable assignment for one who can qualify. Apply 11 a.m. Hotel Bard. Ask for Mr. Morley.

Kenyon read it over again and grinned. Down on the corner a jeweler's pedestal clock said ten minutes of eleven. The Bard was four blocks away. *Well why not?* he thought, and got up off the bench and started away, his chin up and shoulders back.

There were eighteen men in the hotel room when Kenyon went in; he counted them because he had nothing else to do. They were parked on the divan and chairs and window sills, two or three of them really well dressed, most of them like himself, a few downright seedy-looking. A gangling, blue-eyed fellow moved away from the wall and grinned at him.

"Wonder what it is?" he said. "Sounds good, don't it?"

"Too good," Kenyon said.

The door to the adjoining bedroom opened and a man stepped out, a blocky figure, neither tall nor short, with a squarish, muscular face and thinning dark hair, combed straight back. He asked them to line up and they did, awkwardly, with a bit of pushing and considerable embarrassment. Someone asked if he was Mr. Morley and someone else said, "What kind of a job is it?"

Morley paid no attention to either question, but backed away and studied them, first collectively and then individually. After perhaps thirty seconds of this he pointed his finger three times and said, "You," three times, and the third time he meant Kenyon. "I'll talk to you three," he said. "The rest of you won't do."

The others went out, some of them muttering softly, and Kenyon's gangling friend grinned sheepishly at him. Morley went into the bedroom and telephoned some instructions to the desk. When he came back he asked Kenyon his name.

"All right," he said. "I'll talk to you first." He followed Kenyon into the bedroom and closed the door. "Toss your coat on the bed," he said, "and stand over there by the window a minute."

Kenyon did as directed and Morley sat down beside the table-desk and looked at him. What he saw was a nicely set-up man, with a good pair of shoulders and medium blond hair inclined to be curly and in need of a haircut. He carried himself well and looked fit in spite of his rumpled clothes; yet his mouth was slack, he wore an indifferent, sowhat manner, and his eyes looked tired, giving him a temporarily beaten look in spite of the good bones in his jaw and the lean, muscular build. Seeing all this now Morley nodded and a crooked grin warped a mouth that had heretofore been straight and hard.

"Okay," he said. "Sit down and tell me about yourself. Live here, do you?"

"No," Kenyon said. "Gainsburg, Indiana."

"Been in the army, haven't you? Drafted? How come you're out?"

"I'm twenty-eight. They used to let you out at that age. I got my release about a week before war was declared."

"You're in the reserve. They can call you back."

"They can but I don't think they will unless things get a lot worse."

"Oh?"

"I wasn't very good at it."

Morley leaned forward slightly, his gaze intent. "You look fit enough. Maybe you're a mental case."

"Call it what you like," Kenyon said. "I just wasn't the type. As a soldier I didn't measure up."

"How about the booze?"

"I can leave it alone."

"You didn't this morning."

Kenyon flushed. "I stopped for a shot on my way over, that's all."

"To give you courage, maybe. . . . How come you're in Los Angeles? Got any relatives here?"

"I haven't got any relatives anywhere."

Morley let his brows come up. "Maybe you're lucky. Well, what did bring you out here?"

Tony Kenyon explained. Bored with the routine of an army camp and training with make-believe weapons, he had put in for a transfer. For some reason he had been sent to the west coast and finished out his term here. Upon his release he had been given carfare back to the point of induction, but instead of using it he had stayed on with the hope of landing a job on some newspaper. He did not explain his reason for not returning home, but told in detail of his search for work, both in Los Angeles and the surrounding towns—Santa Monica, Hollywood, Pasadena.

As he spoke of these things he was aware of Morley's interest. It showed mostly in his eyes. Light brown, almost amber colored, they seemed shrewd and speculative, cataloguing every detail, every gesture, and as he went on, Kenyon noticed other things and began to wonder what sort of a job he was applying for. Something told him that this would be no ordinary assignment, yet there was nothing tangible to verify his hunch. Morley's suit was good and tailored conservatively. His hands were well-kept, the fingers square-ended and powerful, and on the little finger of the left one was a small star-sapphire. He was chewing gum slowly, nodding his head from time to time, and his crooked smile was quick to come and go; yet always Kenyon's glance came back to the man's eyes and it was this steady, speculative regard that made him wonder—

"Oh, pardon me," he said, aware that Morley had asked another question.

"I said, how long have you been out? Three months, huh? And how've you been living?"

Kenyon's smile got warped and bitter. "Not very well. I put ads in the papers like you, chiseled a few dollars ghost writing, did a few stories for the Sunday editions."

"You could get a job in one of the aircraft factories."

"I will if I have to. Just what is it you're looking for?"

"For someone like you," Morley said, and went into the other room, dismissing the two men waiting. "Any objections to flying back to Connecticut with me?"

Kenyon looked at him, not daring to grin. Connecticut? Well, why not. New York was right next door. There ought to be a newspaper job there.

"No," he said. "Only what do I do when I get there?"

"Pretend you're somebody you're not—for two days."

"Oh."

"I'm a private detective." Morley leaned across the table, speaking in measured tones. "For two months now I've been looking for someone. You're going to take his place. It's only a week's work altogether but for you there'll be new clothes, expenses, and two hundred bucks."

Kenyon thought it over and felt his spirits sink to nothingness.

"And where's the fellow I'm supposed to impersonate?"

"Dead."

"Oh."

"Killed in a traffic accident." Morley grunted softly. "Two months I look for the guy and then that has to happen."

Kenyon let his breath come out. That put a dull ache in his chest and suddenly he felt tired and beaten again. He thought about the past months, the months to come, sitting in Pershing Square reading the want ads, doing a feature piece when he could at space rates—or working in a factory. He thought about New York and two hundred dollars to start out with. Finally he stood up, knowing that it was not a question of any scruples that decided him but the simple possibility that he might wind up in jail.

"No," he said. "I guess not."

Morley waited, not rising, just sitting there watching through narrowed lids.

"Afraid?"

"Um-hum. They throw people in jail for that sort of thing, don't they? Especially people like me."

Morley produced a card. On it was his name and a New

York City address. "I've been in business quite a while. I sort of figure on staying in business. If there was any chance of jail I wouldn't be doing it."

Kenyon shook his head. "Sorry, but it still smells. You'd better get yourself another boy."

Suddenly Morley was on his feet. The crooked smile pried at his mouth and he spread his hands and reached for Kenyon's coat. "All right," he said. "You'll never get another chance to make two yards any easier, but you're the doctor, chum."

He held the coat while Kenyon slipped into it, walked with him to the door. "If you change your mind," he began, and left the rest of it unsaid.

Kenyon trudged sightlessly down the hall to the elevators and pushed the button irritably, for it dawned on him now that he might have been too hasty in his refusal. He could not get the thought of New York out of his mind, nor the two hundred dollar stake he would have had. A man could live three months on that, long enough for anyone with any ability to get a job. And since when had he been particular about how he earned his money?

Doubt still harassed him as he stepped into the elevator, but as he rode down he was glad the decision was behind him. He had started to walk across the lobby when someone spoke close by.

"Hold on, there."

A burly, heavy-faced man bore down on him, breathin hard.

"You just come down from Mr. Morley's room?"

Kenyon studied him curiously. "Yes, why?"

"Let's go back up."

The man took hold of his elbow, steering him toward the elevator. Kenyon took a step and stopped, trying to free his arm.

"Wait a minute," he said. "What is this?"

"Come on," the man said, and flashed a shield.

Kenyon stared at it, anger stirring and his mouth tight. "All right, so you're the house detective. What do you want?"

"You, mister."

They were at the door of the elevator now and people stepped past them and others waited for them to move. "Come on," the detective said, "we're blocking traffic."

Morley was standing in the door of his bedroom as they came down the hall. For an instant Kenyon thought he saw a smile flicker in the amber depths of the man's eyes; then he was speaking in apparent relief.

"Got him, did you? Nice work. I was afraid you might be too late. Didn't notice it was gone until—"

"Listen," Kenyon said.

"Inside, bum," the house detective said, and, no longer bothering about persuasion, pushed him through the doorway.

"Where is it?" Morley asked.

Kenyon squinted at him, color rising and blue eyes smoldering. "Where's what? What the hell is this, anyway?"

"It was on the dresser there," Morley said. "I should have been more careful. He was one of the lads I was interviewing and—"

Listening, not knowing what it was all about, yet feeling a gradual contraction in his stomach and a curious sense of suspicion and alarm, Kenyon jammed his hands into his coat pockets. That was when he felt it, though for a second he did not know what it was, but only that it did not belong there. Then he had pulled out his hand and was staring at a pigskin wallet and hearing the exclamations of the others and letting it be snatched from his fingers.

For another moment he could not think, but stood there mutely, staring, hearing Morley explaining what must have happened. Then anger struck through him. His fists clenched and he started to protest, catching himself in time, forcing down his rage in an effort to think clearly. The house detective was watching him with one eye and Morley was counting bills and all at once Kenyon knew he had been neatly framed, that nothing he could say could offset the evidence of that wallet in his pocket. He tightened his lips, gave Morley a nasty grin, and waited.

"It's all here," that worthy said, "thanks to you." He looked at the house detective and became visibly thoughtful, his brow furrowing and his gaze cloudy. "Look," he said finally, "I don't want to be too tough about this. I don't like to send a guy to prison just because—"

"That's where he belongs, don't he?" the house detective said.

"Maybe, maybe not. If I hadn't left it right there in plain sight—" He broke off, turned to Kenyon. "Is this the first time, son?"

Kenyon took a breath and held it. He concentrated on just one thing: keeping his mouth shut. He focused on the point of Morley's jaw and measured the distance to it; then he stood perfectly still because he knew what would happen if he swung. Morley wrinkled his forehead at him and his mouth twitched, as though suppressing a grin.

"Look," he said to the house detective, and took his arm. "I don't want to be hasty about this. Suppose I talk to the guy. Maybe he—"

"I think you're making a mistake," the house detective said sourly. "The guy's a bum. Anybody can see that. If he gets away with this he'll only try it on somebody else. I ought to call the station."

"I know," Morley said. "But if this is his first slip—" He had the door open now and was easing the disgruntled house detective into the hall. "Anyway, I'd like to talk to him. Wait here. I'm not going to sign a complaint until I know all the facts."

He closed the door, took out a stick of gum and folded it

into his mouth. He sat down and very carefully folded the wrapper into a compact square. All this took perhaps a full minute and during that time Kenyon just stood there, still clinging to his self control. Finally Morley cocked his head and looked up through his brows.

"There were two hundred bucks in that wallet. That makes it grand larceny." He put the square of paper in an ash tray. "If you had some relatives or friends in town maybe they'd stand up for you and get you out of this."

"If I had any relatives you wouldn't have tried the frame."

"The thing is, I need you. I might have to look a long time before I found anyone that filled the bill so well. A week, that's all. No rough stuff. And you wind up in New York with two hundred bucks in your kick." He sat up, his voice curt. "Either that or spend the next couple of years in the clink. . . . Well? Do I talk to our pal in the hall or do I sign a complaint?"

Kenyon thought it over and found in place of his anger nothing but a smoldering resentment. Then, suddenly something happened inside and all the old bitterness rolled over him. All right, if that's the way it was. Why should he be choosy about what he did? What did it get you when you were choosy? A seat in the park. Suppose the assignment was a little off-color—and he wasn't entirely sure it was—what difference did it make? A bum was what the house dick had called him—and it was time for a change. Any change. *So what are you waiting for, Tony? Speak up and tell the man.*

"Okay, mister," he said. "But not for two hundred."

"Two hundred is all."

Tony let his lips come down and his smile was mirth-less. He made his voice clipped and convincing.

"Five hundred or nothing. And don't kid yourself about the frame. Sign that complaint and I'll make you follow through just for the hell of it."

Morley's mouth flattened to a thin hard line and his gaze was stony; then, abruptly, the crooked smile came.

"Okay, chiseler. Five hundred—but no return fare." He slapped Kenyon's shoulder as he passed on his way to the door. "You and I should get along."

Chapter Two

Phony Heir

THE RIDE FROM THE STATION to the Kingsford Hotel gave Tony Kenyon a chance to look over the business section of the town, and from what he saw he put the population at eighty thousand or so. A manufacturing town, he guessed, with busy streets and blocks of parking meters, and in the background drab, age-crusted buildings and an atmosphere of permanent senility.

The hotel was on a corner, a four-story, red-brick structure with white-painted trim and a flat-roofed marquee extending out across the sidewalk. Four wide stone steps led upward to the lobby floor and while Leon Morley paid for the taxi, a bellboy came down and got their bags. At the desk Morley asked for rooms on the same floor. The clerk said certainly and Tony Kenyon wrote, *Joseph A. Comstock, Jr., Los Angeles, Cal.* across the registration card.

He was given a large room on the third floor, facing the rear, and when the bellboy had gone he stood looking out the window. Between taller buildings on the right and left he could see factory smokestacks and a bridge across the river; farther out were the railroad yards and what looked like a roundhouse, and in the distance, wooded hills that looked dark and inaccessible in the morning shadows. When he turned away he caught sight of himself in the full-length mirror on the bathroom door and what he saw brought a wry grin to his lips.

Clothes, he decided, made a difference. For when you had the right clothes a man made the necessary physical and mental changes to round out the impression created. Seventy-eight dollars this brown shetland had cost. Morley had screamed but he had insisted that he have something really good. There was another in his bag, a dark-gray, pin-striped, double-breasted. The shoes had nicked Morley for sixteen-fifty. Yes, it made a difference, especially if you had some money in your pocket. And he had. Not much, but enough to remind him that things had changed greatly for Tony Kenyon in the past three days. He had enjoyed the plane trip; he was proud of the pigskin traveling-bag. No longer had he any misgivings about this adventure, for he had new confidence now with which to see it through. His lean face was smooth and fit-looking, his eyes had sparks in them. Maybe he was about to become a first-class heel, but so far his decision to come had caused him no regrets.

Morley came in without knocking. "I just called the old man," he said. "He's on his way down. How do you feel?"

"I feel all right."

"You look all right." Morley sat down. "You look swell. Just remember that this thing can't miss. You've got nothing to worry about. You don't even have to feel sorry for him. He kicked his wife out in a jealous rage when you were four years old. He's only seen you once since then— when you were ten—in New York. But nobody in this town has seen you since you were a baby. You've got the right coloring and you're close enough to the right age— you should be twenty-six—and you've got a birth certificate, that locket, and the letter he wrote you four years ago to prove it."

"Don't worry," Kenyon said.

"I'm not. I'm telling you. All you have to do is stick around two days and give me time to get my bonus check cashed and then you can walk out. The old guy's no worse off, is he? My job was to bring you back, not to make you stay. I talked with him long distance and made him understand that. He's satisfied. His own son was so bitter toward him he refused to come back in spite of the old man's dough. So when you walk out it won't be any worse for him than if you'd never come. Only you'll have five hundred bucks—and three hundred worth of clothes, damn it."

Kenyon grinned and then the telephone rang and the clerk told him Mr. J. A. Comstock was on his way up. He glanced over at Morley, swallowed, and found his throat was dry. The knocking at the door jarred him and he watched Morley step over and turn the knob; then he was face to face with the man who was supposed to be his father.

Kenyon waited in the center of the room. Comstock took a step and stopped and Morley closed the door behind him. For a long moment they stood that way and Kenyon forced himself to meet the other's gaze with steady eyes, remembering only what he had to do. What he saw was a gray-haired figure, spare of build and slightly stooped, with a high, thin nose topped by rimless glasses and the pasty, slack-skinned look of one who is not well. He saw emotion work upon that face, and behind the glasses the eyes filled, and none of it made any difference now. There could have been a time, not so long ago, when he would have responded to that emotion, for he might have liked this man, had he allowed himself the opportunity. But three days of his new philosophy had changed things greatly. He looked right at Comstock, his face impassive, feeling nothing he did not want to feel.

"Hello," he said.

Comstock came to him quickly then, and took his hand, and for an instant seemed about to embrace him. Then he stopped, as though his eyes in their hungry search had seen something in Kenyon's face that denied him that right. A hurt, defeated look flicked across his features and he put his other hand on Kenyon's shoulders and squeezed hard.

"It's been a long time, my son," he said. "Much too long. I—I was afraid that— but never mind. You're here.

That's all that matters, isn't it?" And he stepped back and turned to Morley, hiding his hurt and embarrassment with a sudden rush of words and a gruff abruptness that fooled no one. "But good Lord, man, why didn't you tell me when you were getting in so I could meet you? Did you have to bring him here? Couldn't you have taken him to the house?"

"Well—" Morley shrugged, and his glance slid away.

Kenyon knew what he had to do then and did it. "It was my idea," he said. "I told Mr. Morley I'd come back, but I didn't guarantee to stay." He inspected his finger-nails so he would not have to meet Comstock's eyes. "Under the circumstances this seemed the wisest move."

"Oh." The word was low, drawn-out, hurt. "Well. . . . You did a good job, Morley. You've done your part. If you'll stop by this evening—" Comstock hesitated and cleared his throat. "We're expecting you for lunch, my boy," he said. "If you'll be happier here for now, why that's all right, I guess. But you'll come along with me, won't you? You've never met Paul or Carl, or Paul's wife. We're sort of counting on it."

Paul and Carl Sherman were Comstock's stepsons, Kenyon knew, one older than he was and one younger, the children of Comstock's second wife, dead these past two years.

"Why, yes," he said. "I'd be very happy to meet them."

There were four people waiting in the drawing-room of the Comstock home when Tony Kenyon walked in. He heard Comstock introduce him and was vaguely aware of the two men he shook hands with: one tall and thin and balding, the other shorter and darker and plump; he bowed to the slender woman who stood next to the tall man and then he found himself facing a slim, dark-haired girl with hazel eyes that looked at him and smiled, and who seemed so altogether lovely that he forgot he was staring and holding her hand until he saw her color heighten and felt the slight pull of her hand as she sought to release it.

Someone said, "Sally has the same effect on practically everyone," and Kenyon saw that it was the plump man and grinned back at him. Comstock was watching, half smiling; the thin man, who was Paul Sherman, and his wife, Marion, gave him a moment of speculative study; then Carl Sherman was moving toward a table laden with drinks and accessories and saying, "Well, what're we waiting for?"

The next hour was not much fun for Kenyon. Aware that he was the center of interest, he tried to let the others do the talking, but there were questions that had to be parried or answered and he strove to maintain a middle ground which was neither effusive nor boorish. He was conscious that Comstock watched him almost continuously, his expression both anxious and pleased; he was aware from time to time of Sally Hayden's smile. Carl Sherman took the lunch and conversation in his stride, but Paul and his wife seemed to accept Kenyon with strong reservations and this he could understand. After all these years the prodigal had returned to change completely their status in the household and apparently to become at once the favored heir. All assumed that he had come to stay and he said nothing to support or deny the assumption.

Morley had coached him well and he knew that Comstock was the publisher of the Kingsford *Sun*, though no longer very active, that Paul Sherman was the managing editor, that Carl ran an insurance office in town. It was not until luncheon was nearly over that he made a mistake, and then, speaking of newspapers to Paul Sherman he said, not thinking, "I worked on one for a while myself."

He realized at once what he had done and kept his eyes on his plate and tried to go right on talking. It did not work.

"Really?" Paul Sherman said. "Where?"

Kenyon had to look at him. He had to cut through the silence and answer, and he saw that of the two evils offered him there was little choice. Either could be checked, yet it seemed riskier to mention some newspaper with which he was completely unfamiliar and so he told the truth.

"The Gainsburg *Star*."

"Oh, yes. In Indiana."

"Of course, that was quite a while back," Kenyon said, and started off on something else. This time it was Marion Sherman who stalled him.

"And what have you done since then? You were working in Los Angeles, weren't you?"

Tall, thin like her husband, Marion Sherman was too straight, and her face too long and angular, to be considered either pretty or beautiful. She was a little too poised, a little too superior for Kenyon's taste, but he put down his annoyance and smiled sweetly at her.

"Yes," he said, and let it go at that. He might have gotten away with it if it hadn't been for Comstock.

"Orchestra work, wasn't it, son? I believe Morley mentioned that you—"

"Yes," Kenyon said. "A dance band."

"Oh. How interesting," Marion Sherman said. "And what is your instrument?"

This time Kenyon had no choice. He had to mention the instrument that the real Joseph Comstock had played in that Los Angeles orchestra under the name of Joseph Anthony. "A trombone," he said, and was glad it wasn't a piano or Marion Sherman would have tried to make him play it.

From that moment he was alert and watchful, choosing every word carefully lest he make some other mistake, and when at last they rose from the table his nerves were ragged and his face was hot and damp. It helped some to move to the drawing-room windows with Sally Hayden and to realize the danger was past.

"Mr. Morley didn't tell me about you," he said.

She looked up across the point of her shoulder, her eyes veiled. "Should he have?"

"He told me about Paul and Carl."

"And Marion?"

"Well—he mentioned her."

"But they're the family. I'm just a sort of secretary."

"A very special sort. Well, it just goes to show you."

"Does it?"

"It happened to a friend of a friend of mine once. He just walked into this party where he didn't know but one guy, and there she was. Young and beautiful, nice disposition, swell figure."

She was watching him now, her smile merry. "Like me?"

"Just like you. That's what I said to myself when I saw you. 'Remember Bill Tenny,' I said. 'Maybe it's going to happen to you.'"

"And did she live happily ever after?"

He grinned. "I don't know. My friend says the husband came and took her away. It happens all the time."

"Oh," she said, wrinkling her nose at him, "but I'm—"

"Joe."

Kenyon heard the voice but it meant nothing to him and he was watching Sally and waiting, and he finally said, "You're what?"

Then, suddenly, he was aware of her curious glance. Someone said, "Joe," again and instantly he was all hollow inside. When he turned he saw them staring at him and felt the blood drain from his face. Instantly he mustered a laugh and an explanation.

"Oh, sorry," he said, aware now that it was Comstock who had called. "I've gotten so I pay no attention to Joe any more. Most everyone calls me Tony."

He could almost feel the tension fall apart. Someone

chuckled and Marion Sherman let her brows drop back in
place. Comstock smiled.

"We'll remember," he said. "I was just going to say
that maybe you'd like to look around. Take him along,
Sally, and show him where things are."

Kenyon began to breathe again, thankful that young
Comstock's middle name had been Anthony but wondering how much longer he could go before he was trapped.

"I'll be in the study," Comstock said, and then Kenyon
was alone with Sally Hayden.

The house was a low-lying building, topping a slight
rise from the street so that, aside from the center section
which was an extra floor in height, the two stone wings
were one story in the front and two stories in the rear. An
acre of landscaped lawn swept down to the street and out
back there was a terrace and a tennis court and a garden.
Eventually Sally brought Kenyon here and they sat down
on a stone bench, and for a little while he forgot about the
part he was playing; for he was young and it had been a
long time since he had known a girl like this.

She was wearing a plaid skirt and a Brooks sweater with
its sleeves pushed up to the elbows. There was a little white
collar poking up through the neckline and her dark hair
fell softly to the yellow wool at her shoulders. She had
long slim legs and even in her sport shoes she had an easy,
graceful way of holding herself that was both poised and
relaxed. Her hazel eyes looked right at him from under
lashes that needed nothing from a beauty parlor; and
before he realized it he was answering questions about the
man whose place he was taking.

At first he found it amusing. It gave him a sort of Jekyll-
Hyde feeling and acted as a tonic to his spirits because he
had to be both quick and careful in his answers. She wanted
to know what he'd done in college and how he happened
to work for the Gainsburg, Indiana, *Star*. She wanted to
know what sort of assignments he had worked on and

why he had given it up. She asked about orchestras, and how long he had studied, and did he hope to have a band of his own some day or what?

Kenyon had answers for everything. Morley had given him a lot of background and what he didn't know he took from his own life, not with any maliciousness or ulterior motive, but simply because this was a new and interesting game to him and he didn't want it to end. She was like a little girl in her genuine eagerness to learn all about him and he found something fresh and solid about her that he had never known in anyone else.

"I guess you'd call me Andy's—that's your father, but I've always called him Andy—secretary," she said finally, as though deciding it was time such confidences became mutual. "You see, Dad was one of his editors and he's known me since I was a baby."

Kenyon sat quietly and let her go on, watching the play of sunlight and shadow across her lovely face, not thinking of why he was here, but only that she was with him. She had caught one knee in her clasped hands, sitting close to him but looking out across the garden, telling him how her mother had died when she was young and how Andy had been an uncle to her ever since. Her father, she said, had died three years ago while she was in college, but there had been enough money for her to finish, and since then she had worked for Comstock.

"At the paper, mostly," she said. "Until he went to the hospital. He was there four months," she said, and looked at him. "He almost died. That's why I'm glad you came back."

That broke the bubble for Kenyon. It jarred him right back where he belonged and left a flat and bitter taste in his mouth. He could not think of anything to say and she, misconstruing his silence, said:

"And you *are* going to stay, aren't you?"

"I—I don't know," he said. "I hadn't intended to." He

put on a grin and said, "Of course I didn't know about
you then," but it was no good. Suddenly he could no longer
kid around and be gay and say the things he might have
said had he met her somewhere as Tony Kenyon.

"Oh, but you couldn't," she said. "Not for a while, certainly. You couldn't let all those things that happened
twenty years ago spoil it now. You can't be that bitter.
. . . Oh, here's Andy."

Comstock was coming toward them from one wing of
the house and they went to meet him.

"Is she a good guide, Tony?"

"The best," Kenyon said.

"He got tired," Sally said. "He had to sit down."

Comstock laughed, and linked his arms in theirs. "I've
been thinking," he said. "I've got to go down to the paper
for a while and I thought I'd drop Tony at the hotel and
he could pack and I could pick him up on the way out."

There was a brief second when Kenyon set his jaw,
determined to make the break now. Instead he wavered.
"Well—" he said, and then Comstock cut in.

"I don't know what your plans are—haven't even had
a chance to talk to you. But while you're in town—"

"Of course he's coming," Sally Hayden said. "And I
have a better idea. Why don't I drive him down in my car
and then—"

Kenyon made a half-hearted attempt. "I'll have to
pack."

"Oh I can wait. I'll take my knitting."

And then she was smiling and he was lost.

Chapter Three

GETTING COLD FEET

WHEN HE SET HIS MIND TO IT, Leon Morley was a reasonably patient man and he listened to Tony Kenyon's recital of what had happened without interruption. He paced the floor of the hotel room and punished his gum with his jaws but he kept quiet until Kenyon was finished; then he made an irritated gesture and sat down.

"Look," he said, "what're you crying about? Getting scruples all of a sudden or are you afraid you'll get caught?"

"Neither. I'm just telling you—"

"Phuie."

Kenyon closed his bag and sat down, his blue eyes brooding. Morley studied him and when he spoke his voice was crisp and incisive.

"Forget it," he said. "You've got a job to do and you're going to do it. I picked you off a park bench. To me you were just another bum but you had what I wanted and I made you a proposition. You took it—and don't tell me you had to. You could have found a way to run out."

"All right, I took it."

"I spent three hundred bucks on you. You knew what you had to do. Now that you look like a man again what do you turn out to be? A slobbering sentimentalist. Well, I'm not having any. Where would I be in my business, feeling sorry for every wife or husband I have to get evidence on?"

"Did I say I felt sorry for him?"

Morley went on as though he had not heard. "Where would the cops be, feeling sorry for every guy that has a sob story? Hell, some of the most vicious killers on record were so sad when the law caught up with them that the sob sisters and the press got hysterical about the injustice done them."

He went over to the window, stared morosely out. "You're getting paid five hundred bucks, aren't you? This guy Comstock kicked his wife out with a four-year-old child. Just once did he try to patch things up—when the kid was ten. He married again and that was the last the first wife heard of him until she died. Four years ago, when the son got out of college, he got a letter from Comstock wanting him to come back and offering to leave him half his estate if he'd do so. The son wanted no part of him. He knew his old man for what he was and he hated him."

He turned, pointing one finger. "Listen. Comstock hired me two months ago, a little over. I spent that two months chasing up that son. When I found him he was playing in a Los Angeles orchestra under the name of Joseph Anthony. Why? Because he still hated his old man so much he wouldn't use his last name. But you—you have to go all to pieces—"

"Who's going to pieces?" Kenyon said hotly.

"You are."

"Nuts."

Morley grinned suddenly. "That's better," he said. "This is a kind of lousy business I'm in. There isn't much dough in it and not much fun. Divorce cases, trying to locate people who'd rather stay hidden, labor cases, once in a while an insurance job. It isn't often I get a spot like this where I can collect a ten thousand bonus. Well, I've done all the hard work and I'm going to collect. I found young Comstock. I even had him about talked into coming back with me."

The grin went away. "Only just then he has to get himself killed in a traffic accident and there's my ten grand out on the limb—or it would have been if I hadn't used my head. The kid lived four or five hours and he talked to me before he died. He gave me the birth certificate and the locket and the letter he'd kept. He told me what to do with his things. All he hoped was that they'd sell for enough so he could be buried with his mother. He didn't even want his body to come to his old man. Anyway, I did what he asked. But I didn't have the ten grand because the bargain with the old man was not that I find him, *but that I bring him back.* That's when I got the idea of putting in the second ad, and that's where you come in.

"For two days you're Joe Comstock, Junior. Actually we're doing the old boy a favor because even though it's only for a few days he'll think he's had his son back for a little while. You're not supposed to feel sorry for anyone, and if you played the part the way his son would, you'd be pretty damn bitter toward him all the time. Maybe every time you see him you'd better tell yourself you should hate him. What is it with you that you can't just look at this as two days' work and then disappear?"

Kenyon thought he had an answer for that too but he couldn't say so. He couldn't say that there was a girl downstairs in a car like no one he had ever known; he couldn't say that she had mixed everything up for him and he didn't know what to do about it.

"Suppose they trip me up?"

"How can they? They've accepted you so far without even asking for the proof you've got. Suppose you did say you worked for a paper in Indiana. Do you think anyone is going to check up in the next two days? Can anyone make you play a trombone if you don't want to?"

Morley came away from the window and Kenyon watched him. He'd learned a lot about the man in the past three days and most of it commanded respect. If there was any great warmth or understanding underneath the muscular face and straight hard mouth, it never cropped out, but he had a keen, perceptive mind and the sort of stubbornness that suggested he could stay with any given problem until he had it whipped. He chewed gum continually, often adding a fresh stick until he had four or five in his mouth; his movements were deliberate and unhurried, and yet there was something about the way he carried himself that told you he could move swiftly and surely when the occasion demanded. A good man to have on your side, Kenyon decided; a bad one to cross. As though to bear him out, Morley tapped him on the shoulder and gave him that crooked grin.

"Just keep one thing in mind, chum. I've had a lot of grief the past two months working for twenty bucks a day and expenses. I'm not going to lose out on that bonus now. A couple more days and you can do as you please—so long as you don't cross me. Maybe I can't do anything now about that frame in Los Angeles, but I've still got the original ad I used to find young Comstock."

Kenyon waited, not understanding the inference.

Morley's grin remained. "I could tell a story about how *you* answered that ad and offered me the birth certificate and things to prove it. You *could* have palmed yourself off on me, you know. It's been done before. And don't forget, you've talked me out of three hundred dollars worth of clothes. They put people in jail for that. It would be your word against mine, but where do you think the odds would be when it turns out that you're a phony?"

Kenyon started to argue. Then he thought better of it and picked up his bag. Morley walked with him to the door.

"Try hating the old man awhile," he said. "You made a bargain three days ago. Keep it. You know what I mean?"

Tony Kenyon did not have much to say on the ride to the house. At first Sally Hayden did not notice this, driving him a roundabout way and pointing out things of interest and telling him how nice it was for Andy that he had come home. Kenyon did his best to sound interested but presently she caught something from his mood and when they finally rolled up the driveway both were silent.

She took him into the wing on the right. There was a doorway at the end which led to three steps going down and then a narrower hall, but the door before this opened into a corner room with casement windows, overlooking the front lawn and the trees. She said she thought he'd find everything he wanted here and he thanked her and she said she'd see him at dinner.

When she had gone he glanced about before unpacking. Outside the windows was a grassy terrace and he saw that apparently an addition had been constructed at the end of the wing and he wondered if this was Comstock's study. The bath, he saw, gave also on an adjoining room. Not sure whether he was to share the bath he knocked at the door and, getting no answer, opened it. When he saw the room was apparently unoccupied he returned to his own, put his bag on the luggage rack and opened it.

He hung up his other suit, put his linen away in the maple chest; then he glanced at the identification Morley had supplied. The birth certificate of Joseph A. Comstock, Junior, was much worn from folding and discolored at the edges. There was an envelope containing a four-year-old letter, also much worn, and there was a rectangular gold locket which held the photograph of a bright-faced woman dressed in a style reminiscent of the early 'twenties. On her knee she held a blond, curly-headed boy who did not appear to be more than two or three. Kenyon looked at this for quite a while, then closed the bag, reminding himself that when he finally left he must see that the locket remained with Comstock.

There was a chair by the windows and he sat down and lit a cigarette. He was still in the chair and dusk was fingering the corners of the room when someone knocked at the door. It was Sally Hayden. She told him Comstock wanted to see him.

They went down the three steps at the end of the corridor and along a short and narrow hall to a door which stood ajar. Beyond this was a room furnished as a study. Standing in front of a desk was Comstock and the moment Kenyon saw him he was aware that some change had come over the man.

"Come in, come in," he said. "Thanks, Sally. . . . Sit down, Tony."

Sally withdrew and Kenyon eased into the leather club chair that Comstock indicated, his glance sliding over the massive desk, the plain-colored rug, the companion leather chair, the other doorway, beyond which, as he was to learn later, was a bedroom and bath. The lamplight was unkind to Comstock's face as he finally twisted the desk chair round and sat down, accentuating its boniness and bleaching the flaccid wrinkled skin to an unhealthy pastiness. There was a new nervousness tormenting him too. His eyes were harried and restless and for a moment he could not decide what to do with his hands. In the end he folded them across his chest, clamping them under his armpits.

"Sorry if I seemed abrupt when you came in. Fact is, something happened a little while ago that sort of unnerved me. You see—someone tried to kill me."

Kenyon sat up. Somewhere in his chest a nerve jumped. He waited, half expecting Comstock to smile, and then he saw something in the pale eyes that told him the man was troubled and afraid.

"What did you say?"

"Sounds preposterous, doesn't it?" Comstock shrugged thin shoulders. "I'm beginning to wonder myself if it wasn't imagination, now that I think of it. But at the time —" He broke off and his face worked in silence. He took another second to think and then, abruptly, he smiled and some of the nervousness fell away. "However, that isn't what I wanted to talk about."

Kenyon sat quite still. The smile wasn't enough, because for one brief instant he had looked into those eyes and seen the fear behind them.

"But—"

Comstock broke in hurriedly, waving away objections. "I'm sure it wasn't anything," he said, "and I don't know why I mentioned it. . . . Tell me, son. Are you sorry you came?"

Kenyon pushed the lingering doubt and uneasiness from his mind. *Remember what Morley said,* he thought. *It will be easier to hate him.*

"I'm not sure," he said. "I'd rather not—"

"All right, all right. I don't suppose it's a change that a man could get used to right off. You're still bitter, aren't you?"

Kenyon looked at him, saying nothing.

Comstock sighed. "I suppose you are. I don't see how it could be otherwise after all these years. You've heard your mother's side of the story and I know now that it was my fault. It is too bad that one does not have more good sense when he is young."

He slid his hands along the chair arms and dropped his glance. "I married Edith in New York when I was thirty. She was a very beautiful woman, your mother, and tremendously alive. I suppose it was dull for her here in Kingsford after New York, and I suppose I was dull too because I was ambitious and working hard and no doubt I didn't give her the attention she deserved. She was born to flirt, I guess. It didn't mean anything, but because she was so beautiful and I felt so lucky to have her, it gave me an inferiority complex. I was jealous because I was afraid. I tried not to be when she went off to New York on trips, but she had admirers here in town and that made a difference because I could not help knowing it.

"We quarreled, naturally. When you came along four years after we were married I thought she'd settle down and she did, for a year or so. But nothing really changed in her. She had time on her hands and she was beautiful

and there were always some to tell her so. Instead of accept-
ing this, instead of realizing that nothing would ever come
of it, I grew more and more jealous. I imagined things that
never happened. I accused her of these things and she was
not a woman who would stand for such treatment without
fighting back. I finally made the mistake of delivering an
ultimatum. I came home from work and found her giving
tea to a young fellow here in town and when he had gone
I told her the next time it happened I would throw her
out. She did not give me the chance. The next day she
was gone—and you with her."

He took a breath and whatever it was he was looking at
seemed a long way off. "It took me two years to find her.
She wouldn't come back. Then I lost track of her and it
was four years before I saw her again. That was the time
I saw you, that was when I knew it was hopeless. A man has
his pride, you know, and I tried to make the best of it.
I married again. When I wrote you four years ago and you
refused to come back I thought that was the end. But
then, while I was getting over my operation, I realized I
hadn't much time left."

His eyes came back to Kenyon. "I didn't mean to talk so
much. You have your own life to live and I've never had
any part in it and you have to do what's best for you. I said
I wouldn't try to influence you and now I'll say no more
about it. I'd like you to stay. If you'd rather not, I'll understand."

He turned to open a desk drawer and Kenyon thought
over all the things that Leon Morley had said, realizing
that you couldn't hate a man just because someone asked
you to. The best he could do now was to try to appear indifferent, and even that was becoming more difficult. What
had happened twenty years ago made no difference to him,
and because his own father had died when he was eight,
because he had never really known what it was to have a
father, he found himself wishing that his father might have

lived to be like Comstock. He found himself wondering what would happen if he stayed, for that was what he really wanted, and then he brought himself up with a start and resolutely put such ideas from his mind.

"Here," Comstock said, and Kenyon saw that in the desk drawer was a small safe which had been opened. There were some new bills in the blue-veined hand and Comstock counted off five, glanced at them, and made a notation in a small notebook. "Always like to keep track of new bills," he said, and then Kenyon saw they were of hundred dollar denomination, realized they were being offered to him.

"No," he said.

"Nonsense." Comstock locked the little safe and closed the drawer. "Of course you can."

Kenyon rose, one part of his mind filled with embarrassment, the other clinging to Morley's instructions. He looked at the money and thought, *Why not? You're still a bum, aren't you?*

"All right," he said. "As long as we understand each other."

"How do you mean?"

"I mean I'll take it if you want me to but it isn't going to make any difference. I didn't intend to stay when I came and this isn't going to change anything, one way or the other."

The lights died slowly in Comstock's eyes and it took him a moment to speak.

"Why, no," he said quietly. "It's all right, Tony. I didn't mean it that way. I—I've pulled you away from your work. This trip was to be at my expense and I wouldn't feel right about it otherwise." He seemed to be trying to find something to add to this, gave up, and glanced at his watch. "Oh, by the way. We eat at seven. Carl is probably stirring up Martinis now. Why don't you go ahead. I'll be along shortly."

Chapter Four

SHADOW OF DANGER

WHEN KENYON WALKED INTO THE DRAWING-ROOM he saw
that Comstock's guess had been correct. Carl Sherman was
measuring gin and vermouth into a cut-glass pitcher and
acting well pleased with his assignment as he talked with
Marion Sherman, who sat on the divan with Sally Hayden.

"Ahh," he said. "Another customer. You're just in time."

"I hope they're dry," Kenyon said.

"Three to one. Okay?"

Kenyon nodded and said hello to the women. Marion
Sherman fitted a cigarette into a long jade holder and
allowed him to give her a light.

"Well," she said, blowing smoke at him, "how do you
like us, or haven't you decided?"

"I haven't decided."

"Serves you right, honey," Carl said above the noise of
his stirring. "It's not nice to be nosy."

Marion smiled faintly, watching Kenyon with enigmatic
speculative eyes. Carl gave her a Martini and poured a glass
of sherry for Sally. He handed Kenyon a glass and held his
own up. "First today," he said, and drank.

"Isn't it time for Spence?" Sally asked.

Carl said he guessed it was and turned on the radio. As it
warmed up Comstock entered and Carl poured him a
sherry, which he took to a chair near the radio. Presently
an announcer's voice swelled out from the loud-speaker
recommending somebody's headache tablets. There was
a station break and then the announcer again, saying:

"*And now, Spencer Arden analyzes the news. . . . Each
weekday evening at this time the Kingsford "Sun" brings
you fifteen minutes . . .*"

"A local boy," Carl said, leaning close to Kenyon. "It isn't enough to have network commentators, we have to have our own." He grinned. "But they think it's good publicity and Spence does a pretty good job."

"Quiet," Marion said.

Kenyon found a chair and sat down. The voice that came over the air was crisp and cheerful and he listened for a while, aware that what Spencer Arden was trying to do was to give as much prominence to local news and gossip as he gave to national affairs. When he glanced about he found the others intent on the broadcast and that gave him a chance to study Marion Sherman.

She wore a dark blue dress, cut rather plainly and having no particular smartness. Her brown hair was worn long and drawn straight back to a bun and this served to make more noticeable the angular length of her face. He guessed her to be about thirty, and while he could not tell whether the air of slight boredom she wore was real or affected, he did not believe her capable of any great warmth or spontaneity.

The sound of the front door closing checked his inspection and presently Paul Sherman came in. He went over to his wife and she offered him a cheek to kiss and a pat on the hand. He said something to Sally Hayden and she smiled and he sat down between the two women, a tired-looking man whose receding hairline and horn-rimmed glasses made him look older than he was. He had a high, intelligent forehead, a suggestion of stubbornness in the slant of his jaw, and a worried, overworked look about him. Kenyon wondered if he had ulcers and when the butler came in bearing a tray with a glass of tomato juice and a cracker, he decided that he had.

Dinner was but a repetition of lunch, with more food. The conversation was about the same and Kenyon was busy turning it away from himself. He asked a lot of questions and learned that Marion Sherman was a dilettante

at writing poetry and a professional in women's club matters. Carl, sleek-haired, dark, and a complete extrovert,
said he was in the insurance business and looked it. He
said business was fine and rates were up, and in the casualty
field premiums were going up too.

They had coffee and liqueurs in the drawing-room and
when he decently could, Kenyon strolled to the far end of
the room and out on the terrace so that he could not be
subjected to any group questioning such as had happened
that noon. He had done a lot of thinking in the past few
hours and he knew now what had to be done.

Morley was right. He had made a bargain. For a trip
east and five hundred dollars he had agreed to impersonate a man now dead. He had no business trying to influence
or change the lives of those here; he had no right even to
think. It was only a matter of two days. He had made no
promises to Comstock, would make none. He could find
excuses for staying away from the house as much as possible and presently he would pick up and leave. As for
Sally Hayden, the only decent thing he could do now was
to avoid her. He did not have to be unpleasant about it; he
could be polite, but always there must be a reserve beyond
which he must not let her penetrate. There were times
when a man had to be tough and this was one of them.

That in itself was a laugh—his being tough about anything. If he had been tough he might have bluffed Morley
back there in Los Angeles. If he had been tough he would
be back in Indiana, doing rewrite and sitting in for old
Mack, the city editor, on his day off. Instead of that he had
been weak about everything, encouraging his weakness
by selfishness and self-pity. He had thought the draft an
injustice. He had a good job and he and Hazel Wainwright
were practically engaged. He remembered their last night
together and how they had gone to the Red Tavern to
dance and then driven along the river in the moonlight.
It had been three o'clock before he brought her home and

they had promised each other that the draft would make no difference. It was a thing that had to be done—there was no fighting in sight then—and a year was a small price to pay for later happiness and security—

"Hello."

He had not heard her come but now Sally Hayden was standing beside the settee and when he started to rise she said not to get up, and sat down beside him. She said wasn't it a grand night and he said it was, offering a cigarette and holding a light.

Remember, now, he thought. *Watch yourself*, and his mind slid back to Gainsburg. At first the army seemed not bad. It was something new and when he had become adjusted to the routine he had to admit that he felt better physically that he had ever felt in his life. But that was before the routine began to cramp him. Now, with the war, it would be different, but then it was the same old drilling, constantly repeated, adjusting itself to the slowest and dumbest member of the squad; mock maneuvers, no ammunition for rifles, stovepipes for mortars and gas pipe on rubber tires for antitank guns. Then the letter from Hazel, who wanted him to be the first to know of her engagement to Howard Lanning and couldn't they, please, always be friends. After that nothing mattered. He got a transfer to the west coast but it didn't make any difference; he got in minor trouble with the men and the officers— because he didn't care, because he wouldn't try—

"You're awfully quiet."

"Thinking," he said.

"About Andy?"

There it was again. He looked at her. Her eyes were in shadow but light from the room caught the sweet curve of her cheek and turned the border of her hair into copper. Seeing this, feeling her nearness, put an ache in his breast and he made himself glance away.

"No. Just thinking."

"Would you rather do it alone?"

"No," he said, and thought, *Why didn't you say "yes," and have it over with?* "Certainly not," he said.

There was a noise behind him and a man came through the French doors, a good-looking blond man he had never seen before.

"Hey," he said, speaking to the darkness. "Where's the long-lost son. Hi, Sally! . . . Oh, there you are. Welcome home, prodigal."

Kenyon got up. "Brash character, isn't he?"

Sally laughed. "Spence? One of the brashest."

Kenyon took the outthrust hand. "You're Arden. I heard you on the radio."

"All right," Arden said, "but no cracks." He reached down and rumpled Sally's hair. "What kind of a guy is he? Is he all right?" Then, grinning, to Kenyon, "Anyway, I'm glad to see you back, though I don't know why I should say that, never having seen you before."

"I think he's very nice," Sally said, "when he's not brooding."

"Oh, the strong, silent type, eh? Well, I'm glad something's wrong with him. I have competition enough as it is. . . . See you later, kids, I want to talk to the old man." And with a wave he was gone.

"I'll bet he eats vitamin pills," Kenyon said.

"He's always that way. Quite mad—in a nice sort of way."

He sat down and once again the silence fell about them. He could feel her arm against his and wondered if she could feel him tremble.

"You talked with Andy," she said finally. "Did you decide anything?"

"Decide anything?"

"About—staying."

Suddenly an odd resentment struck at him. He did not know what brought it on, or even that he had it, until he heard his voice.

"No. And being reminded of it all the time doesn't help any."

He felt her turn and fought against the pressure of her gaze.

"You *are* bitter, aren't you?" she said.

"If I am it's only at myself."

When she spoke again her voice was strangely quiet. "I'm sorry."

"For Andy."

"Yes. Because he waited so long and asked so little. I was afraid at first, when I heard you were coming. Because in his mind he had this picture of his son—I suppose we all did—and sometimes a person one has dreamed about does not turn out to be that sort of person at all. Then, when I saw you, I was glad. I thought I knew what you were like and I could see how proud Andy was, and this afternoon in the garden I thought—" Her laugh was abrupt and she rose quickly. "But then I don't suppose it matters, does it?"

He reached for her arm as he stood up, held her. He did not know why, nor could he explain what happened next. Perhaps it was because this was something he had so desired ever since she sat down beside him; perhaps it was simply that he knew there would never be another chance. Whatever the reason, he pulled her roughly to him and, not meaning to, not even realizing why, kissed her hard on the mouth.

She neither fought him nor responded to his embrace. When he released her and stepped back she caught her breath and stood looking at him.

"Did you have to do it that way?"

"Yes," Kenyon said, and stepped past her into the lighted room.

Marion Sherman was alone, stretched out on the divan, a book in one hand, the cigarette holder in the other.

"Have fun?" she asked idly, and then, seeing Kenyon's white, set face, "Maybe I shouldn't have asked."

Somewhere a doorbell rang, saving Kenyon the necessity of a reply. Ignoring the woman he continued to the hall, reaching it just as the butler opened the front door. Leon Morley came in, handing over his hat and coat, and Kenyon waited for him.

"Good evening, Mr. Comstock," Morley said, his voice holding just the right deference. "Your father around?"

Kenyon glared at him, but this was wasted on Morley, who continued to the butler. "Will you tell Mr. Comstock, Senior, that I'm here, Hilton?"

"Yes, Mr. Morley."

Hilton went away and Morley moved up, amber eyes thoughtful. "How'd it go? Any more mistakes?" He paused, cocking his head. "Come on, chum. Snap out of it."

"Everything is perfect," Kenyon said, biting at the words.

"It better be. . . . Ah, Mr. Comstock. Good evening."

"Hello, Morley."

Comstock came through the doorway to the wing. Spencer Arden was a step behind and as Comstock moved up to Morley and Kenyon, Arden went on past without a word. He picked his coat from a chair in the entryway, adjusted his hat brim; then, seeing Kenyon watching him, he winked and went out.

Comstock and Morley were in the living-room when Kenyon wandered in a minute later. "I'll have your check for you tomorrow," Comstock was saying. "You can pick it up at my lawyer's. The other one—for your last two weeks' expenses—is in the study. . . . Oh, Tony." He put his hand on Kenyon's shoulder. "Would you mind getting it for me? I think you'll find it on the desk. . . . No, wait. I remember now, it's in the bedroom, on the chest. . . . Will you have a drink, Morley?"

Kenyon heard Morley say he would and then he was

going slowly down the hall, past his own room to the three stairs at the end. The passageway beyond was lighted; so was the study. He went in, leaving the door open, and turned toward the adjoining room, which was dark, stopping just inside the threshold and groping along the wall in search of the light switch.

Just what it was that warned him, he never knew. It could have been a noise, though he did not identify it as such; possibly it was some movement which stirred the air, or a matter of instinct, the premonition that danger was close; whatever it was, he stiffened, his hand still on the wall and every sense alert, seeing against some reflected light coming through the casement windows, the silhouette of a floor lamp, the corner of a chest, the post of the bed.

"Who's there?" he called, and then he really heard something, a soft brushing sound like a shoe drawn across a rug. He called once more and started toward the sound and then there was a shadow between him and the windows. Too late, he tried to duck and draw away. Something hard slammed against the side of his jaw, knocking him against a chair. He knew then that it was only a fist, but the chair was in the way and he went down before he could recover his balance.

He heard the window bang open as he rolled to his knees and for a fleeting instant a man's figure was silhouetted there; then the space was empty again and a curtain bellowed gently inward with the breeze.

Chapter Five

PROWLER WITH A GUN

BY THE TIME KENYON GAINED HIS FEET his head was clear, but it was anger rather than any conscious thought that drove him toward that window. It was but a three-foot drop to the grassy terrace and when he hit the ground he hesitated, orienting himself, wondering which way to turn.

The window was at the end of the building. The prowler could have turned either way and Kenyon took a chance and ran to his left, circling the corner of the wing and starting along the back, running hard. He was on a slight downgrade for a moment and he could see, stretching out above him, the main floor of the house, the lighted living-room and the iron railing that enclosed the narrow, flagstone porch outside the windows.

Later, when he thought it over, Kenyon knew it was luck that kept him on the right course. He could hear nothing but the thudding of his feet, and though his eyes were accustomed to the darkness, he saw nothing until a swiftly moving shadow cut across the projected light from the living-room windows. Directly ahead, hunched low so that he was but a vague figure in topcoat and hat, the prowler had apparently swung wide to avoid this lighted area and then cut in too soon.

One instant he was there, the next he was gone, but Kenyon was closer to him than he expected to be and knew he was gaining. A gravel walk circled out in his path and he ran along it. He never knew whether he called out again or not. He was directly opposite the living-room when he saw flame stab the darkness up ahead; then a shot hammered in the night and there was a funny sound at his feet and gravel kicked about his legs.

He slid to a stop and froze, breath held as he waited for a second shot. Highlighted in reflected illumination, he wanted to throw himself flat and could not, and as he waited there was a sudden noise above him and he glanced up. A French door was open and Morley's blocky figure was at the rail.

"Who's that?"

"Me," Kenyon yelled. "I found a guy in the study and he—"

Morley didn't hesitate. It was a good eight feet to the ground but he put one hand on the low rail and vaulted, hitting the ground on both feet and staying erect.

"Which way?" he demanded, and Kenyon saw that already one hand held a flashlight, the other a gun.

They went swiftly ahead then, following the beam of light that Morley sprayed ahead of them.

"We'll never get him now," Kenyon said.

Morley's answer was a grunt.

"I didn't know he had a gun."

Morley grunted again, then slowed down abruptly, putting out an arm to make Kenyon do likewise. They had nearly reached the end of the opposite wing and now there was some new light spilling out on a gravel parking space. As they turned the corner Kenyon saw that the light came from a four-car garage under the house, one door of which stood open. Morley slid around the edge of it and stopped. He lowered his gun and snapped off the flashlight. Carl Sherman was standing in front of a sand-colored convertible, staring, a briefcase in his hand.

"W-What's up?" he stammered one eye on the gun.

"See anybody go past here?"

"No."

"Didn't hear anybody either, huh?"

"I thought I did. I was digging this out of the car"—he held up the briefcase—"and I was just coming out to look. I thought somebody ran past."

Morley looked at him, eyes half closed and jaw hard. He put his gun and flashlight away and turned abruptly. "Come on," he said to Kenyon.

"But what—" Carl Sherman began.

"I ran into a prowler in the study," Kenyon said. Sherman had neither coat nor hat. His hair did not seem mussed. He seemed a little flushed, a little excited, but his breathing was silent and controlled. "He took a shot at me out back," Kenyon said and followed Morley.

They entered the living-room from the terrace at the front and as they started across, Paul Sherman came in from the hall. He had his glasses in his hand and was rubbing the bridge of his nose with thumb and index finger, and that gave his eyes a naked, worried look.

"Is something wrong? Didn't I hear a shot?"

"You could have," Morley said. "Where were you?"

"Why—in the library." Sherman gestured across the hall.

"I guess maybe you did, then."

Comstock and Marion Sherman, who had been out on the rear balcony where Morley went over the rail, came up.

"What is it, Tony?" Comstock said. "Are you all right?"

Kenyon said he was all right. "Someone was in your bedroom. He went out the window and I chased him and —" He broke off, held by the quick transformation of Comstock's face. The eyes went wide, the jaw slack. One hand went to his breast, pressing there for a moment before it fell away. Then, as though reassured by something, he went on. "Yes, yes," he said. "And then what?"

Kenyon told them, his fingers touching the slight lump on the side of his jaw.

"Well, it doesn't surprise me," Marion Sherman said. She shrugged and glanced at her husband. "Now you know why I've insisted on upstairs bedrooms. All one would have to do down here would be to step through a window. I'd as soon sleep in the open."

She said something else but Kenyon did not hear it, for he had suddenly realized that Sally Hayden was not here. He turned. She was standing to one side and slightly behind him, but he had not heard her approach, nor did he know from which direction she had come.

"You might have been shot," she said.

A quick, energizing warmth streaked through him. There was no resentment in her face or in her voice. Her eyes were wide and concerned and if she had been hurt by what he had done to her she did not show it now.

"I don't think so," he said. "He fired low. I think he just wanted to stop me."

"Well," Morley said. "Do you want to report it?"

"Report it?" Comstock had been staring beyond Kenyon with vacant, troubled eyes; now they snapped back to the detective. "Certainly not. What good would that do now? He couldn't have been there long. I hadn't left more than a few minutes before."

"But what could he have wanted?" Marion said.

"What does any prowler want?" Paul Sherman said wearily, and put on his glasses.

Comstock wheeled abruptly and started toward the wing. Morley watched him take two or three steps and then he started after him. As though by some pre-arranged signal, Paul waited a second and followed, and Marion said, "Wait for me," and caught up with him. Carl, who had come in with his briefcase, tossed it on a chair. He sighed, and grinned at Kenyon and Sally.

"Well, come on," he said. "We might as well all go."

"You didn't see who it was, Tony?" Sally said, moving beside him down the hall.

"No."

"Well—" She paused and he watched her from the corner of his eye. She was walking with her head bent, her hair falling forward so that it covered the sides of her face. "I'm glad," she said. "I mean I'm glad you didn't

see him because if you had—there in the room—he might
have—"

"Yeah," Kenyon said, knowing somehow that she still
liked him and wondering how this could be.

Comstock was standing at his desk opening drawers
when they went in. The others stood about, watching,
keeping out of his way. There was an angry impatience
about his movements now. His mouth was pinched and
his eyes, behind the rimless glasses, were hard and fixed.

"Anything missing?" Paul Sherman asked.

"No," Comstock said, and stepped into the bedroom,
snapping on the light.

Kenyon moved up to the doorway, watching him look
the room over. It was plainly furnished, with a heavy
wooden bedstead, a heavy Lawson chair, a high old chest,
and a bedside table holding a lamp, a telephone, two or
three envelopes, and a letter opener. He went first to this
table, glanced at the envelopes, then stepped to the chest
and picked up a slip of paper that had been anchored
there by a leather clock.

"Here's your expense check, Morley."

The detective took it, said, "Thanks," and folded it
carefully, nothing showing in his face.

"And would you mind waiting awhile? I'd like to talk
to you later." Comstock examined the others, as though
seeing them for the first time. His gaze finally moved back
to Paul Sherman and stopped. "I'd like to have a few
words with you now," he said. "If the others will excuse
us. . . . And, Carl, I'd like to see you too—when I've finished
with Paul."

The rest trailed back to the drawing-room and Carl
pushed a button near the doorway. "I don't know what
this is all about," he said, "but whatever it is, it has certainly upset the old boy. Funny, too. Anybody else get the
impression that this wasn't much of a surprise to him?"

"It wasn't that so much," Marion said, screwing a

cigarette into the long holder, "as that he knew what the prowler was after."

"Maybe that's what I meant. . . . Oh, Hilton," he said as the butler appeared. "Stimulants, please."

He gave Marion a light, wandered over to the radio and turned it on. Kenyon became aware of Sally Hayden's quiet inspection and found it discomforting. He finally gave her a passing glance and a grin and was rewarded with a faint smile before he busied himself with his pack of cigarettes.

"You two guys can mix your own," Carl said when Hilton came in with a tray.

"None for me," Sally said.

"I'll make yours short and weak," Carl said.

Kenyon and Morley moved up to the tray and presently the detective caught his eye and gestured toward the hall with his head. When he had tasted his drink he wandered in that direction. On the opposite side of the hall was the dining-room, facing the front, and behind this, the library. Morley had already gone in and turned on the light when Kenyon got to the hall. He followed the detective and closed the door.

"What do you want?"

Morley looked at him and sat down; then he looked at him again, his lids half-shut, his squarish face impassive.

"How much of that yarn was on the level?"

"All of it."

"You didn't see the guy at all?"

"I told you what I saw." Kenyon's voice was curt, irritable. "He had a coat and a hat and a pretty fair punch. That's all I know." He paused, conscious of Morley's cold appraisal. "Except this. You get your check tomorrow morning. Tomorrow afternoon I'm on my way."

"No." Morley shook his head. "That might look a little phony."

"Of course it isn't."

"You'd better stay an extra day," Morley said, ignoring the sarcasm. "I'll get mine tomorrow and if you wait around till the next day it'll look much better." He tipped his head and his crooked smile started to come. "What's the matter? Getting scared?"

"A little. I don't like any part of this and—"

"It's a little late for that, isn't it? What else?"

Kenyon finished his drink and put down the glass. He went over to the window, his eyes darkly brooding and his jaw set. He put all thought of Sally Hayden from his mind and tried to analyze the other things that troubled him.

"I don't know. That gunman tonight for one thing. I've got a feeling something is happening around here that we don't know about, something that has nothing to do with us."

"What is that, intuition?"

Kenyon let it pass.

"Two more days," Morley said. "You think anybody's going to bother checking up on you in that time?"

"If something happened that—"

"Like what?"

"How do I know?" Kenyon turned on him, brows twisted and his mouth hard. "What was that gunman doing in Comstock's bedroom? Maybe he was just a prowler—but suppose he wasn't?" He hesitated and then, suddenly, he knew what was back of his worry and uncertainty. "But it isn't all my imagination. Comstock told me this afternoon that somebody tried to kill him."

Morley sat up. "Say that again."

"That's what he told me."

"Ahh—"

"Okay. I'm making it all up. That's all I've got to do."

Morley rubbed his jaw with his thumb and stood up. He started to turn away, stopped. He lowered his lids a little more.

"What did he tell you?"

Kenyon repeated what he remembered of the conversation. "He said maybe it was his imagination but he was going to find out."

"That makes it different. This guy tonight, I mean. Maybe he wasn't a prowler. Maybe he was waiting for Comstock and you walked in on him." He began to pace the floor. "Maybe that's what he wants to see me about. . . . Well, watch yourself. You've got nothing to worry about. He's fallen for the setup and that's enough. Look. If he doesn't say anything to me about this story of his I'm going to say you told me. That'll give me a chance to question him. He's probably crazy but, by God, nothing's going to happen to him until I get that check."

When they went back to the drawing-room, Carl Sherman was gone and Paul was at the tray, making a drink.

"You'll regret that, darling," Marion said.

"Maybe," Paul said, "but not until later at least."

He glanced at Kenyon and Morley and took a swallow. His face was flushed and his high forehead was shiny and presently he brought out a handkerchief and wiped it; he seemed to have trouble knowing what to do with his eyes and when they got around to the radio he stepped toward it.

"Do we need this?" he said, and cut off the dance orchestra in the middle of a chorus that was hot and brassy.

Morley went over to Marion and asked her if she'd like a refill. She said she guessed not and he made a fresh drink for himself. Then the silence closed down on the room. Paul Sherman sat down near the radio and streched his legs, morosely studying his crossed ankles. Morley joined Marion on the couch and she looked him over carefully before selecting another cigarette. Sally Hayden gave Kenyon a little smile but it was apparent now that there would be no more laughter that night. Comstock was cracking his whip and the rest of them had to sit by and wait to see what was to happen next. It wasn't very pleasant and the silence rapidly became more gloomy and depressing. It was Marion who finally broke it.

"I think I prefer the radio to this," she said, and then there was the sound of footsteps in the hall and Carl came in followed by Comstock.

Carl headed directly for the tray and put ice in a glass. His round face was flushed. His eyes avoided the rest of them and there was a grim and sullen twist to his mouth as he poured an unusually heavy drink.

When the doorbell rang no one paid attention to it. Comstock had advanced a few steps and now he stood with his hands at his side, running his thumbs nervously across his finger tips. Hilton glided down the hall and Kenyon could hear the front door open. Sally Hayden stood up.

"Will you want me any more tonight, Andy?"

"What? Oh." The tightness of the man's face dissolved and his glance softened. "No, my dear. I don't think—" He broke off as Hilton appeared in the doorway and coughed politely.

"I beg pardon, sir." He coughed again and his eyes came around to Kenyon. "But there's a young woman here who says she is Mrs. Comstock."

For just an instant the silence was crushing. Eyebrows were lifted and glances exchanged. Comstock squinted at Hilton and thrust his head forward.

"Comstock?" he said, as though he'd never heard the name. "What the devil are you saying?"

"That's what she said, sir." Hilton remained unperturbed, his glance moving again to Kenyon. "Mrs. Comstock, *Junior.*"

Chapter Six

UP AGAINST SOMETHING BIG

KENYON KNEW THAT EVERYONE WAS LOOKING AT HIM, but for that first interminable moment he could do nothing but stare. Sudden panic rushed at him and he fought it desperately, unable to think, unable even to breathe, yet knowing that he must do something, that he could not stand here and let disaster come to him.

With a tremendous physical effort he made one leg move and pulled the other after it, cold all over now, his stomach a vacuum. His face felt as if it were made of parchment and he could feel it crack as he tried to put on a grin. Then he found he could walk and kept moving, not knowing what he was going to do, but only that he must meet this woman in the hall and not here before the others.

She was standing in the entryway, a fox cape over one arm and an envelope purse in her hand. She had on a sheathlike, black jersey dress which gave her a sleek, curvesome figure, and her hair was red and topped by an idiotic little hat which somehow looked all right on her. That was about the picture he got in his first glimpse, because the light was bad and his brain was whirling and other details escaped him.

He remembered coming to a stop and groping for words. She stood with most of her weight on one leg, the other thrust slightly forward and to one side so that her knee was bent and one hip bulged outward. She was waiting, her eyes obscure, and then he heard steps behind him and knew that the others, curious, had come out to see for themselves. That made him move and, since there was no trap door in the floor through which he could fall to oblivion, he did the best he could, the only thing he could.

"Oh, hello," he said, his voice falsely hearty, and walked up to her, wondering if she could see that he was praying. "I didn't expect to see you here."

He held his breath and waited and then, miraculously, something happened to her eyes—brown eyes, large and deftly accented with mascara and shadow.

"Darling!"

She threw her free arm around his neck and kissed him on the mouth; then she put her head alongside his face, hugged him once, and whispered, "The name is Nora. Suppose you take it from there."

Kenyon backed up. His face was damp and he was trembling a little, and his mouth tasted of lipstick. He straightened himself and turned. They were all there, every one of them. He slid his arm through Nora's and drew her along. He actually smiled, so great was his relief.

"This is Nora," he said, his voice no longer faltering.

"Well." Carl Sherman grinned and his mouth wasn't grim and sullen any more. "Holding out on us, eh, Tony?"

"Yes." Comstock cleared his throat and as though realizing he had been remiss in his duty as a host, stepped forward with hand outstretched. "Come in, my dear. Let me have your wrap. I'm Tony's father but"—he gave Kenyon a reproachful look—"he hadn't told us about you."

"I don't wonder," Nora said. "I haven't seen him in a year. As a matter of fact, I didn't even know that he was here."

That stopped them for another moment, but then Comstock had her by the hand and Hilton had taken her cape and bag and she was being introduced to the others.

Kenyon saw that his hands were still trembling and jammed them in his pockets. He made himself look up and as soon as he saw Morley he knew that Nora was as big a surprise to the detective as she was to him. One by one the lumps and wrinkles in Morley's face went away until there was nothing left but the stunned and puzzled expression in his eyes; when no one was looking he lifted one brow at Kenyon and fashioned a silent whistle with his lips.

Only then did Kenyon become aware of Sally Hayden. She had acknowledged Nora's introduction and was standing in the doorway watching him while the others went past. There were tiny spots of color in her cheeks and in her eyes there was something he had never seen before. He did not think it was anger; he did not know what it was. When he started toward her she turned and went into the drawing-room.

Already Carl Sherman had poured a drink for Nora and attached himself to her, and though the talk that followed did not seem to bother her, the next half hour was a nightmare for Kenyon. He did not know what to say or quite what to do and always he was listening for some statement by this woman which would refute the story he had told. And yet it did not come. She said quite frankly that she had not known where Tony was and had come here to see if anyone could tell her where to get in touch with him.

If she was at all embarrassed by the admission that all was not quite well between them, she did not show it. Her smile was quick and bright, there was no bitterness in her manner or voice, no sarcasm. She would, she said, be very happy to stay a few days, if there was room, and since it was clear that she did not expect to share a room with Tony, she was offered the room adjoining his bath and presently went away.

"Well." Comstock looked Tony up and down and his gaze was both irritated and puzzled. "You might at least have told us."

Kenyon fell back on his original attitude. "I didn't intend to stay but a day or two. What difference could it make?"

"She's a colorful creature," Marion remarked dryly. "I'll say that for her."

"She seems very nice to me," Paul Sherman said.

"Me," Carl said, "I think she's swell."

Sally Hayden stepped up to Comstock.

"I'll run along now, Andy," she said.

"All right. That copying you can do any time tomorrow. I'll get your case for you."

"I can get it."

"Nonsense," Comstock said and started away.

Sally went into the hall. Kenyon watched her and presently followed her out. She was putting on a tan sport coat and shaking out her hair, glancing over her shoulder at him as he approached, but not stopping.

Kenyon stood beside her. He felt pretty low. He felt worse about this than anything that had happened yet. It put him in the spot of a married man who made passes at another woman and he didn't want her to think that. He could leave, he could fade out and let her think he did not like her well enough to stay, but he didn't like this other.

"Sally."

She looked at him, her hands still at her hair.

"I—I didn't think she'd be here," he said, and knew as he spoke that this wasn't what he had wanted to say.

She glanced back in the mirror. "That's rather evident, isn't it?"

"What I mean was—well you heard her say I hadn't seen her in a year. We don't even—well, we don't live together—"

Footsteps behind him cut him off and he saw Comstock coming up, a tan attaché case in his hand.

"Here you are, Sally. Good night, my dear. . . . Oh, Tony. Will you step into the library?"

Sally opened the door. As she closed it she looked once more at Kenyon, her face composed, a little pale, revealing nothing. He stood there miserably, watching it close; then followed Comstock into the library.

Morley was already there. He was slouched deep in a

leather chair, unwrapping a piece of gum. He gave Kenyon a quick sidelong look, nothing moving but his eyes, and directed his attention to the gum.

"This thing that happened tonight has upset me." Comstock sank down on the divan and exhaled noisily. "I don't know whether it has anything to do with this other matter I mentioned this afternoon or not. I suppose it has and yet—You didn't see him, Tony? You haven't any idea how he was built?"

"No. I only really saw him for an instant when he was running and he was sort of hunched over."

Comstock stared ceilingward. "Something funny happened this afternoon, Morley. That's why I wanted you to stay. I mentioned it to Tony this afternoon—"

"He spoke to me about it," Morley said. "Why don't you tell us about it? Where did it happen?"

"On the street, not far from the *Sun* building."

Comstock paused and Kenyon watched him. He looked utterly weary now, the skin sagging from the bony framework of his face and his mouth drooping. He did not say anything for quite a while and Morley prodded him.

"That makes it sound like an automobile."

"It was. It would have gone as a hit-and-run case. I don't know whether you know it but the building is on a narrow one-way street. It isn't long and there are no shops on it and so it doesn't carry much pedestrian traffic. I was crossing from our entrance, diagonally toward the corner. I don't know what made me look round, though I guess it was the sound of the motor."

He paused again and sank a little lower on the divan. "Looking back, I've come to the conclusion that the car had been parked back a way, waiting, and that's why I heard it. It didn't come along silently as a car would that had been in high gear, but noisily, as though it was in second and still accelerating. In any event, I glanced about and saw it swerve, and leaped for the sidewalk. The thing

that saved me was a steel light pole. Had it been ten feet
one way or the other that car would have gone over the
curb after me and for forty or fifty feet there a blank wall
backs up the sidewalk."

Morley unfolded the gum wrapper and carefully re-
folded it. He had his chin on his chest so that his brows
hid his eyes and the overhead light showed up streaks of
pink scalp through his thinning hair. He said, not looking up:

"Could you be mistaken?"

"Not that the pole saved me. I swung behind it instinctively and I heard a tire squeal as it squeezed along the curb-
ing. I couldn't see because my back was to it, but I heard
it. I couldn't be mistaken about that; it's possible that the
swerving could have been accidental, I'll have to admit."

"Let's take it that it wasn't. Let's make it deliberate.
Why?"

"Why?"

"Yeah. Do you know any reason why it should have
been?"

Comstock had been resting the nape of his neck against
the back of the divan; now he pulled his head forward and
stared down at the blue-veined hands on his knees.

"I think I do."

Morley was intent on his wrapper. After a few seconds
he said, "But you're not saying so. Okay. Let's go back.
Were there any witnesses?"

"I don't think so. Some people passing the intersection
but none close enough to have seen the attempt. They saw
the car as it lurched around the corner but it probably
didn't mean anything."

"You didn't see who was in the car?"

"A man was driving, that's all I know. And yet"—he
hesitated, frowning—"I seem to have an idea he was a
husky, thickset man. As broad as you are, broader if anything, with an old felt hat and a massive head. I couldn't

swear to it; I'm not even sure I could identify him."

"But he wasn't like anyone you know?"

"I've been trying to think ever since. I don't believe I ever saw him before."

"What did you do after he missed you?"

"I ran to the corner." Comstock's voice was suddenly weary and remote. "I was too angry right then to be frightened and I ran to the corner. By the time I got there—"

"What about the license number?"

"I couldn't make it out. It was dirty and I think it had been bent upward. I never got very close but that's the way it seemed to me."

Kenyon watched the old man a moment, then glanced over at Morley. The detective dropped his folded gum wrapper in an ash tray and sat up, leaning forward slightly, his amber eyes narrowed and intent.

"That brings us back to why," he said.

"I'd like you to stay here tonight," Comstock said. "That's why I told you this other. I believe I know what's behind it but I can't be sure and it's a thing I'd rather not discuss tonight. I can have the study couch made up for you. If you have no objections you can run down to the hotel and get your things." He rose slowly, glancing at his watch. "It's ten now. If you're back by eleven it will be time enough."

He opened the door for them and Kenyon moved along the hall with Morley. Comstock remained in the study and when the detective saw they were alone he spoke softly.

"I don't know what this is, but I don't like it."

"What did I tell you?" Kenyon said.

Morley seemed not to have heard. "And that dame? If she's on the level—hell, I didn't know the guy was married—she can ruin us." He stopped, his hand on Kenyon's arm. "Go in and talk to her. Find out what the score is. I've come this far, I'm not going to miss out on that dough now."

Kenyon eyed him sardonically. "And what am I supposed to tell her?"

"How do I know? How do we even know she's his wife?"

"She knows damn well I'm not the son," Kenyon said, and told Morley what Nora had whispered to him when she kissed him.

"Find out. I don't know. Maybe you'll have to tell her the truth. She didn't come up here for the ride. If she is Comstock's wife—and I said *if*—maybe she knows he's dead and maybe she doesn't. Either way she's probably out for what she can get and that's all right with us so long as she don't crab our act—and why should she?"

"Well"—Kenyon grinned and spread his hands—"keep your fingers crossed."

Morley's crooked smile came back at him. "On both hands," he said. "Take it easy and be nice. That hadn't ought to be hard." The smile broadened. "She might be all right, you know?" He reached for his coat. "I'll stop in when I get back and see how you made out."

Kenyon walked to the door with Morley and when he came back Comstock was standing in the library doorway waiting for him. He beckoned and Kenyon went in.

"There's something I want to ask you, Tony," he said, and sank down on the divan. "I didn't want to ask it in front of Morley because—well, it may sound funny and —" He broke off, glancing down at his blue-veined hands. It was several seconds before he continued.

"I haven't any right to ask this," he said, "but I'm going to. I told Morley if he brought you back you wouldn't have to promise to stay, but I do want you to stay for a while because you're the only one I can trust."

Kenyon's lip curled. *Is that a laugh?* he thought, and waited, wondering what was to come next.

"I have an idea of what's behind the attempt to search my room, and that near-accident this afternoon," Comstock said. "It's big, Tony. Bigger than you think. Tomorrow we'll have someone here to take on the job of finding out how big, but even with help it may not be an easy thing to crack. It may take time. That's why I'm glad you're here."

He glanced up, eyes dark and intent now behind his rimless glasses. "Whoever is behind this is close to me, perhaps a member of this household. As my son you will live here and keep your eyes and ears open. You may have to do a little detective work, but you'll be glad to do that when you know why it's necessary. I could be wrong. We might get to the bottom of it quickly but I'm not counting on it. That's why I want you to promise to stay here until we're sure we have the answer."

Kenyon didn't like it. He kept thinking of his resolve to leave in two days.

"There must be someone here—" he began.

"No. That's just it. I can't be sure of anyone, not even in the house. There's Morley, yes. He'll be here tonight and for that sort of thing he's all right. I don't want you as a bodyguard, you know. What I have to say tomorrow cannot be said to anyone now. Morley's a good man, but he's a private detective, a stranger who works for a fee. I need someone close to me and that's why—" He hesitated, his smile a little sheepish. "Sounds pretty impossible, doesn't it? And yet it isn't, Tony. It's real. I wouldn't ask this otherwise. But I do ask it. Will you stay and see this thing through with me? It may not take long and after that— Will you stay, Tony?"

Kenyon was surprised at his answer. Intending to stick resolutely to the course he had chosen, intending to shake his head and refuse to become involved in something that was not his business, he was about to say so when, suddenly, inexplicably, a new thought struck him.

"Yes," he said, and now the idea was well rounded and satisfying, and he understood and was grateful for whatever alchemy of mind was responsible. Disgusted with the part he was playing and the weakness that had made him accept, he now saw a way to give a little something in return.

It was far too late to do anything about Sally Hayden, but it was not too late to do something for his conscience. It would, he realized, make no difference to him or to Morley whether he stayed two days or two weeks. And if by staying he could give some comfort to Comstock, if he could help him over this crisis—whatever it was—then later when he remembered this unpleasant chapter in his life he could at least say that he had given something of value to the man who paid the fee. He did not know what this was all about and there was a question in his mind as to whether Comstock's fear were real or fancied; there was no doubt, however, about the man's sincerity. He was afraid of something and he had hired Morley to stand guard tonight. In his own mind he was up against something big and needed help. If he, Kenyon, could do anything to make it easier, to pay off in this way for the fraud he was living, he would be glad. "Yes," he said. "Sure, I'll stay."

"You will? You promise?" Comstock rose quickly, eyes shining and new vigor in his face. "I knew you would."

"Until this—whatever it is—is over," Kenyon said.

"I understand." Comstock stopped at the door, smile fading. "But there's one other thing. If anything should happen to me, you'll have to carry on alone."

Kenyon put on a grin. "I don't imagine anything—"

"Probably not. I just wanted to make sure you understood." Comstock put a hand on Kenyon's shoulder and looked right at him. "But if anything should, it might also touch Sally. It'll be your job to see that no harm comes to her. I know I can depend on you."

Chapter Seven

YOUNG WIDOW WITH PLANS

NORA COMSTOCK was reclining on a chaise longue doing things to her nails with a brush and liquid polish when Kenyon knocked at the bathroom door and stuck his head around the corner. She wore a black chiffon negligee and under it a tea-rose nightgown, and when she saw him she reached down and flipped the negligee skirt about her crossed ankles.

"Come in," she said. "I've been expecting you."

Kenyon advanced slowly, assured by her smile and deciding that her hair was not red but auburn, though with more red than brown in it.

"Sit down," she said, indicating a chair; "unless you've got a drink in your room you could bring in."

"I could get one," Kenyon said.

"That would be fine."

He went through his room and down the hall to the living-room. There was no one here, but the tray remained, and enough ice to make two drinks. Nora had finished with the nail polish and was blowing on her fingers.

"Ahh," she said gratefully, and took a long swallow.

Kenyon sat down. He put his elbows on his knees, leaning forward with the glass in both hands. She smiled at him and he saw it was a pretty nice smile. Her teeth were good and so was her skin, which seemed very white and delicate in contrast to the dark red mouth.

"Now," she said, "tell me about it, Joey."

He angled a brow at her. "Tony."

"I always called him Joey."

"Well, anyway, thanks for the lift. Why did you do it?"

She lifted one shoulder. "You gave me my cue. I knew

you weren't Joey, but I could see the rest of them thought you were."

She hesitated, studying him openly. Ever since she had come to her room she had been asking herself just why she had not exposed him. In that first instant when she saw him coming toward her she had been too utterly astounded to do more than stare. She had been prepared for almost anything but this, and then when he spoke, begging with his eyes for co-operation, she had been both intrigued by the situation and attracted by the man himself.

He was, she decided now, better looking than Joey. He was taller, straighter, with an air of muscular fitness and a way of wearing his clothes that impressed her. His hands, she noticed, were well cared for, and he was scrupulously clean. She liked his smile and there was just enough embarrassment and uncertainty in his manner to reassure her about other things. This was an impostor, but an interesting one. There was nothing brazen about his attitude, no hardness in his eyes; rather there was a shyness and something that seemed to her like shame, and all these things served only to make his impersonation more intriguing. She put some of her thoughts into words.

"I just couldn't figure it at all. I knew I could expose you whenever I liked and I also knew that once I had it would be too late to be sorry for it." She smiled. "Or maybe I'm putting it badly."

"No, you're not." Kenyon sighed, and sipped his drink. "You merely decided to wait and see what the score was before upsetting the applecart."

"Yes."

"And that sort of means you weren't sure what you were going to get out of this trip, either."

"Not only that," she said. "I don't know yet. You're not Joey—"

"But you're his wife."

She eyed him coldly for a moment and then something tugged at the corners of her mouth and the coldness went away. She stood up, twitching the negligee about her, and went to the dresser. When she had opened her purse she took out a sheet of paper and gave it to him. He unfolded it and saw it was a marriage certificate dated two years before.

"Have you anything that does as much for you?" she asked. "It looks like they've accepted you for now, but—"

"I've some things in my room."

Kenyon went through the bathroom and not until he opened his bag did he see that she had followed him. He showed her the birth certificate, letter, and locket.

"I've seen the locket," she said. "Where did you get them?"

He put them back and she started toward her room. He went in with her and closed the door, knowing now that he would have to tell her the whole thing, but no longer quite so worried about it. In some curious way he could not analyze, she inspired confidence. He did not think she would give him away. He had an idea she had come here to do a little promotion work of her own and so long as he did not interfere he thought she would let him carry out Morley's plan. The thing to do was to convince her that by doing so he would not spoil her own routine—whatever that was.

"I'll tell you," he said, "if you'll tell me why you came?"

"It's a deal." She finished her drink and sat down.

Kenyon started at the beginning and told her the whole thing, omitting only the part about Comstock's fears and the incident of the prowler searching the bedroom. It took him perhaps five minutes and not once did Nora move anything but her eyes. When he finished they held a curious blending of amazement and respect.

"Well," she said, blowing out her breath, "is that something? So Morley was the one who took care of the burial?"

"You knew about it?"

"I knew something about it."

"Anyway, that's it. Tomorrow he'll collect the check and the next day I'm on my way."

She sent her eyes up at him, speculating. "And what happens to me?"

Kenyon grinned at her. "That depends on what you wanted to happen in the first place."

"Yes." She glanced at her fingernails, wrinkling her smooth white brow. "Doesn't it?" She stood up and walked over to the door, holding the negligee more tightly about her waist. She turned, still frowning, finally looked at him and smiled.

"All right," she said. "Since we're letting our hair down you can listen awhile and then we'll see where we are. You've probably already got the idea that I wasn't brought up in a convent or educated at Vassar. I wasn't. I was brought up in a Massachusetts mill town and I learned very young that life is not always kind and good. If I ever had any illusions I've forgotten what they were about, because the way it seemed to me was that if you didn't look out for yourself and get what you could, no one would be likely to do it for you. I was born on the wrong side of town and grew up in a dismal little cottage that was never warm enough in winter and not always dry when it rained."

She leaned back against the wall, arms still folded and her smile a little bitter.

"Even now it's hard to remember much about my father. I suppose he did the best he could, and if he got drunk too often I guess he had a good reason. There were four of us kids and I was the youngest, though not by much, and my mother died when I was pretty small, so when it got time to run away I guess it didn't matter to anyone but me. I was fifteen then. I'd finished two years of high school and had worked evenings to pay for some tap-dancing lessons, and I had a few dollars hidden away so I'd be ready when the time came."

She laughed abruptly, no longer looking at him. "There was another girl. Her name was Callahan and she lived on the street in back of ours. She'd had about the same sort of life and the same sort of ideas and it gave us courage to know that there would be two of us going instead of one. Well, we hitchhiked to New York one Saturday morning and I've never been home since. I don't even know what happened to my girl friend. She got work first—behind a counter in an uptown dime store—but I looked older than I was and I had nerve and a figure that had matured early. I wanted to dance but I hadn't had any experience. At that I was lucky. I got a job as a cigarette girl in a hole-in-the-wall night club down on Ninth Street. The Montmartre, they called it. It was a dump. But not to me. Oh, no. It was the stuff dreams are made of—glamorous and exciting and a little mysterious.

"Of course it was a living, too. They put me in tights up to here and a tight black jacket, and that was all right with me. I had what it took, and I knew I looked well and after the first night I forgot to be modest. I did all right."

She pushed away from the wall, still clinging to the negligee, and Kenyon could see what she meant. The trailing skirt covered her ankles but it outlined revealingly the lines of her body. She was tall for a woman, and she had a sort of rounded, full-blown torso that would have delighted Maillol.

"I don't want to bore you with details," she said. "I married Joe Comstock two years ago when I was dancing in a night-club line and he was playing the sliphorn in the orchestra. Right after that I had a chance to do some modeling and I took it. I liked it better than anything I'd ever done and I learned some things I should have learned a long time ago. I got so I could walk right and wear clothes the way they should be worn. I learned to talk—when I put my mind to it—and I made enough money to get by.

"The only thing was, our marriage didn't go so good. We didn't hit it off at all. I was working days then and Joe was out most of the night and"—she tossed one hand and let it fall—"well, to cut it short, one day he just up and left. I never saw him again."

Kenyon waited. When she did not continue he prompted her.

"Then how did you know he was dead?"

She walked toward him, saw his glass on the table. There was an inch or so of drink remaining and she finished it.

"I had a chance to go to Hollywood with some other models. It was only a couple weeks' work and expenses but it looked like the only chance I'd ever have of seeing the place so I took it. We were supposed to provide the atmosphere for some picture about a fashion photographer. It was fun, too, but when it was over that was all for little Nora. I had carfare back to New York and a few new rags and that's all. So that's how I happened to look up Joe—or try to. I'd heard he was playing somewhere on the coast, and then I ran into a trumpet player I once knew, on the studio lot. That was only about three days or so after Joe was killed. He told me about it, and how some fellow—some member of the family, he said—claimed the body and arranged for burial. That was your pal, Morley."

"Yes," Kenyon said. "It must have been."

"So that's when I got the idea."

"You knew Comstock was rich?"

"I spent most of the year I lived with Joe telling him he was a dope not to go back. He told me about the letter his father had written some years before and how he could inherit half the estate but—well, he'd made up his mind and that was that. Now he was dead. And I got to thinking about it. Where did I come in? I was his wife. His old man was rich. I didn't have anything else to do."

Kenyon got up and stretched. Her eyes followed him, a

suggestion of a smile lurking behind the mascaraed lashes, and he decided that he liked her. Her acid self-reliance intrigued him and he believed what she had told him. He liked the way her auburn hair swept up from her neck, the way she looked at him. Maybe she was a little obvious, but she was a good-looking woman and he had the idea that if she liked a person she would go all the way for him. She'd long ago made up her mind that no one was going to give her anything for nothing and she had come here simply on the chance that she might be better off doing so.

"I get it," he said. "If the old man liked you—"

"Why not?"

"Were you going to tell him Joe was dead?"

"I don't know what I was going to tell him. I wanted to see what the old man was like. I could be the perfect picture of a deserted wife throwing herself upon the family's mercy or, if it seemed better, the widow."

"Either way you hoped to be taken care of?"

She folded her arms, her smile challenging. "One way or another."

He buttoned his coat and then a very obvious thought that had somehow escaped him struck hard and he stood still.

"But if you wait for me to clear out—I mean, how can you say you're a widow now?"

"I wondered when you'd get around to that." She leaned back and clasped her hands behind her neck. Her skirt fell fell away from her nightgown and calves but she did not bother with it. "If I'm going to act the widow I've got to tell the truth now. Tonight. It isn't too late because I can say I played along to find out what the game was. But if I wait—" She paused, inspecting him. "Have you got any money?"

"No."

"You could ask for some."

Kenyon started to deny this and then he remembered

the five hundred Comstock had given him that afternoon.
He made his eyes narrow and put his fists on his hips.

"I'm listening."

"Sometimes it's better to have a little and be sure of it
than get big ideas and wind up with nothing but the ideas.
If I keep my mouth shut you say you'll walk out in a couple
of days. I'll be the deserted wife again. Probably Comstock
will feel sorry for me—I hope—and that may be all right.
On the other hand, if I expose you maybe he'll be just as
grateful, and then again, maybe he won't. Maybe he'll be
so disgusted with the whole thing that he'll—"

She broke off and sat up, watching Kenyon pull some
bills from his pocket. He fanned them out, the five new
hundred-dollar bills. He stepped over and dropped them
in her lap.

"Let's get it straight," he said. "That's all I've got and
that's all I'll be getting until Morley pays off. I didn't come
here to chisel from Comstock and I don't intend to. I
agreed to put on an act but no one says I have to like it.
Only that's all, whichever way you play it."

She had been folding the bills as he spoke; now she
looked him over coolly, rose, and put the money in her
purse.

"All right," she said. "Maybe I'm crazy but somehow
I believe you."

He watched her, not sure he understood.

"Well, which way is it?"

"Your way. It can't make any difference to Comstock.
He'll think his son's been with him a few days, which
is better than never having seen him at all. It doesn't make
any difference to me." She laughed, a soft but somehow
derisive sound. "I'll be getting board and room and even
if the five is all I get I'll be better off than when I came."

She came over and slid her arm through his. She turned
him toward the bathroom door, opened it. "I can think of
worse things than pretending you're my husband for a few

days, and in a way the old man is getting a break. From what little I've seen, you're a nicer sort of guy than Joey ever was. The only funny part of this whole business is how you let yourself get mixed up in it in the first place."

He hadn't expected anything like this from her and it embarrassed him. Before he could reply she had given his hand a pat and started to close the door, still smiling, and with some deep-down look of understanding he had never seen before.

"Good night," she said. "Nora has to get her beauty sleep."

In his own room, he shut the door and took the chair by the windows, staring out into the darkness, seeing nothing. So she thought he was a nice guy? She should have met him four days ago, or last month. She wouldn't have wasted a second look at him, and she would have been right. By her own admission she was not quite the person she led Comstock and the others to believe, but at least she was honest with herself.

He could understand her asking for money. That, after all, was what she had come for; what she had been struggling for since she was fifteen. Now she was out to better herself if she could, and he had paid her for services rendered—with Comstock's money. The thought of this filled him with a sense of loathing. Only luck, an incredible luck in the form of Nora's own attitude, had saved him from exposure, and he could no longer blame Morley for anything. Morley, like Nora, was out for what he could get and made no attempt to disguise his motive. He had no compunctions about what he was doing; if he had resorted to trickery and unscrupulous tactics he still could see no harm in the plan.

But then, in Morley's case there was no Sally Hayden. With Kenyon it all came back to that. He could not forget what had happened on the terrace earlier. In fancy he could feel her in his arms, the sweet pressure of her lips, and always, when he closed his eyes, she was there, slim and dark and vital, her gay laughter ringing in his ears.

He heard a car coming up the driveway and saw the reflection of its lights. The sight of something tangible helped him to think reasonably. Two days more and then he could go. Unless the promise to Comstock should delay him. And that would not be for long. That was the thing to think about; that and the hope that some day he could forget these days and perhaps feel clean again.

He was still sitting there when he heard footsteps in the hall and the sound of his door opening. Morley's blocky figure paused on the threshold. He had a small bag in his hand, and though his face was in shadow there was a suggested urgency in the thrust of his neck.

"What about her? Okay?"

"Okay."

"How much does she know?" He moved forward a step, keeping his voice low.

"Everything," Kenyon said, and suddenly he found himself too weary to explain. There was no point in mentioning the money, no point in anything. "She's not going to bother us. She's got plans of her own."

"I thought she would have. . . . Well, be seeing you," Morley said, and backed out.

Chapter Eight

A POLICE CASE

IT WAS SOME MINUTES before Tony Kenyon found the strength to haul himself out of the chair. He was trying desperately not to think at all and he moved slowly as he removed his coat and vest, knowing that what he wanted most to do was to go find a bottle of whisky and get drunk. That he did not follow up the idea was due mostly to stubbornness and a certain perverse pleasure he found in denying himself this relief.

He sat on the bed to take off his shoes and remained there until he remembered to continue his undressing. He slipped off his shirt and tossed it in the bag on the luggage rack. He got rid of his undershirt and was standing in front of the chest when he heard a faint knock on the door. Not turning, but seeing the door in reverse in the mirror, he watched the knob move and the panel swing inward; then a bathrobe-clad figure moved forward and Kenyon saw it was Comstock.

"Saw the light under the door, Tony."

Kenyon did not look round but grinned into the mirror as best he could. "I was just going to bed."

"I came up to—well, just wanted to say good night."

"Good night," Kenyon said.

"In the morning—"

The next word never came. Kenyon was opening the traveling-kit on the chest. In the mirror he saw Comstock's mouth open and close, but he thought the other was feeling for whatever it was he was about to say, and looked at the kit again, dumping out toothbrush and paste. When he turned to wait for the rest of the sentence the door was closing and Comstock had gone.

The latch clicked into place and silence settled down again and Kenyon said, "What do you know about that?" softly, and ran his fingers through his hair. He stood that way, scowling at the door, until an answer came to him; then he knew that he had offended the old man by his lack of cordiality and that, sensing he wasn't wanted, Comstock had taken the easiest way out.

Telling himself it was just as well, Kenyon shrugged and went into the bathroom. The less cordial he was now the less Comstock would mind his going, and that was that. *You can be a heel for a couple more days, Tony,* he thought bitterly. *With you it shouldn't be any trouble at all.*

When he had finished in the bathroom he slid out of his trousers and shorts and tossed them on the chair. He got his pajamas on and slipped on his cotton robe and sat down on the bed, lighting a cigarette and staring morosely at the curling smoke. He was about to grind it out in the ash tray when for the third time he heard someone at the door. He sat waiting, seeing it open until Morley's head appeared round the corner.

"Why don't you go to bed?" he said good-naturedly.

"Why don't you?"

"I'm going," Morley said. "In a minute. The old guy's in bed so I sneaked out for a nightcap. How about you?"

Kenyon shook his head and said he guessed not.

"You know where there is any?"

"There are some decanters in the dining-room," Kenyon said, and snapped off the light.

Morley closed the door and Kenyon, remembering that he had not opened the windows, slipped off his robe and opened them. Presently, when he had stretched out again, he thought he heard Morley coming back along the hall.

Later, when asked how long the interval was between this and what happened next, he said about three minutes. That, he realized, was nothing but a guess. He made no

conscious effort to keep track of time. He remembered that
he had started to think again, that he had not closed his
eyes but was staring upward through the darkness. He
remembered also that the sharp explosion of sound made
him sit bolt upright, startling him in those first seconds
but otherwise meaning nothing.

It was not until he had slid from bed and stepped to the
window—for it was from this direction that the sound
apparently had come—that the overtones of the explosion
registered in his consciousness. Then, with shocking clarity, he knew he'd heard a shot, and he was standing rigidly
with the night breeze sliding up his shanks and something
cold and frightening coiling tightly about his heart.

He opened the window and leaned out. Except for the
study, the front windows of the house were all dark. There
was no other sound but his breathing and the pounding
of his heart, and he caught up his robe, went quickly to his
door and stepped out, scared now, moving automatically.

A night light burned dimly over the three stairs to the
study wing and he hurried to them and started down, the
tightness still about his heart and every nerve end tense.
At the study door he paused, realized he was hesitating,
and went in swiftly, saying, "Morley!"

The study looked different now. The divan had been
converted into a makeshift bed and Morley's clothes were
on the chairs and the remains of a drink stood on the desk.
Kenyon saw all that in the first instant, just as he saw that
the room was empty; then his heart stopped.

"Morley!" he said, his voice hoarse, "Morley!"

Only then did he think of Comstock and the reason for
Morley being here, and then fear streaked through him
and he leaped toward the open door of the bedroom
which had been partially hidden by an intervening chest.

Kenyon did not get far, and for a while he did not think
any more. He saw the sprawled figure on the threshold
and dropped to one knee, shaking a shoulder before he

remembered the light. He stumbled erect, kicking something hard as he stepped back to the switch. What he saw when the light came on was stamped so indelibly on his brain that years later he could remember each single detail of that first glance.

Morley lay on his face, his gun a foot or two from one outstretched hand and blood oozing from an ugly gash on the back of his skull. Near by—the thing he had kicked —was a bronze statuette, and on the bed—

He stepped to the foot of it before he realized it and when he saw what was there he grabbed the bedpost. For a moment he could only stare, incredulous, a sudden sickness rising inside. He took two or three fast breaths and fought the nausea; then the moment passed, and he made himself go on until he could look down at the still, pale figure with the wet red stain across its chest and side.

The covers had been thrown aside, as though Comstock had tried to get out of bed, and he lay at an angle, one foot dangling over the edge. Kenyon did not touch him. It was as though he knew instinctively that nothing so still and small and pitiful could any longer hold a spark of life. He was still standing there with his stomach knotted and the sickness starting all over again when the groan behind him gave him a chance to seek relief in action.

Morley, still face down, was trying to push up from the floor. Kenyon went to him and helped him turn so he could sit up. He got an arm about his shoulders and steadied him, taking the handkerchief from his robe pocket and holding it to the gash on the back of Morley's head.

"Take it easy."

"I'm all right," the detective said thickly. "Just give me a second or two."

"Hold this," Kenyon said, and guided Morley's hand to the handkerchief. He picked up the statuette and put it on the table; he took the gun too, slipping in in his pocket.

"What happened? Can you stand?"

He gave the detective a hand and Morley stood swaying on his feet, and then, suddenly, he jerked free and his face contorted. "Comstock!" he said wildly, and stepped to the bed. For a second or two he was silent while he lifted a limp wrist and felt for a pulse; then he was cursing with a vicious and horrible intensity, not moving, just standing there with his face chalky and knotted into a mean, hard mask.

He stopped as suddenly as he began, stepped to the window, which was open as it had been when Kenyon had been surprised earlier. He came back, his eyes hot and bright and looking in all directions at once. When he spoke his voice was still savage but controlled.

"How did you get here?"

"I heard the shot."

"Shot?" Morley squinted at him suspiciously. "Where's my gun? I had it when I—"

"Here," Kenyon said, producing it.

It was a short-barreled revolver and Morley flipped out the cylinder. There were six cartridges and one bore the imprint of a firing pin.

"Oh," Morley said slowly. "Must have gone off when I fell." He put the gun in the pocket of his robe. "What did he hit me with?"

Kenyon indicated the statuette and Morley glared at him.

"Was it there?"

"No. On the floor."

"And you picked it up? Oh, swell. If there were any prints—well, it doesn't matter now. If there were you've gummed them." He started to pick up the statuette, noticed Kenyon's bloody handkerchief in his hand and pressed it to the back of his head. "Here," he said, giving it back, and looked at the bronze figure.

It was a nude about fourteen inches high, mounted on

a round base with a sharp edge. Morley put it back and
went into the study. He passed his hand across his eyes and
shook his head as though to clear it. There was a swallow
or so of drink remaining in his glass and he finished it.

"Well," he said, his voice no longer savage, "it's a police
case now and we're in it up to our ears. I'd better get at
it." He picked up the telephone, nodding at the glass
before he gave his number. "See if you can get me a refill.
. . . Better bring the bottle; you look as if you needed one
yourself."

Chapter Nine

POWDER KEG FOR TWO

LIEUTENANT NASH, of the Kingsford police, was a chunky, sandy-haired man with a ruddy complexion and a slow, deliberate way of speaking. Arriving with three men within fifteen minutes after Morley had called, he had spent most of this time in the bedroom with the medical examiner; now, coming out with the doctor, he closed the door behind him and spoke to Morley.

"You'd better let the doc fix up that cut."

"It'll be all right," Morley said.

"Let's have a look, anyway," the doctor said, and led him to a chair in the corner.

The rest of them sat and stood around, waiting for Nash to say what he had to say. The blanket on the makeshift bed had been pulled up and Marion and Nora sat there in nightclothes and robes, both smoking nervously. Paul Sherman, what hair he had tousled, sat on the edge of the desk, face pale and more worried-looking than ever; Carl had a drink in his hand and his hair was still smooth and he did not look as if he had been to bed at all. Kenyon leaned against the wall, watching Morley and trying not to think.

"How long were you out of the room?" Nash said finally.

Morley sat on the arm of the chair, his chin on his chest so the doctor could work on the back of his head. The position made his voice thick and muffled.

"Three or four minutes. Maybe five. I found some liquor in the dining-room but I had to look around for a glass. Got one in the pantry."

"And how long had Comstock been in bed? How long since he had gone in and closed the door?"

"Fifteen minutes maybe. Could have been longer, I guess."

A heavy-set, gray-haired man with a cigar between his fingers and an Elk's tooth on his watch chain came in from the hall.

"They don't know a thing," he said, and Kenyon knew he was referring to the servants. "They all sleep in the other wing."

"All right, Sergeant," Nash said, and jerked his thumb toward the bedroom. "Keep looking for the knife."

"Did you find a letter opener?" Marion Sherman asked.

Sergeant Bauer stopped with his hand on the knob, looking at Nash. He shook his head.

"No," Nash said.

"He had one," Marion said. "I saw it tonight when we were all in there before. It was on the bedside table."

Nash said, "Umm," and Bauer went into the bedroom.

"There," the doctor said. He had cut the hair away from the gash and applied a dressing. "That should do it. You're lucky he didn't connect squarely."

"I guess I'd started to duck," Morley said. He rose and flexed his shoulders, his face grim and ugly lights in his eyes. "I guess I sensed what was coming."

"I think," Nash said, pushing out his lips, "I think we'd better make a session of this. Time is an important factor in any murder case; it is particularly important in one like this. It may take a while. If you want to get some clothes on—" He glanced at Kenyon. "Perhaps we could use some other room."

"That would help." Marion rose and folded her arms across her breasts as though she were cold. She looked thinner than ever now and her face seemed all angles.

"One thing more," Nash said. "Was there anyone else here tonight—earlier?"

"Yes," Paul Sherman said, and spoke of Spence Arden and Sally.

"It might be a good idea to have them come over."

"Arden will be over, anyway. I've already phoned him."

"Oh?"

Paul colored. "You don't expect to keep this out of the newspapers, do you?"

"And the other one, this Miss Hayden?" Nash said.

"Surely you don't want us to call her now," Marion said.

Nash looked at her, spoke patiently. "I think she should be notified. We can't make her come, under the circumstances. But if you phoned and told her what had happened and said that if she felt up to it we'd like to—"

"Oh, all right," Marion said petulantly, and went out.

Tony Kenyon did not start to dress right away. He stood at the window of his room, looking out, seeing nothing. He was still sick with the shock of it all and he could not shut out the picture of Comstock lying there on the bed. Only within the past few minutes had he begun to consider his own position, and the more he understood, the more he realized what it meant, the blacker his despair became.

The soft knocking at the door came to him as in a dream and he called, "Come in," without turning round. He heard the door open. When it did not close he glanced over his shoulder and saw Nora at the bathroom door, her hand still on the knob.

She wore the black negligee and mules, but this was a different Nora. Her auburn hair was pinned up, and since he had talked with her an hour before the make-up had gone from her face and her eyes were devoid of shadow and mascara. All this would have made her look younger had it not been for the pallor in her cheeks and the pinched lines about her mouth.

"What are you going to do?" she said, her voice a husky whisper.

Kenyon looked at her, not knowing what she meant.

"You know what this means, don't you?" She took a step and stopped.

"It means someone murdered him."

"No." She shook her head. "That isn't what I mean. Whatever he left to his son, you'll get. Joey once told me that he had been promised half of the estate if only he would come back. Suppose that—"

She stiffened visibly as the hall door opened. Morley came in with a rush and when he saw her he stopped suddenly.

"Sorry," he said. "I didn't know—"

He started to back out. "It's all right," Nora said. "I should be getting dressed, anyway." She glanced at Kenyon, her eyes eloquent in some appeal he could not analyze; then she had slipped into the bathroom and closed the door.

Morley's narrowed gaze slid to Kenyon and back to the door. He moved up to it quietly, listened, opened it a crack and glanced inside. He closed it just as quietly.

"What did she want?"

"I don't know."

"No?"

"She didn't have time to say. She had only just come in."

Morley rubbed his chin. He had on trousers and shirt under his robe now, and slippers on his feet. His thinning hair was combed, and viewed from the front there was no evidence that he had been hurt.

"We play this just the same as before."

"No." Kenyon had a hard time keeping his voice down. "Not now, we don't. I'm telling the truth."

"Like hell you are!"

"You think I'm not?"

"I think you're out of your mind."

"But—"

"But, hell! Can't you see where you stand? Even as the son you're bound to come under suspicion. Where do you think you'd be if they found out you were a phony?"

Kenyon stared, grappling with Morley's question and getting nowhere.

"Why should they suspect me?" he asked. "It was an outsider, wasn't it? The same one that was in the room before?"

"Who knows? And what do you mean by an outsider? Somebody came through a window—unless he sneaked in the other way while I was getting the drink—and anybody in the house could have done the same thing." He jabbed with his index finger. "I'm not saying anyone did. It looks like an outside job and the cops are going to think so—at first. But until they *find* that outsider they're going to consider every damned one of us."

Kenyon wanted to sit down. He wanted a chance to think the thing out for himself.

"We can't get away with it," he said tonelessly. "They'll check back on me now."

"Not if you satisfy them in the beginning. Convince 'em once and you're set. So far you've got by at face value, but now it'll be different. And that's what you've got those credentials for. . . . You've got them here, haven't you?"

"Certainly."

"That's all you'll need—that and a little guts. You've got an old birth certificate, a letter from the old man, and a locket your mother had. That's proof enough for anyone. And listen"—he paused as Kenyon started toward his bag on the luggage rack—"if they don't ask you for any identification I think it would be a good idea to offer it. Think of some good approach and flash those things before anyone gets thinking about other possibilities. Give 'em a chance to ask but if they don't—"

Kenyon never heard the last few things Morley said. He had opened the bag automatically as the detective made his suggestions, had lifted the soiled shirt he had tossed there earlier, and then, in that same instant that his eyes

focused, his heart stopped and his blood turned to ice.
For there in the bottom of the bag, next to the letter and
the locket and the birth certificate, was a red-stained handkerchief; protruding from it was the roughly hammered
bronze handle of the letter opener.

As though from a long way off, he heard the drone of
Morley's voice. He was vaguely conscious of the ensuing
silence, of some movement beside him; then he was fighting desperately to break the grip of fear and dismay that
had struck him rigid and breathless.

He felt himself shouldered aside, and saw Morley look
into the bag, heard him suck in his breath. He saw his
hand dart inside the bag and close upon the handkerchief
and hold it up, the knife handle still protruding, and still
he could not make himself believe it, nor find an explanation.

Morley grabbed a shoulder, his voice savage. "Well?"

Kenyon found an unrecognizable whisper deep in his
throat. "No," he said. "No, I tell you."

He had his breath back now and the stiffness was gone,
and all over his body the sweat pores were opening. His
shoulder ached and he wrenched it free.

"I didn't put it there. You've got to believe me, Morley!"

Morley unwrapped the handkerchief, and the thin blade
gleamed in the lamplight. The handkerchief fluttered
open except for the matted and dried center, and at one
corner the letters JC had been initialed. Morley looked
at them a long while and when he raised his head his
amber eyes were cold and cruel.

Then, suddenly, a change came over Kenyon and he
made no other protest. It was as though he had expected
something like this from the very beginning and now that
it had come there was nothing left with which to fight.

"All right," he said. "Think what you want to."

What happened then lived afterward in Kenyon's memory. There was no warning, no time to prepare himself

for what was to follow. One moment he was watching
Morley, waiting to see what he intended to do; in the next,
the silence and his new-found resignation were shattered
by a loud knock on the door, and instant panic was upon
him, freezing him to immobility and helplessness. For
what seemed like minutes he looked at the knife and handkerchief, knowing there was nothing he could do. Vaguely,
he heard Morley grunt, and pulled his eyes from the knife;
then, standing stock-still, he saw the other's head jerk
about and something come to life in the tight hard face.

Then Morley moved. He had been standing near the
window and now he whirled and took one step, covering
the knife blade with the handkerchief in a quick, wiping
stroke. Leaning out, still holding the knife in handker-
chief-covered fingers, he threw it away, not straight out,
but nearly parallel with the line of the house. Then, with
a continuation of the same movement, he slid the bloody
handkerchief inside his shirt and called:

"Come in."

Sergeant Bauer entered with a plain-clothes man. He
looked over the room casually and brought his glance back
to Kenyon. "You ought to be gettin' dressed," he said.
"Unless you want to sit around that way."

Kenyon beat back his lingering incredulity. By swallow-
ing he found he could speak. "Right away," he said. "We
got to talking and—"

He made no attempt to finish the sentence. His voice
did not sound right to him and his hands were damp and
trembling. He moved over to the bed like a man in a
trance, slipping off his robe.

"Thought we'd have a look around," Bauer said. "Take
the bath, Tom—if that's where that door goes."

The plain-clothes man started for the door.

"That's where it goes," Morley said. "No knife?"

"No knife."

Kenyon dropped his robe at the foot of the bed and

pulled off his pajamas, watching Bauer open the drawers of the chest and look through the clothing folded there. He got into his shorts and shirt and then stopped to watch the sergeant opening the traveling-bag. He could see him reach down, as though examining what was inside, then straighten and lower the lid.

"This ain't going to look so good for you, is it?" he said, glancing at Morley.

Morley's face was still grim. His voice got flat and remote.

"It can be made to look better."

Bauer examined his half-consumed cigar, now out. He took a match and brushed ashes into a wastebasket.

"Yeah?"

"If I help nail the guy that did it."

"That would help," Bauer said, striking a light. "That would help a lot."

He went on with his inspection. Kenyon tried to read Morley's face. He might as well have tried to read a mask. The detective had leaned against a wall, his hands thrust in his pockets. Without appearing to, he was watching every move that Bauer made.

The plain-clothes man came out of the bathroom. "Nothing there," he said.

"Maybe Morley'll let you frisk him," Bauer said.

"Maybe Morley won't," Morley said.

"What is it with you private snoops?" he said, sounding as though he did not especially care. "Always hard to get along with. Or maybe you're the sensitive type."

"Maybe I don't like insinuations from cops."

"I've heard that before too," Bauer said. "Maybe Mr. Comstock won't mind," he said, and was already going through Kenyon's coat and vest.

Kenyon felt a lot better now. He had his confidence back for the moment and he could breathe again and act as if nothing Bauer did could matter.

"The pants?" he asked.

Bauer looked at him, practically undressing him with his eyes. "No, I guess not," he said. "Okay, Tom." He ordered the plain-clothes man out with a jerk of his head and then, passing the bed, picked up Kenyon's robe and felt of the pockets. He had the bloody handkerchief out before Kenyon remembered it was there.

"Looks like blood."

Bauer's tone was the same but under his bushy brows his little eyes were suddenly bright and cold.

"It is," Kenyon said.

"From the back of my head." Morley pointed to the dressing on his head. "He found me, remember? That's what he used to stop the bleeding."

"Oh," Bauer said, a note of disappointment in his voice. "Well, I'll take it along anyway. Okay? . . . And snap it up, will you, Mr. Comstock? The lieutenant's waiting."

Morley moved as the door closed, stepping to the panel and listening before he turned to Kenyon.

"I'm in this thing now, and I'm staying in."

"I didn't kill him," Kenyon said.

"I'll string along with that until I find out different." Morley pulled the bloody handkerchief from under his shirt, folded it, and put it in his left hip pocket. "I don't think you'd be dope enough to hide that knife where you did. But that wouldn't help your neck any if Bauer'd come a little sooner."

"But who—"

"Never mind who, now. Someone did. Either because he wanted to frame you—and that would mean somebody in the house—or if it was an outsider, he just stepped through the window, not knowing whose room it was, and left it as a red herring. But the point is this: Comstock's son was known to have hated him for years—motive number one. If it happens that he's left you a lot of jack—"

"But I'm not the son and if I tell them so now—"

"Look." Morley became elaborately patient. "We've got to go see the lieutenant. If you still don't know why you're in a worse spot being a phony than you would being the real son I'll explain it to you when the police go. Just remember this. You're the son and you're going to stay the son until I get my ten grand."

He cursed under his breath, stepped back. "If I'd been paid this morning like I should have been, I'd've been gone now. I'd've cashed the check this afternoon and been on my way. I'd have my dough and I wouldn't be in the spot I'm in now. A private dick letting a client get killed right under his nose! How do you like that? What does that make me? How do you think it's going to read in the paper?"

"But you'll get your money, Morley," Kenyon said. "The check—"

"I'll get it if you don't crab it for me, yes. But when? Hell, in a case like this the bank freezes an account until they get authority to pay off. Maybe the lawyer'll be reasonable and maybe I'll have to get a court order."

His face was white and stiff as he reached for the doorknob. "Come on, let's get this over with. You're sitting on a powder keg now—and so am I. But it's not going off if you keep your nerve. It's not going off at all until I've got the killer—or someone has—because that's the only thing that will really pull us out. . . . Come on."

Chapter Ten

MOTIVES FOR MURDER

KENYON COULD HEAR Lieutenant Nash talking as he approached the drawing-room with Morley, and guessed that the questioning had been going on for some time. Nash, standing in front of the fireplace, stopped as they went in, and then Kenyon saw Sally Hayden.

She was one of the four sitting on the divan and next to her was Spencer Arden. She wore a plain, dark woolen dress and a coat had been thrown about her shoulders and Arden's arm was holding it there. She had her head back against his arm and she looked white and sick. Kenyon could tell she had been crying, and when he entered her glance slid past him as though he was someone she had never seen before.

He heard Nash ask him to sit down and took a straight-backed chair just inside the doorway. Then Nash started to question Morley and Kenyon knew vaguely that the questioning finally centered on the story Comstock had told them earlier about the attempt on his life. He did not follow it closely. There was too much weariness inside his head just then and he sat relaxed and motionless, glancing at the others, inspecting each in turn.

Paul and Marion Sherman were on the divan with Arden and Sally. Nora, in a quilted housecoat now, sat in an overstuffed chair, and Carl, in slacks and sweater and looking sleeker than ever, sat on the arm, his fingers resting lightly on her shoulder. Nora had a wadded handkerchief in her hand and looked very tragic with her big eyes and faraway look. With her, Kenyon decided, it was acting; with Sally it was the real thing, and what he saw in her face served only to increase his despondency and hopelessness. He brought his attention back to Nash and kept it there.

"It could have been his imagination," he was saying.

"On the contrary," Spencer Arden said, "I got the same impression Andy did."

"You did," Nash said, accenting the *you*. "How did you—"

"I saw it—or part of it. I was just coming out of the building when I saw the car swerve." Arden paused, watching Nash. "I don't say it was deliberate because I don't know what happened before, but I did see it swerve. By the time I could move, Andy was already chasing it."

"You caught up to him?"

"He stopped at the corner. He was pretty scared then— and so was I, for that matter—and asked me if I saw it and I said I did. But when I started to question him, he shut me up. Said nothing could be done now and asked me not to mention it."

Nash put one elbow on the mantelpiece. He kept looking at Arden, though more absently than not, and so did Kenyon, finding him a tanned, blond man of about his own age, with a tweedy, pipe-smoking look about him and regular, handsome features, no longer bland and grinning but sober and worried.

"It's been done before," Nash said. "It's a form of murder that happens more often than we know. But this thing —I don't know. Generally it happens at night. If the victim survives he sees nothing. And generally it's in a spot where the killer can get out and find out if the guy is dead —just hitting him doesn't always do it—and if he isn't, he runs over him again."

"How ghastly," someone said, and Kenyon saw it was Marion Sherman. She was wearing slacks and a pull-over and cardigan. She was sitting on her feet, and her angular face was slack and gray.

"Yeah," Nash said. "That's why I wonder about this

one. It doesn't look so much like murder as it does an attempt to put him out of the way. Murder could result —a man of his age—but it looks as if the idea was to clip him and put him in the hospital. However"—his glance came over to Kenyon—"that's only a guess. What about this prowler?"

Kenyon repeated the story he had originally told and Nash nodded and sucked his lips and looked thoughtful.

"Hmm," he said when he had heard it all. "Well, I guess we can reconstruct what happened later." He looked at Morley. "You were already undressed when Mr. Comstock came up to say good night to this Mr. Comstock"—he indicated Kenyon—"and when he got back he went into the bedroom and shut the door. Then what?"

"I got in bed and turned out the light. But it was a strange bed and not very comfortable and it was fairly early. I knew I wasn't going to sleep right away and I got thinking about a drink. Finally I decided I'd get one. I got up and turned on the light and started out and then I thought I'd better tell Comstock in case he called."

"You didn't hear anything in the other room during this time?"

Morley thought this one over. "That depends on what you mean by hearing. I don't remember anything out of the ordinary—if I had I'd have investigated—but I did hear sounds, like a person moving about, a window opening, maybe a bed creaking."

"So?"

"So I rapped on the door and he said, 'Yes,' and I said, 'I'm going down the hall a minute; I'll be right back.' When he didn't answer I went along."

"You sure it was his voice?"

Morley grunted softly. "No. Not now, I'm not. I was then. It was just a voice, muffled by the door. If nothing had happened I'd swear it was his. Now I can't ever be sure."

"You went down the hall and stuck your head in Mr. Tony Comstock's room and asked him if he wanted a drink —and where you could find one. From that point until you got back to the study it was three or four minutes?"

"Just about."

"Then what?"

"I took a pull at the drink and lit a cigarette. Maybe I sat there a couple of minutes. I took some more of the drink and started to put the light out and then I thought maybe Comstock didn't hear me come back and that I ought to tell him. I stepped to the door and knocked and said, 'I'm back.'"

He paused and his voice got sardonic. "I've told you all this before and you can ask me from now until Christmas and I still won't be able to explain why I went in. Somebody said, 'All right, good night.' I don't know whether it was the voice I had heard before or not. Maybe it was different. Maybe that's what did it. Maybe it was because I'd been gone five minutes or so and wanted to be sure, and maybe I felt guilty about leaving him alone at all. I don't know. I'm a detective and some times in this racket you practically think with your instincts—"

"Yes," Nash said. "If you're any good you do."

"This was one of the times. I decided to be sure. My gun was on the desk and I picked it up and opened the door. I called to him and stepped in, and wham!" He flipped his hands apart. "That was it. I guess maybe there was an instant when I knew something was wrong because I must have tried to duck or else the guy's aim was poor. I know I didn't fire while I was conscious because I didn't have anything to aim at."

Morley found a pack of cigarettes in the pocket of his robe and took one. Nobody said anything for several seconds. Nash shifted his position at the mantel and ended up by putting his hands in his pockets. Carl Sherman tossed Morley a paper of matches and he got a light. It was then that Sergeant Bauer came in. When Kenyon saw he carried something in a handkerchief he felt the tension coming over him.

Bauer unwrapped the handkerchief and Nash glanced at the knife without touching it.

"Where'd you find it?"

"In some bushes a few feet from the house. Near the study windows."

"Oh?" Nash's brows drew down. He looked at the knife, finally tipped his head. "I thought you looked there before."

"Tom did. He must have missed it the first time."

Nash nodded and Kenyon waited, unable to find anything in the lieutenant's face or in his voice to indicate whether he believed this or not. He asked Bauer to see if any of them could identify it and Marion Sherman did so at once.

"It was on the bedside table when we were in there before."

Nash nodded to Bauer, who wrapped up the knife again, and then Hilton came in, pushing a tea wagon and looking as impeccable as ever.

Carl Sherman said, "Ahh," and slid off the chair arm. "Thank you, Hilton," Marion said, and then she was pouring coffee from a large percolator and asking about cream and sugar. With the coffee and the two plates of sandwiches, it was ten minutes or so before Nash could get back on the subject which interested him. He had coffee but refused a sandwich and smoked a cigarette and paced about, glancing covertly from face to face.

Kenyon was well aware of this inspection. He knew there were a lot of points about which Nash was not satisfied and he was not surprised when the lieutenant cleared his throat and gave him his attention.

"Sergeant Bauer tells me there were some things in your traveling-bag. A birth certificate and—"

"Yes," Kenyon said. He felt all right now that the knife business was past, and he knew how he was going to play the rest of it. For the next few minutes he was going to be Joseph Comstock, Junior, and he was going to convince Nash of that fact. "I must say I resent the interference but—"

"I know," Nash said dryly. "And you'll not be the only one." He glanced about, continued evenly. "There'll be others that do some resenting before I've finished, but unfortunately there isn't much we can do about it. This is murder. It's a thing the average person finds hard to imagine—outside of newspapers and books and the movies. You all know it happens but it's a tough thing to imagine happening to you or your family. I guess I know how you feel. I don't like it any better than you do and the more co-operative you are the sooner we can crack it—and the sooner you'll get rid of me. . . . Now, Mr. Comstock, if you don't mind—"

"Bauer can get them, can't he?" Kenyon said, pleased with the cool indifference he was able to simulate. "He knows where they are."

The sergeant went away without being told. Nash put his cigarette out and continued.

"On the face of it, it looks as though we have a murder pattern that points definitely to an outsider. The attempt this afternoon—real or imagined—the prowler in Mr. Comstock's bedroom, and then this other. The killer made a clean getaway and tossed the knife away as he ran. All right. That's the way it looks but it also could be *made* to look that way. We haven't much to go on. No description of the man, no witnesses. Maybe we'll find some fingerprints but I doubt it. There were a lot of smudges on the statuette"—he glanced at Morley—"but you've told us about those. I have an idea there won't be anything on the knife. The handle is too rough to take them and if the man was smart he probably wore gloves, anyway."

He paused as Bauer came in, took the articles from him and went on without looking at them.

"But"—he accented the word—"it's not a question of getting out the word to look for a killer as we are usually able to do, because in this case we don't know who we're looking for. That's why I'd like to get every bit of information I can. That's why I asked for these." He tapped the letter and birth certificate, continuing as he inspected them.

"No one here could possibly identify you, Mr. Comstock. After twenty-odd years you've come back to Kingsford."

"Now, wait a minute," Morley said.

Nash was imperturbable. "Go ahead," he said; "I guess you've got a right to be sore."

For a moment Morley's jaw was hard and ugly; in the next instant the grin came and he sat back.

"Okay," he said. "It's your job. If Comstock's a phony I'm probably guilty of complicity."

"Something like that." Nash started to put the papers and locket on the mantel. "There have been cases—but these are good enough for me." He nodded to Kenyon. "I was just trying to show you that I have to be careful."

"May I see the locket?" Sally Hayden was leaning forward on the divan. Nash gave her the locket, and when she opened it she said, "Andy used to carry a picture just like that in the back of his watch. I wondered if this would be the same one."

Nash came back to Kenyon. "You hated your father," he said bluntly.

Kenyon blinked. He started to protest, caught himself in time. "That's true. For many years I did."

"But Morley convinced you to come back."

"He said, ah—father was afraid he hadn't much longer to live. I—I finally agreed to see him."

"I see." Nash was very casual about it, all except his

eyes. They were not suspicious, but simply steady, prying, and shrewd. "But if you hated him that long, and you still hated him— What I mean is, hate makes a wonderful motive for murder."

Kenyon had to say something. He could feel them watching him.

"Well, you ought to know," he said, as though it did not matter.

"Furthermore, your father was a wealthy man. . . . Do you happen to know the provisions of the will, Mr. Sherman?"

Paul Sherman frowned. He took off his glasses and massaged the bridge of his nose with thumb and forefinger, glancing at his brother.

"You don't have to tell me now, of course," Nash said.

"What difference does it make?" Sherman shrugged. "As far as I know, Tony was to get half—after a bequest to Sally and various minor ones—and Carl and I shared the other half."

Kenyon sat very still, unable any longer to ignore the overwhelming weight of motive now presented. He heard Nash ask if the will was a recent one, heard Paul say that it was not.

"He made it four years ago. I don't think he changed it. The way it stood, Tony was to receive half if he could be found or appeared to claim it within one year from the date of Dad's death. Otherwise his share went to us."

"It makes a difference, doesn't it?" Nash said, and brought his gaze back to Kenyon. "I would be a pretty lousy police officer if I overlooked motives like that. And until I'm sure of where I stand I'll have to go right on digging up all the motives I can. . . . By the way, Mr. Sherman, you had some sort of an argument with Mr. Comstock this evening, didn't you? After that business of the prowler?"

For a moment Paul Sherman glared at Nash and his

cheekbones got white; then he put on his glasses and shook his head.

"Nothing of the kind."

"One of the servants says different."

Sherman lowered his eyes. When they moved up again they were defiant but no longer glaring.

"It was no argument. We were merely discussing business."

"Business?"

"Just that. We didn't always agree on the editorial policy of the paper. I ran a piece and he didn't like the tone of it."

"I see." Nash nodded and looked at Carl. "And you had a session too, didn't you? What was that about?"

Carl stood up and gave Nash a steady, ten-second look. "That, I'm afraid, is none of your business."

Nash's ruddy face got ruddier. "Maybe I can make it my business."

"You can try," Carl said. "But not now. Not any more tonight, you can't." He had a funny little smile on his mouth, but there was no humor in it and his round face did not look smooth and soft any more. "I'm going to bed. I think I've had enough."

"Carl," Sally said, trying to catch his eye.

"Someone who had been here before came back and killed Andy—either while Morley was in the next room or when he was out. You've practically admitted it and you've got the knife, and no amount of snooping into our personal affairs is going to change anything. Any time you and what's-his-name"—he jerked his head toward Bauer —"find out different you'll come back and say so. Until then—"

He stopped, watching Nora. She had risen while he spoke and had started toward the hall, walking slowly, head down. Carl took another look at Nash and went after her.

The others rose one by one and Nash, his cheeks flushed with resentment, blew out his breath and nodded to Bauer. Kenyon sat where he was for a while, watching Sally Hayden. Arden helped her with her coat and then turned to say something to Paul Sherman, and when Sally moved into the hall without so much as a glance at Kenyon, he got up and followed her.

"Sally."

She took another step and stopped, not turning around. She had her head down and was struggling with her gloves, and her dark hair all but hid her lovely profile.

He came up beside her, knowing what he wanted to say but not knowing how to do it. She looked so small and brave and miserable that he wanted to touch her and make her look at him so he could say something to comfort her, to tell her that everything would be all right. Then, thinking this, the bitterness came again. How could anything ever be all right again?

"Sally."

"Please, Tony. Not now."

"I'm sorry," he said, and then Arden was there taking her arm.

"Come on, angel," he said. "I know how it is, but you can't let it get you. I'll drive you over."

Chapter Eleven

Night Callers

Nora Comstock was sitting in the chair by the window smoking a cigarette when Tony got back to his room. She had her knees crossed, kicking her leg idly up and down; seeing her here now annoyed him.

"Couldn't it wait until morning?"

"Is that nice?" She stood up, mashing out her cigarette and coming toward him. "Well?"

"Well, what?"

"You heard what Paul said. Joey would have inherited half the estate, and now you're Joey."

He turned away and sat down on the bed. He put his elbows on his knees and the heels of his hands alongside his jaws, knowing what she meant and yet, for the moment, unable to think clearly about anything.

"And if I'm Joey's wife," she said presently, "and I am, you know—"

"If you're thinking about getting a cut—"

"Of course that's what I'm thinking. But that's not all. I'm scared. I don't know what this is all about. I thought I could play along and then after you'd gone the old boy would be sorry for me and probably I'd make out all right. But now he's dead and how much chance do you think I'd have of getting anything out of the rest of them? That's the only thing that stops me."

Kenyon looked up. "Stops you from what?"

"Stops me from telling the truth. That and the fact that I rather like you." She hesitated, dark eyes speculative. "You didn't kill him, did you? . . . All right." She spoke quickly when she saw his face darken. "I was just asking. The thing is, if I told the lieutenant you were an impostor, what do you think would happen to you?"

"I'd probably get pinched," Kenyon said morosely. "But that's all. I didn't kill Comstock and—"

"All right. But look." She folded her arms, pulling gently at her upper lip with thumb and forefinger. "I didn't tell the truth and I don't think I'm going to, because if I do that makes me a widow and then where am I? But with you it could be different. . . . Well, I guess that's all. I just wanted to tell you that I think you'd better keep right on playing Joey."

She slid her fingers along his jaw and patted it softly; then she turned and went out, her mules clopping and hips swinging.

Kenyon was still sitting on the bed when Morley came in. He had a full whisky bottle under his arm and a glass in his hand and he sat down wearily and stretched his legs.

"Those cops," he said disgustedly. "You know that bottle you brought to the study? Empty. Not a lousy drop. I got another. The way I feel, I need it. Get a glass."

"I don't want any."

"Nuts. Get a glass." He put the bottle and his own glass on the floor. When he came back from the bathroom he had another glass. He poured two drinks and handed one to Kenyon. "To crime," he said, and drank.

"Yeah," Kenyon said. "To a nice easy two-day job. Just pretend you're some other guy. There's no chance of anything going sour, no chance of going to jail. Hell, no! This is a cinch." He glanced up, his mouth twisted. "Well, how do you like it now?"

Morley watched him narrowly, shrugged. "Go ahead and beef," he said. "You've got a right, I guess—if it makes you feel any better. But don't get the idea I'm quitting. The thing curdled on us, that's all, and we've got to watch ourselves until we know what the score is." He studied his glass for some seconds, turning it in his hand. "Was that dame in again?" he said finally.

Kenyon took a swallow of whisky and said she was.

"I had an idea she would be," Morley said. "That's why I waited a while. What did she say?"

"She said I should go on being Joey Comstock."

Morley grinned. "She's no fool." He finished his drink and poured another; then he got out a cigarette and slid farther down in the chair. "She's all right, that Nora. She's good-looking and she's built and I'll bet she can multiply and add without any help. You know, I think I could go for her myself if I didn't have so damn much else on my mind."

Kenyon watched him moodily, saying nothing. For the first time since he'd known the man he could see the marks of fatigue on Morley's face. His hard, square jaw was relaxed and so was his body, and along with the wrinkles at the corners of his eyes were others underneath them. His smile came and went quickly as always, but now it seemed more genuine, as though there was no need to impress here and he could afford to be more human.

"She's got it figured, all right," he said. "If she squawks she gets nothing now and if she doesn't—"

"She's still got nothing, because I'm not going to be Joey."

"You are, until we nail this killer." Morley pulled himself a little higher in the chair. "Look. I'm going to draw you a diagram. You heard what Nash said about hate being a motive for murder?"

"But, damn it all, if I'm not the son there can't be any hate."

"Sure," Morley said. "But there's another motive. Murder for gain, or profit. It's the commonest of all, aside from crimes of passion. Ask Nash, ask anybody who knows. And in your spot, as a phony, that motive is a hundred percent stronger than if you really were the son. Listen."

He sat up a little more, folding his hands across his chest. "As the son, that motive isn't worth much because if the kid wanted money he could have had it any time he asked for it. He's been the heir for four years. He wanted none of it. But you—you know how it'll look, don't you? You're a friend of young Comstock's, say. He gets killed, and knowing about his old man it's a cinch for you to get the necessary identification and pass yourself off as the son. You come here and maybe there's a slip or something and you kill him to get the estate."

"But if I tell the truth," Kenyon argued, "then I'll get nothing and where's the motive?"

"Right where it was. Because here's what the cops will contend: that you hoped to get away with murder and collect as the son, that having bungled and being under pressure, you got scared. Now, rather than take a chance, you confess to the impersonation, hoping to throw them off, hoping to show them you had no motive. You see? The thing is exactly the same to them. Confess now, admit you are a phony, and you're worse off than before. If you had told the truth while the old man was alive, yes; but now—" Morley shook his head, his lips compressed. "Un-unh. It's too late. The motive was there at the time of his death, and that's what counts."

Kenyon put his glass aside. He took his time lighting a cigarette and spoke in measured tones.

"Maybe you're right. I see what you mean and I guess maybe the police would look at it that way—if it weren't for one thing. I didn't know young Comstock and it wasn't me that figured out the impersonation, but you. Maybe you've forgotten that."

Morley leaned back again. "No, I haven't forgotten. I've got myself in a sweet little mess but I haven't forgotten that." He was silent a moment, and seemed to be watching the smoke curl upward from Kenyon's cigarette. "Things have never been too easy for me. I was brought up in Brooklyn and my old man worked around the Bush Terminal and I kicked around with the other kids in the neighborhood. I got kicked around plenty too, not by them so much as by my old man. But my mother had courage and an idea and she worked on it until I finished high school. I might have been a bum at that if I hadn't had an uncle who was a cop. He helped out here and there and kept me out of trouble and fixed it up so I could take the police examinations.

"To make it short, I finally worked up to be detective, first grade, and maybe I'd still be at it if I hadn't got in a jam. I was tough and independent and I didn't care who you were if you got out of line. I plugged a kid in a stolen car when he tried to run me down and it turned out his old man was a little two-bit politician with friends and it wound up with me back in uniform. So I got out. I got a job with the Ames Agency and stuck it for a couple years until I could open my own office."

His glance came back to Kenyon and his grin was wry. "What I'm leading up to is this: it's been upgrade for me all the way. I told you before I never had a job as good as this one or a legitimate chance to make some real dough. For over two months I worked for that bonus and but for the lousiest kind of break I would have had it. But I still want the money and I can't see how ringing in a phony son is going to do any harm so I find you and act as nursemaid for three days and buy you enough clothes to last you two years. I get away with the gag too, until a few hours ago, and now somebody not only knocks off my client but in doing so holds up my dough. Well, I told you once before and I'm telling you again—I'm going to get it. The only way I can get it now is for you to keep on playing your part. And you're going to."

The grin went away and hardness came slowly into his features. "I covered up for you with that knife. Not because I like you, understand, but because if they put you on trial for murder I'm damn sure I'll never collect. If you knocked him off I'll have to get you for it, but I don't think you did and so I covered up. But if you try to crawl on me now, Kenyon, if you think you can keep your own skirts clean by squawking, you're out of your mind. This was my idea and I haven't forgotten it. But no one can prove whose idea it was now. No one can identify me as the fellow who went to young Comstock's apartment while he was in the hospital—with his key—and got those things I gave you."

Kenyon stood up. "You told me before."

"And I'm telling you again. You can say I hired you, and I can say you got Comstock's things and sold me a bill of goods, that you presented yourself to me and convinced me that you were Comstock. It'll be your word against mine—with this difference. With the old man dead you stand to gain maybe a million dollars; I stand to gain nothing. As far as the old man went—and his lawyer, who was going to give me the check—I earned my ten thousand. So how do you think it'll stack up and who do you think it's going to be toughest on?"

He stood up, corking the bottle and putting it aside. "I'm going back to the hotel but I thought I'd better let you know how it is. Talk and you can gyp me out of my ten grand; that I admit. But if you do, if you talk before we find the killer, you'll probably hang. Because you're a bum and everything in your record since they drafted you will prove it."

"Finished?"

Morley, half turning toward the door, turned back, squinting at the tone of Kenyon's voice. He lowered one lid and inspected the grimly smiling face as something he had never seen before.

"Yeah. Why?"

The twisted smile fought its way through the disturbed darkness of Kenyon's eyes. He had an answer for that. He had a lot of answers. Before, when he had talked to Morley about this thing, he had been too unnerved, too shocked by the death of Comstock and the finding of the murder weapon in his bag, to think clearly. All he could see then was the danger of his own position. Now there was something else.

He had done a lot of thinking in the past hour. His own personal position was no less dangerous but there was still a promise to be fulfilled. A crazy promise. A promise that did not seem real in a way, yet was real because he had given it sincerely as a way to expiate his fraud and cleanse himself. He had recalled it back in the drawing-room while Nash was talking and, remembering, had made up his mind to do what he could to fulfill it. He had promised to stay with Comstock until the danger that threatened him was passed; he had also promised to carry on in case the man could not do it himself.

That he had never expected this would be necessary altered nothing. He had given his word for what it was worth and he could not forget one other thing Comstock had said—that this danger might also touch Sally Hayden. Now the thing that Comstock had feared had happened.

It was nothing he could tell Morley and he had argued with the man now to see what position he would take and how the odds were stacked. Now he knew. There was no point in telling him what had changed his own mind, for it was a thing—this promise—that might not stand a logical inspection in any eyes but his own.

Even so, he realized the danger of delay. Every hour he put off his confession weakened its effectiveness and yet, thinking back to what he had said to Comstock, he saw no other choice. To tell his story now meant instant arrest, if not for suspicion of murder at least as a common swindler. Once arrested he had no hope of being able to fulfill the promise or of finding out who murdered Comstock. That was why he had made up his mind to wait, to say nothing, to cling to his freedom regardless of the personal risk until he had a chance to find out what this thing was

all about. . . . He thought all this in the few seconds that
Morley watched him and the grim smile still warped his
lips when he answered.

"I just wanted to be sure I had everything straight," he
said. "You're in this thing and I'm in it with you."

"That's what I said, chum."

"Okay, who's arguing?"

Morley's eyes opened, mirroring disbelief. It took him
five seconds to speak. "I thought you were. I thought—"

"Forget it," Kenyon said. "I'm staying in. Until we find
out what's behind all this I'm Joe Comstock."

Morley looked relieved. He gave Kenyon's arm a light
jab. He reached for the doorknob, turned back. He put on
the crooked smile and once again his voice was weary.

"Now you're talking my language. Let's get this murder
thing cleaned up first. They've hung more than one innocent man and don't let anybody tell you different."

Kenyon went over to the bottle and poured a mouthful
into his glass, a curious sense of satisfaction upon him now
that he was alone, now that he had made up his mind.
There had been a chance once, that afternoon, to tell the
truth and pull out. Now the chance was gone and he had
to do what he could to make up for it. Morley didn't worry
him one way or the other. Morley wanted his money and
if he could nail the killer he'd do it.

He took the drink and began to undress, his thoughts
sliding back and some of his confidence oozing away, not
because of his position as an impostor, but because of the
things he did not understand. The murder itself. The
knife and handkerchief in his bag. What would have happened had the knife been found? Why should anyone want
to see him arrested for murder? There was no answer to
this and as he glanced out the window he remembered
what Morley said and realized how easy it would have been
for some outsider, wanting to confuse the police and lead
them to suspect someone in the house, to have stepped

inside and, seeing the unlocked bag, slipped the bloodied evidence there.

He shivered unconsciously, thinking about it now, and suddenly his palms were damp. He turned off the light and stretched out in bed, remembering Nash and his questions. The others in the house had been friendly enough but what would they think now that Comstock was dead? Should they be able to expose him, Carl and Paul could double their inheritance, and seeing this point as some new and heretofore unrecognizable factor, Kenyon realized how alert and careful he must be until he found out what Comstock had been afraid of, until the murderer had been caught. . . .

Kenyon did not know he had been asleep until some mental alarm clock went off in his brain and told him so. Even then it was seconds before he began to think. He seemed to be coming out of a dream and it was a rather frightening dream so that when he opened his eyes the feeling of danger remained.

He lay there stiffly, his nerves keyed high, his senses sharply tuned. He wondered why. He wondered why he should imagine that he smelled some faint but cloying odor which reminded him of a hospital or sickroom.

He could see nothing but the vague outline of the ceiling and he did not turn his head then, but waited for the moment to pass, listening, summoning a mental grin to push aside the mood. That was when he heard the clicking sound near by and knew that there was a reason for his nervous tension, that he had been awakened by instinct and the intuitive warning that some danger lurked within the room.

Slowly, so as to make no sound, he moved his head on the pillow. The windows were sharply outlined against the night sky and he could see the side of a chair and the vague shadow of the chest. Then something moved in the corner of one eye, a shadow blacker than the rest, that slid noiselessly past the outline of one window and stopped in front of the chest. Instantly, the tension hit again and the memory of that other darkened room came back to him.

He did not know whether this was the same man, nor did he care; all he could think of then was that he must not call out, that this time he must keep the element of surprise in his favor. A curious tingling ran along his neck as he lifted his head. Fear was mixed up in it, though not the fear of bodily danger so much as the thought that he might fail again.

He got one elbow under him and waited, resting, listening, hearing a drawer open softly, an odd thrill of excitement and elation crowding out all uncertainty.

He could see the shadow clearly now and measured the distance as he sought to fold the covers back so that he could spring to the floor in one movement without tripping. He got that far when he heard a soft grunt, a warning sound that came not from the man at the chest but from the head of the bed; then, all caution gone and trying only to gain his feet, he felt an arm circle his throat, and something soft and moist was clapped across his mouth and nose, and the sickish smell he had wondered about was filling his head.

Even without the man from the chest who came to help, Kenyon could not have freed himself. Caught from behind, his neck and chin clamped in a strangle hold by a powerful arm, he was pulled from the bed. Before he could roll aside, his hips were caught in between legs that were like solid oak. When finally, he had to breathe, the giddiness came almost at once, and as he felt himself slipping into unconsciousness he had time to note one detail that he remembered long afterward.

Still trying to escape the chloroformed pad, he got hold of the hand that held it, tried to pry it free. That was how he noticed that on that broad rough hand the third finger was missing.

Chapter Twelve

Suspicion of Evil

SOMEONE had Kenyon's head in a vise and his first semiconscious thought was that he had a frightful hangover. The pressure was excruciating and there was a feeling of nausea at the pit of his stomach and he turned over, seeking sleep, until, with stunning suddenness his brain began to function.

He sat up, grabbing his head so it would not fall off, not daring to open his eyes yet, but just trying to steady himself. He put his hands down and felt for the night light, pulled it on; then, experimentally, he opened his lids and let the brightness enter a little at a time. When he saw the open drawers of the chest the whole fantastic sequence came back to him.

He was pretty shaky when he stood up but he forced himself to inspect the room and looked, finally, at his watch. It was three-forty. He tried to figure out a time sequence that would tell him how long he had been unconscious. It had been two-thirty when Morley had left him, and he had been asleep for a little while at least when he awoke to find the men in his room. When he finally realized it did not matter, he went into the bathroom and bathed his face in cold water. Then, deciding that he could not possibly feel worse, he looked around for the whisky bottle Morley had left.

"I'll be damned," he said presently.

There was no whisky bottle in the room, and thinking about it served only to confuse him more. He remembered the hand with the missing finger, recalled that it was the left hand. Well, that at least eliminated anyone in the house. But what kind of prowlers were these? There had been but one in Comstock's room. A search was being made when he interrupted it. A second search had been made either before or right after the murder; now his room had been searched.

"For what?" he said, half aloud.

He was moving barefooted back and forth across the room as he considered these things, his lean face pale and tight across the cheekbones, his blond hair tousled. Only once did he think of calling the police. They could do nothing now, and another question and answer session was the last thing he wanted. What he wanted was a drink and some sleep.

He slipped into his robe and slippers and put cigarettes in the pocket. He stood by the window as he belted the robe, anger churning within him and his blue eyes darkly brooding. The cool air felt good on his face and he put his hands on the frame and leaned out, breathing deeply. Ahead of him the tree-studded lawn was black, the sky above leaden and cloudy, and far down the slope a street light blinked through the faintly moving branches of a tree. Off to the left there was a pale, yellowish patch—

Something thumped against Kenyon's ribs and his hands tightened on the window frame. He leaned out, his glance darting along the line of the house to the left.

The study wing, set back slightly from the original foundation, was partially visible and though he could not see the windows, Kenyon knew instantly where that faint yellow patch came from.

He drew back in his room, thinking hard, the muscles bunching at the hinge of his jaw. Someone was in Comstock's study, and it was four o'clock in the morning, and he knew he was going to have a look and find out who that someone was.

Halfway to the door he stopped. Something, he did not know what, made him look about for some weapon, and then he knew he wasn't going to walk into that room until he knew what he was walking into. Wheeling, he went to the window, threw a leg over the sill, and stepped down to the grassy terrace.

The foundation planting was thick here and he scratched his hand on a barberry bush as he pushed past to the lawn. From this angle he could see the light, not much light, for there was no real brilliance behind the two windows, but enough to tell him his hunch had been right. Then he was moving silently across the turf, swinging closer to the study wing as he approached, until, when he reached the window, the wall was at his shoulder.

Leaning sideways, he looked into the room. The light came from a desk lamp, all illumination focusing downward so that the rest of the room was in shadow. In a chair, his back turned and practically blocking the light from this side, was a man.

Kenyon waited, his nose touching the pane. It took him a while to get all the details but he could see that a drawer stood open, that the man was going through some papers under the lamp. His head was obscured by his hunched shoulders and not until he lifted it did Kenyon know who it was. Then, checking the impulse to knock on the window, he retraced his steps, went through his room and down the hall to the study door. Knocking once, but not waiting, he opened it.

Paul Sherman started visibly, his body stiffening so that his elbow knocked some of the papers to the floor. He half rose, eyes peering behind the thick-lensed glasses, his jaw slack.

"Hello," Kenyon said.

"Oh." Sherman dropped back in the chair. "It's you."

He continued to stare as Kenyon approached. The papers in one hand trembled violently and his forehead was shiny with perspiration.

"I guess you startled me," he said.

"I saw the light," Kenyon said. "Up late, aren't you?"

"I couldn't sleep."

"Neither could I."

Sherman remembered the papers he had knocked to the floor and retrieved them. Kenyon just waited, watching, saying nothing. Sherman straightened the papers. He stood the silent treatment as long as he could and then looked up, exasperation curdling his voice.

"Is there something here you want?"

"No," Kenyon said.

Sherman seemed about to speak, closed his mouth. He put the papers back in the drawer, pushed it shut. He hesitated, giving Kenyon a sidelong glance and then, defiantly, opened another drawer and started to examine its contents.

Kenyon put his hands in his robe pockets and watched, knowing he was exasperating the man and doing so deliberately. A few seconds ticked by and suddenly Sherman leaned back and looked up at him, his glance cold and uneasy.

"I was trying to see if I could find anything here that might help us understand what happened tonight. If you want to help, pull up a chair and sit down."

"You're doing all right," Kenyon said. "You know more about things than I do. I'd only get in the way." He paused, thinking rapidly. He'd been given an answer. Whether it was the right one or not made no difference now because it was the only one he'd get. "I'll shove along. I was looking for a drink when I started out and I guess I'll keep looking. Sorry I startled you."

Sherman mumbled something about it being all right and Kenyon went out. He climbed the three steps to the main hall and started toward the drawing-room, wondering about Sherman until he realized there was no point in it.

It was dark up ahead, but he did not bother to turn on the lights. He reached the entrance hall and stairway without barking his shins and with the soft leather soles of his slippers making no noise on the hardwood floor, then went into the dining-room. He could see a little better now and found a glass in the pantry without trouble. There was some whisky left in the decanter on the sideboard and he poured a good jolt, not caring whether it turned out to be Scotch or rye. He went to the pantry sink and added water and then went back to the hall.

His head still throbbed, but he was wide awake now and knew he would have difficulty getting to sleep. Deciding that a book might help, he turned toward the library, seeing the blacker outline of the open door as he approached and wondering if he smelled tobacco smoke. The smell seemed more pronounced when he paused on the threshold, and then he heard a faint noise ahead of him and stiffened, aware that someone waited there in the darkness. For a second or two he listened, hearing nothing but the pounding of blood at his eardrums. Suddenly a voice struck at him from the shadows.

"Who's there?"

He had not known how tight his nerves were strung until he felt the quick relief that followed.

"Me," he said. "Tony. Is that you, Marion?"

"Oh." The word was a drawn-out sigh and it was another moment before she spoke again. "You frightened me. I thought I heard something but—"

"I was in the dining-room getting a drink. I don't know why I didn't turn on a light." He hesitated and when she did not answer he said, "I couldn't sleep and I thought maybe I'd get a drink and a book."

Still there was no answer and he was about to apologize and move along when she spoke.

"Sit down and talk to me. I couldn't sleep either. . . . There's a chair there on your left."

He felt for it, settled himself. He could see the glowing end of her cigarette now and he found her sitting between

him and the window, her head and part of her shoulder
silhouetted against the sky outside.

"I could get you a drink," he said.

She said she guessed not and would he like a cigarette?
He said he had one and lit it, the match flame blinding
him so that he could not tell anything about her face or
how she was dressed.

"I envy people who can sleep through a night without
waking," she said. "Paul is one. It takes him a long time
to drop off but once asleep he's good until morning. I'm
just the opposite. Five minutes and I'm dead but the least
noise wakes me and then it's frightfully hard to find any
sleep at all."

Kenyon sipped his drink and waited, wondering whether she knew her husband was up.

"He doesn't know how lucky he is," he said. "Here we
are prowling around waiting for morning and he's up
there pounding his ear."

"I know. Sometimes just the thought of it infuriates me.
It seems so unfair."

Is she lying? Kenyon thought. *Or doesn't she know?*

"That's why we decided we had to have separate rooms.
I'd fall asleep and he'd be tossing around for hours and
wake me and then he'd eventually get to sleep and there
I'd be."

She said other things along the same line but Kenyon
did not attempt to follow her. All he could think of at the
moment was that, without realizing it, she had destroyed
any alibi her husband might have had at the time of the
murder. If he could get downstairs now without her knowing it, he could have done the same thing shortly before
midnight.

He was at once aware that this did not prove anything,
and going back over the maze of incident and facts that
had come to light during the past twelve hours, he tried
to sort them into some recognizable pattern. That was

when he saw how little he really knew about this family and its background. . . . He realized Marion was silent and he thought of something else.

"Have you always lived in Kingsford?"

"Oh, no. Not until three years ago." She put her cigarette out and Kenyon waited. Morley had told him that the Shermans had been married ever since Paul got out of college, but from this new information it was evident that he had not always worked on his stepfather's paper. "You see, Paul worked for the New York *Press* when we were married and later he was their Central-European correspondent."

"Oh. I had no idea he had that sort of background. Did you like it? Were you there long?"

"I liked it. Until near the end. I think we were in Berlin two years altogether. I was in Paris a while and Paul spent some time in Vienna and Budapest; that was before we went to Berlin. We might have been there a few months longer if it hadn't been for Spence Arden."

Kenyon took a long pull on his drink and put the glass on the floor, knowing that there was more to come.

"You probably wouldn't think so to hear him talk now, but he is a Belgian—though he spent most of his life in England and seems more English than Continental—and he was a correspondent too and we met him in Berlin. We got to like him very much. He used to argue continually —he was a rabid anti-Nazi—and he wasn't always discreet about the things he wrote, and when Hitler moved into the Low Countries it looked bad for Spence because he'd been on the suspect list. The Gestapo was looking for him and he was missing for three days, and then one night, late, he came to the apartment."

She moved in the chair and he heard the crackle of paper and presently a match flame flared and he could see her face. It was quite without make-up now, the cheekbones highlighted and the eyes in shadow. Caught in the soft glow of the flame, her features in repose, her face seemed to him both pleasant and distinguished-looking. It was not pretty and never would be, but it would survive the years well, and he decided that, when he had stripped her of the pretense and brittleness she so often chose to affect, he liked her.

"Paul got him out," she said when the match fluttered into blackness. "I don't know exactly how but he did. He sent me out of the country that same morning by plane and three days later Spence was across the border. That's why Paul was later given twelve hours to leave the country. They knew he was responsible, of course, but they could prove nothing and so they had to let him go."

"Arden came here with you?"

"No. He didn't come for several months. In fact we didn't even know he was in this country until we saw him."

She went on, explaining how Arden developed into one of the paper's editorial writers and how he had worked up the idea of the daily broadcast. Kenyon finished his drink and listened to her with half his brain while the other half examined the motives, possibilities, and personalities of those in the house.

His head no longer ached and his stomach was steady. He felt relaxed in body if not in mind, and through the window he could see a faint lightening of the sky and knew that dawn was near. There was, he decided, no use in thinking more about what had happened. He could tell Nash about the man with the missing finger; that, at least, would give the police something to work on. He started to say he guessed he'd go to bed and then, not knowing quite how it happened, he found himself saying:

"You don't happen to know a man who has a finger missing on his left hand, do you?"

Marion Sherman gave no sign that she had heard. Her slim figure, more sharply outlined in the growing light, did not move and the room seemed very still. Somewhere in the distance a cock crowed and was answered by some acquaintance a block or two away; a truck rumbled past on the pavement out front and then, as the silence came again, she moved her head.

"What did you say?"

"I asked if you knew anyone with a finger missing."

She sat up, turning toward him and leaning her fore-arms across the side of the chair.

"Why do you ask?"

Something in her voice held him. The light was at her back and he could not see her face but he felt the pressure of her gaze and for a moment was taken aback by her question. He repeated his own.

"Do you?"

"No."

"Oh."

"I don't know anyone like that but I *saw* a man with a finger missing tonight."

A cold breeze slid lightly up the back of Kenyon's neck. He got his feet under him, kicking over the glass, and then leaned forward, hands grasping the chair arms.

"Tonight?"

"This evening. Just before dinner—before you came in for cocktails. In fact, I'd only just gotten back."

Kenyon sat there stiffly, not believing, yet finding nothing in the low breathlessness of her voice to warrant that doubt. He let her go on.

"There's a mailbox on the corner that I often use, and this afternoon I'd written some letters and forgotten to ask anyone to post them. I remembered them as I came downstairs and I knew Hilton would be busy just then so I took them down myself."

She stopped, as though this explained everything and Kenyon said:

"What about the man?"

"He was in a car. It was practically dark but there is a

street light and this car was parked so that I passed close by when I crossed the street to the mailbox. Going over, I thought nothing of it—"

"What kind of a car?"

"Oh—old. A sedan, and dirty. This man was sitting behind the wheel. The window was lowered and he had his elbow resting on the lower ledge and his hand propped up against the front part. . . . Oh, I don't know how to describe it, but it's where the glass is."

"I know," Kenyon said.

"Well, that's all. I looked right at his hand—I don't know why—and the third finger was gone. I remember distinctly."

That did it. If there had been any doubt in Kenyon's mind it vanished when she named the finger. He let his breath come out and sat back, knowing now she would ask him why he wanted to know all this and that he would probably have to tell her.

Chapter Thirteen

Enter the FBI

IT WAS AFTER TEN when Kenyon got up, and when he went into the dining-room twenty minutes later in search of some breakfast he found Carl and Nora having coffee together.

"Good morning, darling," Nora said.

Kenyon said good morning, as he took a place opposite them.

Nora wore a flannel skirt and a white pull-over that did things to her figure and her make-up was just right. Her lips were red, but not too red, her dark eyes were bright and sparkling and her fine white skin did not have a line in it. Whatever she and Carl had been talking about had temporarily eliminated any thoughts of the night before and her smile was warm and friendly.

Carl, too, had weathered the night very well and if he had any lingering feeling of worry or sorrow it did not show on his smooth round face. There was a freshly scrubbed look about him, every hair was slicked in place and his slacks, sleeveless cashmere sweater, and brown sport coat were immaculate and expensive-looking.

"You look as if you'd had a tough night," he said.

"I did," Kenyon said. "I didn't get to sleep until mornlng."

"I took a pill," Nora said.

"Pills are bad for you," Carl said, grinning.

"Not the kind I take."

"They're habit-forming."

"Rubbish."

"First thing you know you'll be taking two. All a person needs is a normally tired body and a clear conscience, that's what I always say."

Nora smiled back at him and said something else that Kenyon did not hear because he found it a little difficult to believe that he was hearing anything at all. Not by word or gesture did these two acknowledge that anything out of the way had happened the night before. Outwardly, at least, the murder had left them quite untouched and for the moment they seemed interested only in each other.

A maid came and took Kenyon's grapefruit away, bringing bacon and eggs, muffins, and fresh coffee.

"Besides," Nora said, "I only take them once in a while. It isn't any habit, is it, Joey?"

"Joey?" Sherman wrinkled his brows at her and then at Kenyon.

"That's what I always called him," Nora said.

"Joey." Sherman rolled the word on his tongue as though he liked the sound of it.

"Is it?" Nora pressed.

"No," Kenyon said grumpily, and attacked his eggs.

Sherman sipped his coffee and blew smoke around the table.

"I was trying to persuade Nora to have lunch with me," he said presently. "That is, if you have no objection."

"Oh, Joey wouldn't care," Nora said. "It's just that, well, it doesn't seem quite decent."

"People have to eat. We can't help what happened and there isn't anything we can do about it."

Nora studied the ash on her cigarette and Sherman studied Nora. He had, Kenyon realized, been watching her most of the time, inspecting her thoroughly and in detail, and apparently liking very much what he saw. Carl, Kenyon decided, had been smitten, and taking another glance at Nora he could understand why. She was, as Morley had said, a good-looking woman.

"There's a place out on the turnpike," Sherman said. "Nobody would pay any attention to us." He looked at

Kenyon. "I think it would do her good to get away from here for a while."

"All right," Nora said, and then someone coughed.

Hilton was standing in the doorway.

"Yes, Hilton," Sherman said.

"There's a man outside, sir. A Mr. Fleming. He asked to see either you or Mr. Paul."

"Fleming? I don't know any Fleming—"

"No, sir. He said to tell you he was an agent of the Federal Bureau of Investigation."

Sherman sat up, the good humor fading from his face. He looked at Kenyon. "What the devil does he want?" He sucked his lips, frowned at Hilton, and finally shrugged. "Well, take his hat and coat and tell him to come in."

Hilton looked shocked. "In here, sir?"

"Certainly. I haven't finished my coffee."

The man who entered a minute later was a neat, efficient-looking fellow of average height, quietly dressed. He wore gold-rimmed glasses and there were good bones in his jaw. He looked a little surprised when he saw them at the table.

"Oh, sorry," he said. "I can just as well wait—"

"No," Sherman said. "Come in and have a cup of coffee." He rose, introducing himself and the others. "Sit down. We can talk just as well here, can't we? Or is one of us about to be pinched? . . . Another cup, Mary, please," he said to the maid who had just come in.

Fleming sat down and Kenyon got the impression that, without appearing to, he was cataloguing each of them and filing away impressions in the back of his mind. He had that sort of eyes, level, observing, and quick.

"I heard about your father this morning," he said to Kenyon, "and I wondered if you knew why he called me yesterday afternoon."

Sherman, in the act of lifting his cup, put it down and suddenly the room was very still. Kenyon's thoughts spun, picking up forgotten impressions and trying to remember others. For a second or two he met that steady gaze and a growing sense of uneasiness began to eat away at his assurance. He was glad Sherman spoke first.

"He called you?"

"He called the office—in New York."

"What about?"

"That's what I'm trying to find out," Fleming said, and his glance slid back to Kenyon.

"No," Kenyon said. "I didn't even know he had called."

Fleming looked at the cup of coffee that had been placed in front of him. He took his time adding cream and sugar and they all watched him, waiting, saying nothing.

"It was around four o'clock," he said, finally.

"But didn't he tell you—"

"He said he had something that he thought we might want to look into. He said he didn't want to go into it over the phone but he intimated that it had something to do with espionage or Fifth Column activities of some sort." Fleming sipped coffee, put the cup down carefully.

"Ordinarily we would want a little more than that, but because of his position here in town we did not press him over the phone. He said if we could come in the morning it would be all right, so—"

He broke off as Sherman looked up at Hilton, who again stood in the doorway.

"Lieutenant Nash, sir."

"Oh, my God," Sherman said. "It's starting again." He pushed his cup and saucer away and sighed heavily. "All right," he said, and looked at Nora. "Now you know why I thought it would be a good idea to get away for lunch —if we can."

When Carl Sherman had given the police permission to go over the study and make a detailed examination of Comstock's desk and papers, he went off in his convertible with Nora. By this time Morley had arrived and he accompanied the others to the study. It was then that Kenyon told the story of the attack on him that morning, and almost before he had finished Nash was on the telephone putting machinery in order that would set every policeman and detective in town looking for a powerfully built man with a finger missing on his left hand.

"That's something," he said, hanging up. "That's a start."

"A guy like that might be found," Sergeant Bauer said. "That finger is something he can't cover up."

Fleming came away from the window. "You think he was a workman of some kind?"

"I don't know," Kenyon said. "His hand felt rough, tough-skinned. That's why I thought about it. As if he were a man who worked with his hands."

Morley, deep in a chair, was carefully folding the wrapper from a piece of gum that had just been added to that in his mouth. His squarish face was somber and the muscles along his jaw were ridged with their chewing. Once, without his moving his head, his eyes slid over to Kenyon, looking troubled and brooding.

"If you hadn't woke up," he said, finally, "you wouldn't have known a thing. They wanted to search your room and the big guy stood by the bed with a saturated pad in his pocket in case you made trouble."

Fleming, at the desk and going through the drawers, looked up.

"If Comstock was right about the man in the car that tried to run him down, it was probably the same one."

Kenyon thought about what Marion Sherman had told him. "It was," he said, and went on to describe the car and explain how she had seen the man with the missing finger the evening before.

"Could he have been the one you surprised in the bedroom when you came to get the check?" Nash said.

Kenyon thought it over. "I don't know," he said. "He could have been but I don't think he was."

"Why?"

"I think he would have hit me harder than I was hit." He paused, thinking, and the memory of his struggle came back to him clear-cut and vivid. "The fellow that grabbed me and held that chloroform on my face had tremendous strength. I could barely move. If he was the one who hit me earlier I don't think I'd have got up so soon."

The door opened as he finished and Sally Hayden stood there looking at them, her eyes wide and uncertain and a little afraid. She had on the tan coat and a dark green dress under it and her young face was pale and drawn. For a moment her glance paused on Kenyon and he tried to smile, to tell her that everything was all right, to reassure her; then, with no indication that she had noticed anything at all, she closed the door.

Nash came forward, saying, "Good morning, Miss Hayden." He introduced her to Fleming and went on. "We asked you to come over because we thought perhaps you could help us."

"I'd be glad to do whatever I can."

"Fine." Nash smiled and rubbed his hands. "Now, do you know why Mr. Comstock telephoned Mr. Fleming's office in New York yesterday afternoon?"

"Why, no. I didn't know that he had."

Fleming's face fell. "Oh."

"I was with Mr.—Mr. Comstock, Junior, most of the afternoon. That is until—"

"This was about four o'clock," Fleming said.

"Then he must have phoned from the paper."

"We can check that," Nash said, nodding to Bauer. He studied the girl a moment, disappointment clouding his face. "We hoped you could tell us about it. You see, we have a theory now about the murder. Whatever it was Mr. Comstock called Mr. Fleming for must have been known to someone else. Comstock might have known this and he might not have. But he did have some idea why an attempt was made to run him down. He must have had an idea who was behind it. Why he didn't tell the truth last night to Morley and Mr. Comstock"—he nodded toward Kenyon—"I don't know. He was worried or he wouldn't have asked Morley to spend the night here." He hesitated, his voice taking on new bitterness. "The trouble was, he wasn't worried enough."

"He probably wasn't sure," Fleming said. "He had an idea—and it must have been pretty serious—but he didn't want to do anything drastic until he was positive. I can understand his not wanting to confide in us over the telephone—and this was before that car tried to run him down. Later, when you found the prowler in his bedroom" —he glanced at Kenyon—"he knew why, but having already called us he must have decided to wait until I came and turn the whole thing over to us."

Remembering how Comstock had acted when he asked for help, Kenyon decided that Fleming's theory was right. But there was something else. Comstock had intended to give his facts to Fleming but he had intimated that the facts might not be enough, that the investigation might take time and that he needed Kenyon's help because he feared someone in the house was involved. Now, wondering if he should pass the idea along, Kenyon listened as Fleming continued to Sally.

"You see, Miss Hayden, what we're really trying to do is decide what it was that prompted him to call us in. It must have been something very definite, something tangible. I say *must* because his bedroom was searched at least once, probably twice, and possibly this study as well."

Kenyon's thoughts slid back to the early morning hours when he had found Paul Sherman going through the desk. He considered giving this information now. What stopped him was the thought that if Sherman were involved, and if the man with the missing finger had not found this thing that Fleming sought, then Sherman had perhaps already found it himself. On the other hand, he had no proof that Paul Sherman had anything to do with the murder. . . .

"We've been going over this room," Fleming was saying. "We haven't finished, but I don't think we'll find anything when we have. I'm not sure this thing was here at all —at least our prowlers did not find it. Otherwise there would be no reason for them to continue their search later in this Mr. Comstock's room."

He indicated Kenyon and Sally Hayden looked at him quickly, her lashes suddenly wide open. Kenyon realized that she did not know what had happened to him, but he made no interruption and let Fleming continue.

"So we were wondering if you knew any reason why Mr. Comstock should call us, if he had mentioned anything yesterday that might help us now."

Sally had continued to look at Kenyon. There was no particular expression in her gaze and she seemed intent not upon him but on her thoughts; now the spell was broken suddenly and she gave her attention to Fleming.

"No." She shook her head. "No, I'm sure he didn't."

"What was he working on?"

"A series of articles about the economic adjustment that must come when the war is over."

"For the paper?"

"A book he was thinking of. The first ones are in here." She rose and went to a filing-cabinet, taking out a manila folder and passing it to Fleming. "But yesterday," she said, "he only worked a short time in the morning. He was at the paper most of the afternoon and there were only a few pages for me to copy."

Fleming was leafing through the manuscript and Nash looked over his shoulder. Morley, twisting the star sapphire ring on his little finger, said:

"It wouldn't have anything to do with that, or they'd have come to Miss Hayden's place instead of Tony's. This wasn't any secret, was it, this writing business?"

"No," Sally said. "He'd been at it quite a while."

"Yes," Fleming said, sounding discouraged. "Well, thanks, Miss Hayden. If you should happen to think of anything—" He broke off and turned back to the desk.

Sally hesitated, looked from one to the other, and finally stood up. Kenyon rose with her. He went over and opened the door for her. When she went out, he followed. She went up the three steps to the main hall before she realized that he was with her and then, though her step faltered, she continued resolutely, not glancing round.

Kenyon moved up beside her and slid his hand inside her arm, pulling her gently to a stop. She did not try to free herself and he let his hand fall.

"Sally."

For an instant he felt a spark of hope and thought she would help him out; because in that instant she examined his face and he thought there was a troubled softness in her gaze. Then it went away and the spark died.

"Yes."

"I've got to talk to you."

She hesitated, then began to walk again, looking straight ahead, her voice now matter-of-fact.

"All right. But I'm afraid there isn't time now."

"It won't take very long."

"I'm sorry, but I don't think I should stop. I'm supposed to be at the paper—"

She did not finish and he walked along with her. They were in the central hall now and he stopped in the foyer, his lean face slack and despondent, his eyes miserable. He watched her open the door and suddenly something snapped in his chest and his face tightened. His jaw set and a grim little smile screwed itself into the corner of his mouth.

She was going down the steps when he went through the doorway. She must have heard his footsteps on the gravel drive but she walked right up to the little coupé and opened the door. When she slid in behind the wheel, Kenyon opened the other door and climbed in beside her. She did not look at him even then but he could see her lips compress and a spot of color touched her cheekbone.

"Now you're being silly," she said.

"Am I?"

"You haven't any hat or coat."

"That's right," Kenyon said, and sat back on the cushions.

For another five seconds she sat there, looking flushed and grim and altogether lovely; then, tightening her lips even more, she snapped on the ignition and jammed her thumb against the starter button.

Chapter Fourteen

Two Such Different Women

KENYON let her get the coupé into high and out on the pavement before he said anything. He was watching her out of the corner of his eye and her color was still high and he had an almost overpowering urge to lean over and kiss her on the cheek. He took out cigarettes and offered her one.

"No, thank you."

He got his own lighted and turned on the seat so he could get a better look at her.

"What're you sore at?"

No answer.

"I know how this thing has hit you. I know how much you thought of him. It's a pretty rough time for you, for all of us, and it just makes it that much worse to have you angry—"

"I didn't know that I was. Last night it seemed to me that you were the one who was angry."

"I wasn't angry. You asked me if I was bitter and I said I was. At myself. I still am."

He stopped, watching her. She kept her eyes on the pavement and both hands on the wheel. Some of the color had gone from her cheeks but the tightness was still there and presently he knew that no amount of talking on his part would do any good. Yet there was one thing more he wanted to say, and he did, regretting it instantly.

"Is it because I didn't tell you about Nora?"

She looked at him then, coolly.

"Is that what you wanted to talk about?"

"No," Kenyon said, and now he began to stare at the pavement ahead. "No, that's not the reason I came. I came because there is something I want you to understand and I knew that the way you felt now it would be the only chance I'd get." He paused, seeking the right way to tell her. "Last night—this morning, rather—a couple of guys searched my room."

She looked at him curiously, as though half expecting that this was some trick of his. "And where were you?"

"I was there," Kenyon said, and explained everything that had happened in blunt, incisive words.

Long before he had finished, Sally Hayden was giving as much attention to him as she was to her driving. She let the coupé slow down to a mere twenty and no longer was there any tightness or hostility in her face. Her lips were parted and there were worried lights in the corners of her eyes.

"But why?" she said. "Why, Tony?"

"Why do you think?"

"They must have wanted something."

"Sure."

"But what?"

"I don't know. The thing is—from now on you've got to be careful. Maybe I'm wrong—I hope I am—but I don't think we've seen the end of this. I don't want to frighten you either, but until we know what's behind this, until the murderer has been caught—"

"But, really." Some of the matter-of-factness came back. They were downtown now and she was giving most of her attention to the traffic and the stop-and-go signs. "I'm afraid you're imagining things, aren't you? How could I possibly be in any danger?"

Kenyon sighed. He wanted to tell her all the things Comstock had said, but he couldn't do it here. Now, the way things were, the promise would sound silly, even more so than his warning. He made his voice patient.

"I guess I didn't make my point very well."

"It's just that I can't—"

"Why do you think my room was searched? Why do you think those two men went to that risk last night?"

"Because they were looking for something," Sally said.

"But I had nothing. Why—what possible reason would they have for thinking I did?"

She was silent. When he saw she still did not sense what he meant he tried again.

"Somebody tried to run Com—Andy down. Somebody was searching his bedroom when I went there for Morley's check. Somebody searched it, in part, at least, about the time he was killed. Obviously he didn't find what he wanted or the search would have been over. But it wasn't. He, or they, came to my room—"

"Because, not finding it, they thought perhaps Andy had given this thing to you for safekeeping," Sally said. "Yes, I see now."

"The point is," Kenyon said, "that they didn't get what they wanted from my room either because I didn't have it. So now where can they look?"

"Oh," Sally said in a still small voice. "You think that—"

"I'm saying it's a possibility. Whoever is behind this— and my hunch is that those two thugs are working for someone—knew I was with Andy yesterday. I was sup- posed—" He caught himself in time and perspiration broke out on his forehead. *Supposed to be his son.* That's what he was going to say and now he went ahead quickly. "I'm his son and I suppose it was conceivable that he would entrust me with whatever it was he was worried about. But he didn't."

"He could have given it to Paul or Carl."

"He could have given it to you, too."

She swung the car down an alley and into a parking space behind the *Sun* Building. She cut the engine and put the keys in her purse.

"Well," Kenyon said. "Did he?"

"No. Certainly not. Wouldn't I have told the police if
he had?"

"I don't know, but whether he did or not might not
stop them from looking."

They walked to the back door. Inside, Kenyon could
hear the rumble of the presses. A conveyor was dumping
bundles of papers out on a ramp and men were loading
trucks, on the sides of which were plastered posters adver-
tising a feature running in the *Sun*. Sally stopped in the
doorway and looked up at him.

"Thank you, Tony," she said. "I'm glad you told me."

"You have to be careful," he said, a little desperately
because he knew there was nothing more he could say.

"I will be," she said, and then she was gone and he was
alone, half his brain telling him to follow her and the
other, the stronger half, telling him that it was useless and
that even if he could make her like him again it could not
possibly bring her anything but added unhappiness.

It was about a mile and a half from the *Sun* Building
to the Comstock home and Kenyon walked it, quite un-
aware of the distance, his surroundings, or the occasional
stare of a passer-by at the grim, straight figure that walked
sightlessly along without coat or hat.

The drawing-room and library were deserted when he
got back, and remembering, finally, that he had had nothing to eat since breakfast, he rang for Hilton, asking for
a sandwich and a glass of milk. Hilton served him in the
library and Kenyon flopped on the leather divan and
closed his eyes. He was still there, some time later, when
he heard voices in the hall which he presently identified.

He glanced at his watch and found that it was four
o'clock. And apparently Nora and Carl had just returned
from lunch. Kenyon smiled sardonically at the ceiling,
getting snatches of their conversation and gathering from
what he heard that Carl was trying to promote a dinner

date as well.

"But it isn't decent, darling," Nora said.

"Why?" There was a brief silence. "Because of your husband?"

"Oh, no. Not that. Joey doesn't care. In fact, I'm asking him to send me to Reno when he decently can."

"All right, then," Carl said blandly. "What are we arguing about? We don't have to go back to the same place. I know lots of places."

"I'm sure you do," Nora said, and then their voices passed out of earshot and Kenyon sat up.

He rose and stretched. When he heard someone going up the stairs he wandered into the hall. Nora was still there, standing in front of the entryway mirror doing something to her hair. She had a hairpin in her mouth and spoke past it, her arms still up and her body arched gracefully.

"Oh, hello."

Kenyon said hello and had turned slowly toward his room when she called to him.

"Wait a minute, darling."

He stopped, watching her put the last pin in place and give a final pat to her thick auburn hair. She smiled and came up to him, linking her arm with his as she walked along.

"I want to talk to you, Joey."

"All right."

They went to her room and Kenyon took the straight-backed chair near the bed. Nora kicked off her pumps and moved to the chaise longue.

"Now," she said. "Oh, damn!" She had plumped both knees on the extension and flopped back, her knees still curled. Now she was sitting up and examining a new run in her stocking. "Look at that," she said, wetting her finger and applying it to the run. "That just shows you the kind of stockings you get nowadays. . . . Well." She smiled at him and he thought it was a nice sort of smile, though perhaps more wise than friendly. "Here we are again."

"Yes. Here we are."

"I'm all in. Completely. I've got to have a nap before dinner—Carl wants to take me out again—but I had to talk to you."

Kenyon watched her yawn and cover it with the back of her hand, wondering what was coming next.

"Carl says that after all taxes are paid you should get at least a million dollars."

"You mean that's what I'd get if I were Comstock's son."

"You will, anyway, now. You can't miss." She studied him a moment, her smile veiled. "You were in the library when we came back, weren't you? Did you hear what we said?"

"Part of it. I heard the Reno part," Kenyon said dryly.

"Oh, did you? Yes. Well, I meant it, Joey."

He pulled out cigarettes and she held out her hand. He got up and gave her one. She curled a little tighter on the chaise longue and blew smoke at him, a sudden thoughtfulness touching her glance.

"Last night I didn't know what was going to happen. I didn't know what to do. It frightened me, Joey. I didn't know what it meant and I guess I might have thought that you did it. . . . Oh, I know how it sounds. And I didn't think so long because I know you're not that kind."

"That's very generous of you."

The sarcasm was wasted. She neither looked at him nor seemed to hear what he had said.

"I told you I liked you; I do. I knew you couldn't have killed him. But at first, before I thought it out—well, you can see how it looked. You coming here and pretending you're the son and making everyone believe it, and then the old man being murdered and you inheriting half the estate. It was almost too perfect."

She flicked ashes on the rug. "And this morning I could

see something else. All my life I've waited for something like this to happen to me and now it's almost too good to be true. I've been going around wanting to ask someone to pinch me so I'll know it's really happened."

"You could get Carl," Kenyon suggested.

She looked at him, smiling. "Yes, I know. Carl likes me. And I like him. I told him all about us—I mean about how you ran out on me and how we haven't lived together in over a year and all that. I told him I'd never bothered to get a divorce because I'd never had time. And about myself I've told him the truth, Joey. He knows I've worked in cheap night clubs, and been a model. He knows all that and yet he likes me. I think he might want to marry me. He hasn't said so but I think he might."

"I hope you'll be very happy."

This time she got the undertone of bitterness and her smile went away for a moment.

"I mean it, Joey. And I mean it about going to Reno. You're going to collect and I'm glad for you. And I'm going to Reno and get a divorce from Joey Comstock—that's you."

"And then I'll give you a big settlement."

"That's right."

"Um-hum."

"It won't have to be anything that's unfair. All I'd like would be enough to make me independent. If you get a million you could give me two hundred thousand. That's what I thought of at first, but now I don't think it has to be even that much. You could give me a hundred and fifty thousand, couldn't you? That wouldn't be too much, would it? Everything considered?"

"No," Kenyon said wearily, "that wouldn't be too much." He listened to her enlarge upon her plans, a little amazed at her simple ingenuity, yet knowing that she really believed everything she said. There was a shining brightness in her brown eyes, reflecting some inner dream that she knew would come true. The elements of fraud involved did not concern her; she accepted the circumstances as made for her benefit and the moral values were something she did not consider. What impressed him even more was the conviction that she not only would keep any bargain she had made, but also, in the event that she should marry Carl, do her best to make him a pretty good wife. It presented such a crazy paradox to him that he finally gave up and brought his mind back within the focus of her voice.

"That way," she was saying, "I'll have something in case the other does not work out—with Carl, I mean. And if it does, it will be so much better." She paused, hugging her breasts, her thoughts a million miles away. "You'll have what you want and I'll have what I want and neither of us will ever tell the truth because we'll never have to."

He let his breath out slowly, unwilling at the moment to offer any argument. Presently some new thought came to her and when she looked at him her eyes were clouded with doubt.

"You will give me the settlement, won't you? When you get the inheritance?"

"*If* I collect," Kenyon said, "you'll get yours."

He would have gone on then but Nora, ignoring in her jubilation the *if*, jumped up, bounded over to him, and throwing her arms around his neck, kissed him hard on the mouth.

"I knew you would," she cried. "Oh, you *are* nice."

And then she did a pirouette, throwing up her arms, her skirt spinning to reveal her rounded knees and thighs. In that brief moment of abandon there was grace and beauty in every line of her and he grinned at her crookedly as he stepped to the door, an odd feeling of sadness passing over him.

"There's only one thing," he said. She faced him, poised, lips parted, and though he knew he must break the bubble of happiness her dream had created, he knew he could not do it violently. "All this is based on my collecting. Hasn't it ever occurred to you that I might not want to collect?"

She just stared at him, her lips still parted, her eyes enormous against the white background of her face. Kenyon went out before she could reply.

Chapter Fifteen

A Sober Binge

In his own room, Kenyon had little time for thought because Leon Morley came in shortly, skidding his hat on the bed, greeting him with unaccustomed cheerfulness.

"How's it?" he said. "How do you feel now?"

"All right."

"How's the courage?"

"Just the same."

"That's not saying a hell of a lot," Morley said, but there was no barb in his tone. He sat down, fanning out his coat and reaching for a piece of gum. "How's Nora? Seen her?"

"Yes. She's all right." Kenyon eyed him sardonically. "Nora's fine—up to now," he said, and went on to tell in detail his recent conversation.

Morley listened without interruption, folding his gum wrapper, his face revealing his interest.

"I told you she was no fool," he said, and chuckled, a sound Kenyon had seldom heard. "Got it all figured out, huh? And good. You know the only dope in this setup, don't you?"

"Me, I suppose."

"You know it. That Nora's all right. She'd go for you too—or would have, if you'd made any kind of play for her. And then where'd you be? I tell you. You could be married to her with a million bucks in the sock—there wouldn't be any settlement to pay, you know that, don't you?—and not a chance of a slip-up. But, no. You don't want a million bucks. Okay, but I hope to God you didn't tell her so."

"I didn't," Kenyon said. "I just gave her a little hint."

Morley watched him narrowly. "A hint? Why? Are you nuts?"

Kenyon shrugged and sat down on the bed. "I just wanted to let her know there was more than one way to figure. Now when I run out it won't be any shock."

"All right." Morley flipped the paper wad in the general direction of the wastebasket. "Have it your way. I only wish I could trade places with you."

"Yes, you do."

Morley wasn't smiling any more. Kenyon did not know when the smile had stopped but it was no longer there and his tone was blunt and irritable.

"You think I'm kiddin'?"

Kenyon let it go. "What about this murder? How do I stand now?"

"You stand okay. You stand even better than the Sherman boys." He leaned forward, elbows on the chair arms. "Did you know that Paul used to be a correspondent in Germany? Did you know that until war was declared he was a rabid isolationist? You didn't know that he and the old man didn't get along and that there was some talk that he might be demoted?"

He sat back. "It's only talk and Sherman denies it now and there isn't any proof. But it's a thought, you know what I mean? And Carl, well, he's something else again. You saw his car? That gives you an idea. It takes a lot of dough to keep a guy like him in spending money and there wasn't any allowance for him either. The mother had nothing to leave and all he gets he gets from the insurance business. Of course, the old man set him up and the name brings in a lot of accounts. The only thing is, he spends too much. The last time he put the bite on the old man he got turned down and when he went to the bank he got the brush-off there too."

Kenyon thought it over, believing all he heard, seeing the motives unfold and wondering if they were enough.

"Do you think either of them could have done it?"

"Certainly they could have. I don't say they did—yet. Because there's something else. We got a line on Missing Finger." He paused and pursed his lips, a gleam of respect in his eyes. "That Fleming is all right. You know what he did? Checked all factories around here working on Government orders. You know how it is, don't you? All workers are photographed and duplicates are made and kept —even after a guy quits. Well, we think your pal used to work for the Seaburn Manufacturing Company. Anyway, his description is right—a thick-necked husky with the third finger, left hand, missing."

Relief flooded Kenyon's face and his spirits lifted with this new corroboration. "Now if you can find him—"

"We will. He's a naturalized citizen, came from Germany originally. Name of Rudy something or other. Once we nail him we'll maybe find out who he was working for and then—" He broke off, shrugging and folding his hands.

Kenyon thought it all over and presently Morley continued.

"The way things look, you'll be out of here before long. I saw Comstock's lawyer and put up a squawk for my check. He's co-executor with the bank. He said he'd talk it over with them. Of course, you're crazy, you know that? But it's nothing to me. I want my ten grand and I'm going to get it. If you want to run out I guess it'll be all right. You can just fade out and write a letter back and be noble and renounce all interest in the Comstock estate.

"You know the kind? You can't bear to accept the inheritance, having hated your old man all these years. You want no part of it. . . . Sure. Go ahead. Be a stupe. They'll believe a letter like that. The two brothers will get the dough and you'll be on your own and nobody'll give a damn what happens to you." He stood up. "The only thing is, for now, you're overdoing it."

Kenyon did not get it. He said so.

"That mournful pan, the sad eyes. It's all right to be sober and a little worried. After all he was your old man even if you hated him, but don't overdo it."

"Nuts. I'm not—"

"I know you're not. I'm just saying how you look. What you need is—say, how about eating with me tonight? Maybe we can find a place with some music and toss off a few. You can get a little cocked if you want. Maybe it would do you good."

It did not take Kenyon long to decide this might be a good idea. Maybe he could look in on Sally. Maybe he could find out more about what Fleming and Nash were doing.

"All right," he said.

"Atta keed. Come when you get ready. I'll be in my room."

It was nearly seven when Kenyon left his room. For more than an hour he had sat by the window, watching the dusk thicken. Always there had been in the back of his mind the hope that he would see Sally's little coupé come wheeling up the driveway. He never got to the point of thinking what he might say to her; it would make a difference just to know that she was here.

Nora was at the telephone behind the stairs when he went through the hall to the dining-room. She wore the black robe and her auburn hair was piled high and there was a certain impatience in her end of the conversation. He thought he knew why. He had heard the water running in the tub and apparently the call had interrupted her bath.

"Certainly," she was saying. "I said I would, didn't I? Yes. . . . Yes, that's all right. . . ."

Kenyon found Hilton in the pantry and asked if he knew where Sally Hayden lived. Hilton lifted a brow and said he did.

"Three-eight-four Monroe Street, sir."

"Which way is that?"

"Two blocks to the left, sir, and one over. It's parallel with Maple Street."

Kenyon thanked him and went out. Nora had finished her telephoning and he got his hat and coat from the closet. It was cool out and very clear overhead. There was no moon yet but the stars were coming thick and bright against their deep blue background.

It was dark here under the trees and he cut across the sloping lawn toward the street light below, wondering if this was the one where Missing Finger had parked his car the evening before, when Marion Sherman saw him. He noticed a mailbox across the street and decided it was, and then he was stepping out briskly with his shoulders back and his stomach in.

The address Hilton had given him proved to be a small three-storied apartment house built in the shape of a block U and having three entrances. He found Sally's card in the one on the right and saw that she had 2-B. He almost lost his nerve then, and looked back out at the court before he finally turned and pressed the buzzer.

What could he lose? He could ask her if she'd have dinner with him, that's all. If she said yes, he'd telephone Morley and if she said no— He shrugged mentally and pressed the button again. He pushed it three more times before he finally gave up and started walking toward the hotel.

Leon Morley was in an excellent mood. He wore a blue-striped shirt, blue tie, and a neat double-breasted suit of dark gray. It made him look blockier than he was, but there was a trimness too that suggested there was no fat underneath. His black oxfords were shining and his hard broad jaw was smooth and freshly powdered.

"You want a shot here," he said, "or shall we go?"

"I don't care."

"You don't want to eat here, do you?"

Kenyon said not particularly.

"Good." Morley put on his hat and adjusted the brim to his satisfaction. "I've got a couple of places the bell captain gave me. If you want a steak we'll go to one or if it's lobster the other."

Kenyon said he'd prefer the steak and they went down and got into Morley's sedan, a drive-yourself that he rented by the day. A ten-minute ride brought them to a dimly-lighted doorway on a street made up of small shops and two- and three-story buildings. The outlook was pretty discouraging, but when they opened the door Kenyon could hear the band and there was a cute little brunette in short skirts to take their hats and coats.

There was a small bar on the right with a lot of mirrors and chromium and leather, and they had two Martinis, taking their time over them and ordering dinner from there. They were on their third when the waiter came to get them.

They had a good table by the wall where they could watch the orchestra and the dancers. The room was about half filled and the orchestra, although boasting but seven pieces, was fairly good, its swing solid but not too loud. It was, Kenyon decided, a pretty nice spot and he amplified the decision when he tasted his steak.

Morley accepted the burden of the conversation and he kept it away from Kingsford and the Comstock case. He had a lot of interesting stories about other jobs he had worked on, and spoke some of his early police experience. They took their time eating, had brandy with their coffee, and Morley indulged in a cigar. By that time it was nine-thirty and, according to Morley, almost time for a drink.

"Here?" he asked. "Or shall we push off?"

Kenyon said he was ready and they drove back to the hotel. Without either of them suggesting it, they drifted

into the tap room and sat down again. Morley ordered rye
and Kenyon took Scotch, his glance following the waiter.
That was how he happened to see Spence Arden at the bar.

"There's Arden," he said.

"Arden? Who the hell is Arden?" Morley turned, his
face clouding and then clearing suddenly. "Oh, the newspaper guy."

He gave his attention to his drink and now Kenyon's
thoughts, which had been kept away from himself by
Morley's chatter, sank back into a morass of despondency.
He finished his drink and was still watching Arden moodily when the other saw him. He had been talking to a
slender, nondescript-looking youth next to him and now
he said something else and came toward the table.

"Hi," he said. "What're you drinking? . . . Dominic!"

A waiter came over and Morley and Kenyon ordered.
Arden said he'd have the same and handed over his empty
glass.

"Hear the broadcast tonight?"

"No," Kenyon said.

"Couldn't take it, huh?"

His teeth flashed in a grin and he looked from one to
the other, and Kenyon, remembering the things Marion
Sherman had told him, began to inspect this blond, good-
looking man with new interest. It would have been difficult to guess that he was a Belgian or, from his accent, that
he had spent most of his life in England. There was something in the cadence of his voice that suggested a background of culture and good schools, but his use of slang
helped to obliterate the impression. He had a quick, easy
way of moving and a bland, unruffled manner, but there
were shrewdness and intelligence in the eyes and Kenyon
got the idea that nobody fooled him more than once. Now,
having pulled up a chair, he was giving his attention to
Morley.

"Anything new?"

"What do the police say?" Morley countered.

"Damned little. All we've got so far is the run-around and the usual hokum about the identity of the killer— or his accomplice—being known, and about the close co-operation of city, state, and federal authorities." He waved one hand. "Naturally an arrest may be expected shortly."

"Nothing about a lad with a missing finger?" Morley said.

The waiter had put down the drinks and Arden, in the act of paying him, stopped. For an instant something flickered in his eyes and then he squinted them at Morley.

"Are you kidding?"

"Do I sound that way to you?"

Arden gave the waiter a bill and shook his head. "No," he said. "No, you don't. It's just that it sounded so much like something out of a penny dreadful." He grinned. "But go ahead. What about him?"

Morley sipped his drink and took his time.

"Nothing. I just asked if the police mentioned one."

Kenyon glanced from one to the other, noticing that while Arden's face reflected some irritation, Morley's reflected nothing at all. Arden tried again.

"And is that right about the Federal men being in on it?"

"They've got an agent up here."

"Hmm. That sounds like something more than murder."

"Yeah."

"But you're not saying what?"

"It isn't my case, exactly. My client got knocked off and I'm cutting in but I'm not talking out of turn. If I get lucky and crack something I'll tell you; until then the police will do the talking."

"I guess that's telling me, isn't it?" Arden stood up and examined his glass. "But so far we've kept you out of it in our stories—I mean about your possibly being derelict in your duty to your client, and so forth. We like to have people play ball with us, Morley, and then we can play ball with them. . . . Well, it's nice seeing you again."

He went to the bar and finished his drink. Presently he went out and all this time Kenyon knew that Morley was watching him. He also knew that the detective's eyes were mean and hard. So was the line of his jaw—until he glanced back at Kenyon; then he was all right again.

"Come on," he said. "I'll get a bottle and we'll go up to my room."

"I think I'll go back to the house," Kenyon said.

"I thought you were going to get drunk."

"Maybe I will yet but—"

"Listen." Morley grinned and became very patient. "I've got twin beds. You can drink as much or as little as you like and if it's too much I can toss you in—and it's not often I offer to buy a bottle, chum."

"Thanks," Kenyon said, "but I guess not."

Morley sighed loudly and shook his head. "Okay. But you're a big disappointment to me. Here I lay out a three-buck dinner and feed you liquor and you're just like you were when you started. . . . Well, I suppose I've got to humor you. Come on, I'll run you out."

Chapter Sixteen

DEATH STRIKES AGAIN

CARL SHERMAN AND NORA were in the drawing-room when Kenyon came in shortly after eleven. Apparently they had just returned because they were standing just inside the doorway and Nora still wore her cape. She had slipped it back on her shoulders and was sort of holding it at the waist to keep it from falling, and underneath she wore a long black dress, cut low and well-filled with Nora.

"Oh, hello, darling," she said casually.

"You're back early," Kenyon said.

"That was Nora's doing," Carl said, and grinned, looking pretty pleased with himself.

"Well"—Kenyon started to turn away—"good night."

"Are you going right to bed?"

Kenyon stopped and looked at her, not sure whether she was addressing him or not.

"No," he said. "I'm going in the dining-room and get one of those decanters and a glass and then I'm taking them into the library."

"Now it comes out," Carl said. "A solitary drinker."

He smiled and glanced at Nora to see if she was, but she wasn't; she was watching Kenyon.

"Well, will you stop in for a minute, Joey?" she said. "If it's not too late?"

Kenyon tried to get some reason for the request from her dark eyes but he was too far away and all he could see was the faint smile on her red mouth.

"Sure," he said, and started for the dining-room.

He got a glass in the pantry and one of the heavy cut-glass decanters from the buffet and came back to the hall. He did not shut the library door, nor turn on the light.

He could hear Carl and Nora saying good night. It was all very proper and Nora thanked him nicely and then Kenyon could hear her heels tapping her away and, presently, Carl's step on the stairs.

He poured a small drink, holding the glass up against the light from the hall, stoppered the decanter, and found a chair. The house was quiet now and with the windows closed there was no noise from outside. He tasted the whisky and found it good. He lit a cigarette and leaned back in the chair, knowing that before he stood up again he must reach some definite conclusion and plan his course of action.

He could see now that his whole problem centered around Sally Hayden. Everything that had happened had been considered in its relation to her, part of every thought had reached out to include her in some way. The feeling of shame and loathing that had so tormented him did not come entirely from the part he was playing, the fraud he was perpetrating; he felt guilty now and sickened with his complicity but he had felt guilty about other things in the past—his weakness and self-pitying reaction to Hazel Wainwright's decision to marry another, his record in the army. But if it had not been for Sally and the promise he had given Comstock he might have gone away and had nothing more to worry about than some momentary pangs of conscience.

Because he had never intended to profit by the impersonation other than through the fee Morley was to pay. Carl and Paul Sherman would have divided the estate had he not come, and they would divide it now. The murder was something he did not understand and therefore he could not feel responsible. It would, he was sure, have happened anyway. As for Nora—well, Nora would get a break after all.

She was out for what she could get but she had something to offer as well. What he did now would not hurt her if, as she intimated, Carl had fallen in love with her. Neither did he intend to double-cross Morley. On moral grounds he should, but on the other hand the Comstock estate would not miss ten thousand dollars, and Morley had put up with plenty of grief in spite of his shyster scheming.

Insofar as these were concerned, the problem was easy. In a day or two Morley would collect, and so long as he, Kenyon, was not under suspicion of murder, he could disappear whenever he chose. . . . He gulped the rest of his drink and put the glass down hard, exasperation riding his thoughts. Like hell, he could! Suppose the police did not find Missing Finger? Suppose they found him and he turned out to be a decoy and not the real threat at all?

How could he go away until he had done something to live up to the word he had given Comstock? That—reassuring an old man who was about to die—was the one decent thing he had done since he arrived, and though he tried to tell himself it was silly to let a thing like that promise influence him now, he could not get it out of his mind.

Well, he was staying. He knew that now. Let Morley think what he liked. Starting tomorrow he was going to keep an eye on Sally whether she liked it or not. He was going to tell Fleming of his talk with Comstock and of the man's suspicions. Later, when this was all over, he could tell the truth to Sally. It would not hurt Nora then; not if he warned her so that she could make her peace with Carl.

He got up, thinking hard. If Carl loved her he would forgive her for the part she played—if she was the one to tell him. She would be smart enough to know how to manage that, once she knew what had to be done. Carl would not kick much, since his inheritance would be doubled. No, that part was all right. The thing now was for Kenyon himself to show something, to do something that would justify the old man's faith in him.

He went into the hall and poked the light switches until nothing remained but a single lamp in the entryway; then headed for his room. He started to open the door before he remembered he was to see Nora, and then went back to her room and knocked, reaching for the knob as he did so.

The knob turned under his hand but there was no answer and he knocked again, opening the door a few inches, seeing then that the room was dark.

"Nora."

He opened the door a little more, believing she had dropped off to sleep and not wanting to startle her.

"Nora. It's Tony."

Suddenly he found himself holding his breath and listening. Driven by some urgency he could not explain, he stepped inside and light from the hall fell across the bedroom floor. Opposite him the windows stood open. Curtains waved gently at him and a breeze slid along the floor and curled up along his ankles, bringing a sudden chill that reached clear to his heart.

He could see the bed and something dark stretched out there, and now he knew that something was wrong, horribly wrong, and called her name again, hoarsely, as he groped for the light switch.

Then the room was bright and he saw her lying on the bed, not under the covers but on top, face down, still clad in the black negligee. He saw other things in that fearful instant before he could move—the disordered state of the room, the open traveling-bags with scattered contents; then he was at the bed, shaking her shoulder and calling her name.

"Nora," he cried, his voice hollow, "Nora."

The point of her shoulder was warm and soft and limp under his grasp. He reached for the other, lifting and turning her quickly on her back. Then he saw her face and panic struck at him. He let go of her and stepped back.

For a split instant he thought about the telephone and the doctor and then he was dragging her from the bed and turning her face down on the floor.

Later he found it difficult to explain how he knew what was the matter. When viewed dispassionately and with suspicion, such things as instinct and intuitive conclusions often fall apart, but now these were the forces that drove him on, that told him Nora had been smothered or strangled in some way—and but a very short time ago. That was why he straddled her and tried in his frenzied, clumsy way to apply artificial respiration.

How long he worked over her he was never sure, for to Kenyon it was but a period of concentration, of frantic effort; a timeless interval in which he was conscious only of his aching arms and tortured lungs and dry, constricted throat.

She was dead. He knew it. It was too late now, and yet something within that was sickness and fear and desperation drove him on. Once he thought he heard a knock on the door. He did not remember calling out, nor hearing it open.

What made him stop was a ragged cry of anguish that struck him mute and immobile. When he looked up, Carl Sherman was standing in the doorway, his face ghastly, his eyes wide open and stricken with horror.

For a second or more Kenyon stared at him, unable to move, unable even to think, yet taking in the picture of the other in his trousers and shirt and silk robe; then Sherman was on his knees, knocking Kenyon aside and turning the limp figure so he could see the face.

The rest was pure nightmare. With exhaustion creeping up on him, he could hear, vaguely, Sherman call her name in hushed and strangled tones. He saw him touch her face once, and then, without warning, Sherman had turned on him, striking out, shouting, knocking him backward.

Somehow Kenyon gained his feet, not trying to strike

back but only to defend himself. Talking, trying to explain but not knowing what he said, he moved in close and grabbed, and in their struggle they tripped and fell and Kenyon rolled, getting, finally, a stranglehold and applying it as it had been applied to him the night before.

"Carl!" he said. "Stop it! It wasn't me, do you hear? It wasn't me. I was trying to revive her. I found her that way."

As suddenly as it began the tempest stopped. One instant Sherman struggled violently against Kenyon's increasing pressure; the next he went limp all over. Kenyon let go and rolled clear.

"We've got to get a doctor," he said. "You stay here."

It was just something to say. A doctor would do no good now. Nothing would. He straightened slowly and felt so weak and shaken that he had to grab hold of a chair back to keep his knees from buckling.

Sherman was sitting on the floor, one hand over his face and the other bracing him. Kenyon looked away but he could not shut out the dry, sobbing sounds as the man tried to get his breath. He stood there another few seconds, taking deep gulps of air and waiting for his strength to come back. He looked about the room, as though at something he had never seen before, and saw again the open drawers and bags, the purse on the floor, its vanity and lipstick and papers spilled out by the killer in his hurried search.

He thought he knew how it had happened. There had been a bruise on her jaw and Nora had struggled, as he had the night before, but this time there had been no chloroform and she had struggled too much and the murderer had held on too long. It made him faint and sick inside to think about it and he went quickly into the hall.

He telephoned the police first and answered questions automatically; then he called the hotel and was connected with Morley's room.

"Get up!" he said. "Get dressed!" He kept talking, not letting Morley interrupt. "Somebody murdered Nora. You'd better come over."

He hung up without waiting for an answer, knowing there was nothing more he could say that would matter. He went into the library and got the decanter and glass. He did not take a drink, but took the whisky back to the room for Carl Sherman.

Chapter Seventeen

A TIGHTENING NOOSE

LIEUTENANT NASH conducted his investigation in the drawing-room and this time it did not take long. The medical examiner's verdict—pending an autopsy—was that death had occurred from asphyxia. There were no marks on the body other than a bruise on the chin which had probably been inflicted during the struggle. Now, having made his preliminary examination, the doctor was questioning Kenyon.

"There was no pillow over her face when you found her?"

"No."

The doctor, a trim-figured man with a black mustache and glasses, glanced at Nash.

"Well, I think a pillow was used. There were no marks on her neck and I don't think a p.m. will show any hemorrhage or fracture in the hyoid bone or laryngeal cartilages. I think she was smothered on the bed."

Kenyon sat staring into the empty fireplace. He had given no details except to say he had found her on the bed and pulled her to the floor in a futile attempt to resuscitate her, and he felt too numbed and despondent to elaborate now.

"Well," Nash said, "if you find anything—"

"I'll have a full report by afternoon," the doctor said, and went out.

Nash walked part way with him, nodding to Fleming, who followed. They could be heard talking in low tones and when Nash came back he said:

"I guess that's about all for now."

"All?"

Marion Sherman sat up, her long face stiff and white at the cheekbones, her voice a little shrill.

"But when are you going to do something about it? Three times it's happened. To Andy and Tony and now Nora. Two of them are dead and—" She broke off suddenly as her husband put a hand on her arm.

He did not look at her, but sat on the divan, his chin on his chest and his jaw hard. For a moment no one said anything. Fleming and Nash were watching her and Morley was watching Kenyon and looking worried about what he saw. Carl Sherman sat alone, motionless, his round face chalky and his eyes vacant and staring.

"I'm sorry," Marion said. "It's just that—that—"

"I know, Mrs. Sherman," Nash said.

"How can we tell he won't be back again—whoever he is? How can any of us sleep?"

"Would you feel any better if I left a couple of my men here?"

Marion blinked, as though the thought had not occurred to her.

"Why—yes. I'd feel decidedly better."

"Fine," Nash said. "I think it might be a good idea, anyway." He pushed his lips out and sucked them back. He looked pretty weary and discouraged and his voice was tired.

"If you had thought of this before, it might not have happened," Paul Sherman said, still not looking up.

Nash's ruddy face got pink. He opened his mouth, closed it; then he shrugged and tried again.

"If you have any idea we haven't been thinking the same thing, Mr. Sherman, you're mistaken. It's pretty evident now that we should have done just that. It didn't seem so today because this was one of those things that became evident only after it was all over."

He looked over at Kenyon, surveying him with steady eyes before he spoke. "By the way, Mr. Comstock, what was the name of the orchestra you played with in Los Angeles?"

Automatically Kenyon told him the name of the organization Morley had given him; then, realizing the significance of the question, he felt as though someone had slugged him in the pit of the stomach. It took another second to collect himself. He had to discipline his voice in order to keep it from shaking.

"But, look here," he said. "You're not suggesting—"

"I'm suggesting nothing," Nash said. "We're still looking for a guy with a missing finger. The way that room was searched tonight follows out the pattern of what happened before, to your father and to you. Nobody around here knows a thing about the case." He paused to glance at the others. "Or if they do they're holding out. But the fact remains, Mr. Comstock, that within twenty-four hours the two people closest to you—your father and your wife —have been murdered. And under the circumstances we intend to keep right on digging until we get what we're after."

He hesitated again, his shrewd gaze measuring everyone in the room. "Until we're sure, every single one of you will remain under suspicion. Not one of you has an alibi that is worth anything, and as far as motives go, we have a few that might stand up pretty well in court, given enough facts to go with them. . . . Well, I'll put two men on the place. If anything else happens in this house it won't come from outside."

Leon Morley was burning. Kenyon had seen the hint of it in the detective's knotted jaws and in the amber coldness of his gaze while he was waiting for a chance to get Kenyon alone. Now, in the library, he shut the door and stepped close.

"Damn you!" he said with quiet savageness. "Why did you have to find her? Why didn't you stay at the hotel and do your drinking, like I asked you?"

"I didn't do any drinking. I only—"

"You know how it looks, don't you? You've got no alibi and Sherman walks in and finds you working over her on the floor. That can look more than one way to a jury." He broke off with a curse, turned away, and came back. "You wouldn't stay with me. Oh, no! You didn't want to spend the night there, you wanted to come home and—"

He cut the sentence short, and leaned close, his face less than a foot from Kenyon's, his narrowed eyes probing and intent. "If I thought you— No. You couldn't be that much of a dope."

He said a lot more things in the same vein that Kenyon heard only with his ears because his brain was working on something even more frightening.

"They're going to check on me," he said finally.

"Check on you? Certainly they're going to check on you. That Nash is going to be a tough baby from now on."

"They'll get in touch with the orchestra."

"Who cares? Joe Anthony played with it and you're Joe Anthony."

"They'll ask for a description."

"Sure, and who do you think that description will fit? What do you think I put that ad in the paper for? They're going to say he was slender and medium tall, with light brown hair and blue eyes—and that fits you."

"They'll check on other things."

"Maybe, but not at first. Checking with the orchestra is a good thing. It's a corroboration that, with what we've already given him, will quiet Nash a little more. Later, maybe, he'll know, but we've still some time."

He pulled out a stick of gum, started to unwrap it, and then threw the whole business violently at the wastebasket.

"Damn it all, it's the motive that'll keep Nash on your tail. If it wasn't for that guy with the missing finger you'd be in a cell now; you'd be as good as on the gallows."

Kenyon sat down. Beaten and bruised by what had happened, he had a hard time thinking straight under Morley's rapid-fire assault.

"Suppose we told the truth," he said finally, forgetting in his despair that it was now too late.

"The truth! Hah! The truth, he says," Morley jeered. "That would be fine, that would be just great. That would be all Nash would need."

"He's going to find it out, anyway."

"Maybe. But can't you get it through that thick skull that until he does we've got a little time? When he knows the truth we're cooked, both of us. Suppose we went to him and told him everything, suppose I said I'd tricked you into taking on this job. Do you know what would happen? I'll tell you. I'd lose ten thousand bucks—but that's all."

He came up and tapped Kenyon's shoulder. "Do you know what Nash's theory about you would be? Do you know what the District Attorney would tell a jury? He'd tell them that you came along with me to make five hundred bucks. Of course he'd make me out a prime heel too, but that I could stand. He'd say that after you got here you talked with the old man and found out you were going to inherit a fortune and saw how you could get it. Somebody wanted something he had and searched his rooms—that much we know—and you took advantage of this to kill and throw suspicion elsewhere.

"And having gone that far there was something else you had to do. Nora played into your hands by pretending she was your wife, but she fell for Carl and you were afraid she would talk and you had to kill her too. You have no corroboration for that chloroform business except Mrs. Sherman's piece about the guy in the car with the missing finger and that wouldn't amount to a damn." He stopped, lips flattening. "You know, if one more thing happened it would be perfect; one more thing and you wouldn't have

a prayer, missing finger or no missing finger. All that needs
to happen now is for somebody to knock me off. That
would do it. The old man, and then the only two people
who knew the truth."

Kenyon listened, bewildered, incredulous, yet seeing
with horrible clarity the soundness of the theory.

"That," said Morley, "is what the D.A.'s premise will be
and I'll be damned if you could refute it, no matter what
either of us said."

Some of the fire went out of him with that. The spring
had run down, and with its tension gone, he looked tired
and restless. His jaw wasn't quite so hard and his thin
lips were slack and presently he went over to the wastebasket and dug out the gum he'd thrown there. Kenyon
watched, trying to think, and when at last Morley had his
teeth working on his gum the detective came up to him
and spoke levelly.

"We've still got a chance. It may take Nash a couple
of days to get the truth about Joe Comstock and he may
not get it at all. But if he does I'm washed up and the only
thing that will save you is for somebody to nail that guy
that chloroformed you."

"We'll find him," Kenyon said.

"We've got to. He's our boy and if he isn't he'll be working for the one who is. If we could be sure of getting him
before Nash cracks this other—" He paused, cocking his
head and closing one eye. "You know, if there was only
some place you could go, I think it would be a good idea
to duck. I mean if Nash cracks this thing of ours."

"No," Kenyon said. "That would be just like admit-
ting—"

"Yes, but there's something else. You don't know how
cops work. If Nash gets the truth he'll throw you in the
can and there won't be any bail. And once he gets you he'll
be concentrating, not on old Missing Finger, but on building a case against you. Oh, he won't quit on the other guy.

But what I mean is, you're going to look so good to him that he's going to use all he's got in making an airtight case."

"Where could I go—even if I wanted to?"

"That's it." Morley shrugged. "No place, I guess. No good hitting the road; they'd only pick you up. If you could get a room, a little apartment maybe, and lay low —someplace where I could keep in touch while we bear down on Missing Finger—" He sighed and turned to the door. "But I guess you couldn't. . . . Well, maybe we can nail him before it's too late."

He opened the door, hesitated, then grinned a crooked wry grin that was reflected in his voice.

"Boy, was that a mistake, picking you up off that park bench?"

The police came back shortly before ten the following evening. For most of the morning Nash and Bauer had been examining Nora's room and asking questions and looking over the grounds, and when they finally left the two men who had been on guard during the night went with them.

Kenyon learned all this from Hilton, since he himself had been away from the house most of the day, and he knew that for him it was only a question of time. Nora's death had destroyed any hope he had of clearing himself and all he could think of now was to make the most of the hours of freedom which remained.

For this reason he had hired a car and when Sally Hay-den left her apartment that morning, he had followed her downtown, parking where he could watch the alleyway behind the *Sun* Building as well as the front entrance. At noon she had come out with Spence Arden and they had lunch together, and shortly after they returned Lieutenant Nash entered with Sergeant Bauer. They had stayed the better part of an hour and later in the afternoon Fleming had arrived, though he had not remained long.

Shortly after six Sally left in her coupé and Kenyon followed, waiting outside a tearoom while she dined alone and putting down the temptation to walk in and join her. By that time he was a man grabbing at straws. Comstock had been afraid something might happen to her. Nothing had. Yet Comstock had been so right in his other fears that Kenyon would take no chance now, and not until she had driven to her apartment and put her car away did he return to the house. Now, as he cleaned up and prepared to go back to the apartment and resume his vigil, Hilton had come to his room to tell him that Lieutenant Nash would like to see him.

Kenyon had heard the two cars come up the drive, and watched them swing to a stop at the front entrance and park with lights on. He felt no surprise when Hilton told him who it was because he'd felt, somehow, that they would come. He had thought about it often that afternoon, sitting in the car and waiting, just as he had thought about Morley's suggestion of flight. That he had stayed was due chiefly to his stubbornness and the desire to vindicate himself and Comstock. He could see things closing in but he couldn't run. While he had freedom he had a chance. If he lost it, well, at least he had tried to keep his word.

There were two plain-clothes men in the front hall and a third was standing in the entryway looking out the glass inserts at the sides of the door frame. The two plain-clothes men looked him over and he looked back, and that was when he saw the long, black-leather case on the floor behind them.

"You'll find them in the library, sir," Hilton said.

Kenyon made some reply, but all he could see was the leather case; all that he silently asked was that his nerves quiet so that he could go in and talk calmly, indifferently, and make them prove each thing they said. For in that long case would be a trombone and Kenyon knew that if

Nash had gone that far he would undoubtedly be prepared to go further.

The library door was open and Sergeant Bauer closed it behind Kenyon and sat down on a chair arm. Nash had leaned his chunky hips against the table and waited, his arms folded and his face a little grim around the lips but otherwise expressionless.

Kenyon said good evening and what was on their minds.

"A few more questions, Mr. Comstock," Nash said, "and this time I don't think it will take long."

"Have you found Missing Finger?"

"No, but we will. We've got a pretty good line on him now—but that's not what I came to talk about. . . . The other day you told Paul Sherman you used to work for the Gainsburg *Star*."

So they finally got to that, Kenyon thought. Aloud he said, "That's right."

Nash gave Bauer a sidelong glance that held a glint of satisfaction. "Mr. Sherman thought maybe we should get in touch with them. We did." He paused, building up for the punch line. "They say that they never heard of anybody named Joseph Anthony—or Joseph Comstock either."

Kenyon found a certain perverse pleasure in prolonging the discussion. He knew it would do no good in the end because they could re-check, but for now he had an answer Nash could not refute. He let his brows climb, spoke mildly.

"You didn't ask them about anyone called Tony Kenyon?"

"Kenyon? No." Nash frowned and glanced uncertainly at Bauer.

Kenyon laughed and it didn't sound too bad.

"You should have," he said. "I don't wonder you were suspicious. When I worked there I used the name of Kenyon—Tony Kenyon. Don't ask me why. I used other names—none of them Comstock—before I got into the orchestra business. You could call the *Star* again. I think they'd remember me. I think they'd even describe me for you."

The flush deepened in Nash's ruddy face and his eyes got unpleasant. He was a good cop, Nash, and he had handled many murder cases in his time and most of them were not difficult to solve. In the majority of them the motive was obvious, the culprit easy to pick out. Often there were witnesses and once he had a suspect he could generally get to work on him with bare hands and no fear of the consequences.

In this case, however, he had been thwarted from the beginning by the personalities involved. These were no little people without money or influence. Comstock was important and the Shermans hardly less so. They had money, position, friends, and a powerful newspaper to back them up and Nash had to be careful. He was still careful, but not in quite the same way he had been that first night. He was still polite but inwardly he was aroused and frustrated. It had occurred to him that he was getting the run-around, and though he kept his voice down it now held an undertone of flat determination and assurance that had not been there before. His jaw was set, his gaze narrowed and relentless, and every move he made indicated that he was closing in, that he had the goods, that nothing Kenyon could say was going to make any difference.

"Okay," he said finally. "We'll check back, Mr. Comstock. Meanwhile, there's something else. We've also been in contact with the Los Angeles police—and the leader of that orchestra."

He hesitated and Kenyon took out cigarettes. He lit one and blew smoke off to one side. When Nash continued his scrutiny without speaking, he said:

"Do they miss me?"

"I don't know. The leader said you were pretty good. He said you were damned near as good as Dorsey."

"That's swell," Kenyon said; "but if you lugged that trombone up here"—he gestured toward the hall—"with the idea that I'd give a few licks you've wasted your time."

"You don't feel like playing, huh?" Bauer said.

"No."

"Maybe that's what they call temperament."

Nash silenced the sergeant with a glance. "It was just an idea," he said, "and I've got another one. The description we got of Joseph Anthony—Comstock—fits you all right, but the police and the orchestra leader say that Anthony was killed in a traffic crash."

Kenyon found a fleck of tobacco on his tongue and took it off with the tip of his finger, a little surprised that he could accept the announcement so calmly. He felt old and tired and beaten but he had been afraid of something like this for so long—it was curious to realize that it was only two nights ago that murder had trapped him—that he had no further capacity for discouragement.

"Really?" he said. "And did it ever occur to you that the Joseph Anthony who played the trombone and the one who was a traffic victim might not be the same person?"

"Yes," Nash said. "It occurred to us. It would be a coincidence but possible. And that's why we're here. We can't make you play the trombone and if you could that might be coincidence too. But there's one more thing, and that you can't explain away. You've either got it or you haven't."

Kenyon waited and when he saw the expression on Nash's ruddy face he knew that, whatever it was, this was it. Nash had something he was pretty damn sure of. These preliminaries just led up to the crusher and now he was ready to apply it.

"Well?" he said.

"The real Joseph Comstock had a birthmark." Nash

pushed away from the table and dropped his arms. "As a four-year-old child it was about the size of a penny and on you it should be much larger. If you've got a patch like that on the back of your left shoulder blade—or a scar— we'll shove along."

Kenyon's face was stiff and he bent it into a grin. "You want me to take my shirt off here?"

"That's right. It won't take but a minute." Nash waited, lip curling. "Of course if you want to be stubborn we'll have to take you down to headquarters. After that we'll see if we can't find some way to take a peek."

"Oh?"

"Yeah. And in case you're thinking about a warrant, forget it. We've got one. . . . Well?"

Kenyon stepped to an ash tray and ground out his cigarette. He kept the grin on and gave it to Nash and then to Bauer.

"All right," he said. "I think I'll go along with you, just for the hell of it—and the ride. I suppose you'll bring me back—after you're satisfied."

Nash's face darkened dangerously and for an instant he seemed about to speak; then he clamped his jaw shut and clapped on his hat.

"We'll bring you back—"

"Maybe," said Bauer.

Kenyon opened the door, holding the knob and drawing back, bowing with mock politeness, extending his hand to signal them to precede him.

Bauer went out. Nash glared and followed. With Bauer it was probably overconfidence, but with the lieutenant it was more anger than anything else. Had he not been furious he might have been suspicious, but now he stalked out and before he could turn Kenyon slammed the door, twisted the key, and wheeled toward the windows.

Chapter Eighteen

Too Late for Truth

Until the very last Kenyon had had no idea of escape. Even when he realized that he was actually to be taken to jail, he had seen no way to avoid arrest. That he had made the attempt at all was largely a matter of impulse, but now, having made the first move, he knew what was behind this desire to break away.

He had a window open as the pounding began on the door, and found himself on the narrow balcony which ran along the back of the house to the living-room. He dropped over the railing as Morley had done two nights before and was running when he hit the gravel driveway, skirting the tennis court and then sprinting through the darkness of the garden.

He heard a window open as he vaulted the shrub border at the rear and he knew someone had reached the balcony through the living-room. He kept on, falling twice when something tripped him. Behind him a car roared to life and then another, their motors blending in a rising crescendo as they tore down the drive; then he was at the back of the lot and running along a fence toward the corner.

It was a stout-looking fence of heavy wire mesh, about six feet high and covered with vines. When it turned back from the corner and he realized he was trapped, he ran right at it, caught the top and pulled himself upward, balancing stiff-armed, then swinging one leg up and dragging the other after it.

He dropped to a sidewalk, scurried across the street. Off to his right he heard a car and looked in time to see it turn the corner. Luckily a two-foot hedge fencing in someone's front yard was close, and he hurdled it and sprawled flat, hugging the ground as the headlights swung past and the car raced up the street.

By the sound of it, it was still in second gear. The driver was flicking a spotlight from side to side, the quick bright beam searching walks and front yards and porches. Kenyon could hear its two occupants talking as it went by, and when it swung left at the corner he jumped up and sprinted for the opposite one.

Here he paused, looking first one way and then another. When he saw no car lights, he took a chance and ran across the street, continuing for half a block before he slowed down and began to pick his way through back yards and alleys. He took his time now, on the lookout for clotheslines and trash barrels, careful that he make no unnecessary noise. Two or three times in the next two blocks he heard cars racing by on the street, and twice his heart thumped his ribs when dogs barked at him; but he kept on, his luck holding, confidence rising.

At no time had he felt any sense of fear. There was a steady tingling along the surface of his skin and inside a thrill of excitement stirred him. It was a new kind of feeling and he found it comforting and stimulating, even though he knew his freedom would be short lived.

Until now things had happened to him and he had been shoved around, and he had done nothing at all to merit the faith Comstock had placed in him. This, at least, was something positive. This was action and he did not worry now about what would eventually happen but thought instead of his temporary success and that he might, after all, be able to do one of the things he had so wanted to do before he was caught.

He approached Sally Hayden's apartment house from the rear and moved along the wall with care until he reached the front. There were three or four cars parked here and he stood awhile, watching them, before he was satisfied that they were empty; then he moved swiftly across the front, and along the court to the first entrance.

The lower door was not locked and he went up without ringing, noting that there were two apartments on each floor. Hers was on the right, a front one, and when he saw the crack of light under the door his relief was so acute that for a moment he felt all weak and shaken. He made himself wait until he had his breath, until his nerves had steadied, before he knocked.

He stood close, watching the doorknob. When it turned he put his shoulder against the panel, moving with it as it started to swing back, shoving one foot in the opening before he glanced up.

His precautions were unnecessary. She did not try to close the door, but opened it wider, a slim dark figure in a quilted house coat, her hair drawn back and her hazel eyes startled but unafraid.

"Oh," she said. "You."

"Hello," Kenyon said, a little ashamed now but still determined. "Can I come in?"

She hesitated, holding to the doorknob, her glance uncertain. "Why—"

"It won't be for long. I don't think I'll have much time."

She did not answer but turned and moved back. He went in and closed the door, locking it behind him.

She was waiting in the center of the room. Her eyes were still wide with uncertainty and there was a certain breathlessness in her manner, but when he saw she was not afraid, when he realized again how small and lovely she looked, a tightness came into his throat and he had to grin to counteract it.

"Maybe you'd better sit down," he said. "I've got quite a lot to say."

She stood right where she was, nothing moving but her eyes, which finally left his face and slid down and focused on his knees. He looked, seeing now the stains where he had fallen, realizing how he must seem to her without his hat or coat.

"Yeah," he said, "I left in a hurry and the way I came it was dark. I don't think the lieutenant liked it."

She answered quietly. "They were going to arrest you?"

"I think that was the general idea. Of course, they still will, but I had an idea that once they tossed me in a cell I wouldn't be having a chance to talk to you." He shrugged, making it sound as though it wasn't important because that was the only way he could do it. "I doubt if you'd be calling on me and so I stopped by to tell you what I've been wanting to tell you for quite a while. Now I can, because it won't make any difference."

"They think you killed Andy and Nora," she said, still not moving.

"Something like that."

"But what about the other man? The one who—"

"Has the missing finger? Oh, they're still hunting for him. But I'm looking better to them all the time. That's why I stopped by. You see, Nash has got the idea that I'm not Joe Comstock. . . . And of course he's right. I'm not. The name is Tony Kenyon."

He waited for some exclamation, watching for the surprise to strike her face. Then it was his turn for surprise because nothing happened. She caught her lip and her eyes were troubled, but that was all. He was still waiting when she went to the sofa and sat down in the corner, drawing her feet under her and revealing yellow pajama legs.

"Was it the birthmark?"

Kenyon stared. "How did you know?"

"I'm the one who told them about it."

Kenyon looked round for something to sit on and found a chair. He was glad it was close.

"Don't tell me you knew I was a phony all the time."

"I didn't know it until you came."

"But—"

"The police came this afternoon. Lieutenant Nash said there was some doubt in his mind about you and did I know of any way he could be sure." She glanced past him, her eyes distant. "I told him he must be mistaken, but I did remember one thing Andy had told me—that his son had been born with a birthmark on his left shoulder. He told me so many things. That was one of them."

"But you couldn't know whether I had the mark or not."

"No. Until you said you had run away from the police. If you *had* been Joe Comstock you wouldn't have run, would you?"

Kenyon let his breath come out and grinned again. "That's nice figuring. . . . Well, now all I'll have to tell you is how I happened to be here at all."

"Where *is* the real Joe Comstock?"

"He's dead."

"Oh."

"He was killed in a traffic accident a couple of weeks ago in Los Angeles."

The distance was still in her eyes but there was a frown at the edges and topping the bridge of her nose.

"Then it was Mr. Morley," she said. "He wanted to earn his bonus."

"He didn't see how it would do any harm. I was only supposed to stay two or three days. I was to say I didn't want to stay and disappear. . . . But before I tell you the rest there's something else. I didn't kill Comstock, Sally. I didn't kill Nora. I'd never seen her before when she walked in that night. I liked her. She was swell. When I tell you about her you'll see what I mean. I didn't kill her and I hope you'll believe that—though I don't see why you should."

"I believe you," Sally said.

Kenyon felt a sudden lift and some new warmth coursed through him.

"Do you know why?"

Her glance came back to him and steadied. "Must there be some reason?"

And then she was sitting bolt upright, looking at the door, then back at him, her eyes wider now and agitated. When he started to speak she silenced him, one hand lifting suddenly. Then he heard it—the sound of steps on the stairs outside.

He stood up, a sinking feeling attacking his stomach. He faced the door. The steps were louder, nearer, now. Then there was a tug on his arm and Sally was close and trying to draw him toward an inner hall. He stared down at her, uncomprehending, and took a reluctant step.

Even though he expected it the knock was loud and startling, the following silence shocking in its suddenness. He found himself taking other steps and wet his lips and might have spoken had not Sally called out first.

"Yes? Who is it?"

"The police, Miss Hayden. See you a minute?"

Kenyon was in the little hall now and she still had him by the arm, steering him toward an open door.

"All right," she called again. "In a moment."

Then Kenyon found himself in a bathroom and she had snapped on the light. "Here!" she said, and pushed him behind the door. He stumbled back in the corner and watched dazedly as she bent over the tub and turned a faucet and the drain lever.

"Stay there," she said, at the same time tossing the bathmat on the floor.

He drew back in the corner, realizing that from the way the door was hung there was a triangle here just big enough. A second later Sally was back, dumping stockings and underthings on the floor.

He could hear, in the hall, the sound of garments brushing the walls and then something yellow fluttered past the edge of the door and helped to make the silken pile larger.

The pajamas didn't make sense then but they did later.

"Coming," he heard her call and then the door closed and he was standing in the corner, stiffly, hearing nothing but the pounding of the water in the tub.

To Kenyon the next two minutes were interminable. Steam floated from the tub and coated the mirror and the heat closed in and he could not tell whether his face was wet from perspiration or only from the steam. When he finally heard the doorknob rattle he drew back and held his breath, and then he realized why Sally had discarded the pajamas. There was nothing underneath that quilted robe and she wanted the policemen to know it so that it would make more convincing the story of her bath.

"You have no right to come here at all," she was saying, indignation in her tone. "The *Sun* will have something to say about this. I was just about to take a bath and if you think I'm in the habit of undressing before strangers—"

"Oh—yeah," a man's voice said, and Kenyon, glancing down at the pile of clothes, knew he could not get in unless he stepped on them. "Well, I'm sorry, but the lieutenant told us to be sure and—" The rest was cut off when the door closed.

She came back a minute later and glanced round the corner, her face a little flushed and a half smile in her eyes. "All right," she said. "You can wait in the living-room." She turned off the water and when he went out she was picking up her clothes.

She came into the room a few minutes later wearing gray slacks and a tan pull-over. Her hair was still back and she wore no make-up and her bare feet were thrust into fuzzy slippers that made her seem even smaller. She looked cute as hell to Kenyon and he nearly said so.

"Thanks," he said. "Thanks a lot, though I don't know why you bothered. They'll get me any way."

She curled up on the sofa again and selected a cigarette from a box on the end table. He stepped up to give her a light and she blew smoke at him and leaned back, her glance speculative.

"That's what you said before. But since you went to all that trouble of running away and coming here to tell me a story I thought I'd better hear it."

He sat down on the opposite end of the sofa, examining his cigarette and wondering where to start. He was still conscious of some inner excitement and he did not know whether it was just being here like this that caused it, or whether it was the thought of what she had done. He could not forget her ready self-reliance, the quick in- geniousness with which she met the problem, and so, presently, he found himself talking, a little haltingly at first, and then easily, with no desire to impress but only to unburden himself of those things that had been torment- ing him.

He told her of Morley's search for Comstock's son, and how, having found him and persuaded him to return, the accident spoiled his chance for success. He explained about the advertisement in the newspaper and how Morley had framed him on a robbery charge.

"But that's not an excuse," he said quickly. "I could have figured out some way of giving him the slip later if I'd really thought it was important. That was the trouble. By then I didn't much care. I may even have thought it was a pretty slick trick. I do know that I was glad to be coming east, and that five hundred he promised me looked pretty big."

He put out his cigarette and his voice got sardonic.

"If you've gathered from all this that I'm a grade-A heel, you've got the general idea pretty well. I was going to walk in, play a part for two days, and walk out. Oh, I rationalized the whole thing every time I felt a little guilty —which wasn't often. Young Comstock was dead and his old man would never see him, so if I acted the part well and then disappeared he would at least have figured that he'd had his son with him for two or three days. You know, it's easy to figure these things when you want to. The fact that Morley was technically gypping the old boy out of ten thousand—with my help—didn't bother my conscience at all."

He waited to see if she wanted to say anything and then went on, not looking at her.

"At no time did I see that I was doing any great harm. I'd be gone. No one would care. Eventually the estate would go to the rightful heirs and that would be that. But all that seems a long time ago now. That was before Nora, and the first murder. I couldn't tell the truth then; Morley made that clear. And now, well, you can see how it is. I'm a phony who came to do a job and saw a way to improve on it. I killed the old man to inherit half the estate and then killed Nora to prevent her from exposing me. It makes a pretty good case when you stop to think of it." He laughed shortly. "And now, after all his grief, even Morley is out in the cold."

"Yes," Sally said. "If it hadn't been for the murder—"

"It would have been okay. Or almost okay. Not quite, though it could have been if it hadn't been for you."

"Me?"

"Yes, you."

She sat up, frowning, lips parted.

"How do you mean?"

"I mean, I was all set to do a job. Conscience all taken care of, no qualms, plenty of confidence. Then I meet you, and talk to you—"

"But why should that—"

"I asked you the same sort of question a little while ago, remember? What did you say?"

Color touched her throat and seeped upward. She got very busy picking fuzz off her slippers.

"I said, 'Must there be a reason?' "

Kenyon grinned, though she did not look at him. "Um-hum. And I'm going to give you one because I guess that's really why I came. What happened was, you knocked me over. I'd never known anyone quite so lovely and before the first afternoon was over my equilibrium was all upset. I was ashamed. It turned out to be a different sort of job entirely. Even Morley got worried, though he didn't know what my trouble was. And then, that evening, I could see how impossible everything was."

"That's why you were so bitter on the terrace."

"And that's also why I kissed you like I did. I knew I shouldn't and I did because—oh, I don't know. Because I knew I never would again. . . . Sally."

She looked up, her cheeks pinker now and something in her eyes he had never seen before.

"I want you to know that," he said. "You've got to believe that. I promised myself then that I was going when my time was up. It was too late then to tell the truth and I wanted more than anything to stay and be Tony Kenyon but I couldn't. You see, don't you? I couldn't stay at all. Even if there hadn't been a murder I wouldn't have tried to live as Comstock's son, and that you must believe."

She was frowning, looking beyond him again. "You didn't have to stay this long. You could have gone yesterday. You could have got away. Then they would know you could not have killed Nora. They would have known it was someone else. You could have gone away."

"Yes," Kenyon said. "I could have gone. If it hadn't been for one thing." And then, not meaning to, the story of his talk with Comstock came tumbling out in hurried sentences that were not always specific and were often confused. When it was all over he realized how the story of that promise sounded and said so. "I guess it sounds sort of silly," he said. "I guess I had an idea in the back of my head that since I had promised maybe I should do something, but when you add it all up I've done exactly nothing—to help myself or anyone else."

She bent her head, watching her hands. He could not see her face nor know what was taking place in her eyes. Then he knew that he had said all there was to say and it was time to go. He pushed out of the chair slowly and adjusted his coat and tie.

"Well, that's it," he said. "That's what I wanted to say —a little more than I wanted to say, I guess—and I'll always be grateful for the opportunity."

He turned slowly and stepped to the door, taking care not to look at her again. He turned the knob and found it locked and reached for the key. He heard her jump up, heard her voice, though there was no word only some sound in her throat; then she was beside him, her hand on his arm.

"Where are you going?"

He started to smile, not understanding. "Going? Why down to see the lieutenant, I guess."

"But you can't. He'll arrest you."

"Sure. What else is there? Where could I go like this? Even if I tried to get away they'd catch me—and I'm not going to try. I didn't kill them and—"

"But don't you see?" she said, and then she was giving him the same argument Morley had offered. "Think how it will look? Those motives. You can't go now—not until they find that other man. He must be the one and when they find him they'll know you're innocent and then—"

He smiled and eased her to one side so he could turn the key. Then abruptly she had shaken off his hand and wedged her body in between him and the door.

"Tony! Listen to me." She caught her breath and looked up, her mouth pale. "You can stay here."

"No."

"You've got to. For a little while. For a day or two. Until they find that man. I can get Paul and Carl to offer a reward. Morley can help. No one will have to know you're here."

Without realizing it he found himself being slowly pushed back. Her hands were on his chest and though he could not understand, nor quite believe it was happening, he knew that he would stay.

"All right," he said, and his throat closed and something was stinging the backs of his eyes. It took everything he had to resist the impulse to take her in his arms, to bend his head and put it on her shoulder; but he did it and swallowed fast to clear his throat. "All right," he said again. "Relax."

"Sit down," she ordered, pushing him to the sofa. "And stay right there till I come back."

Chapter Nineteen

DANGER IN A NOTEBOOK

KENYON WAS STILL ON THE COUCH when Sally Hayden came back with a blanket in one hand, a sheet and pillow case in the other, and a pillow under her arm. She dumped them in a pile at one end of the sofa and sat down.

"I don't need all that," Kenyon said. "The blanket'll be all right."

She gathered the two couch pillows and piled them on a chair and then shook out the pillow case.

"You've told me what happened *after* you'd seen Mr. Morley's ad," she said, "but you haven't told me how you happened to be there—on that park bench."

Kenyon had been watching her. He had an idea she didn't want to look at him yet from the way she busied herself with the pillow case. So he hauled out another cigarette and leaned back and told her how he had been drafted and about Hazel Wainwright; about the army and what had happened afterward.

"And why did you say you were a bum?" she asked when he had finished.

"I don't know. Probably I felt like one."

"Was it the girl?"

"Maybe. I guess that started it. I guess I couldn't take it. If I'd had any guts it wouldn't have mattered."

"I think it would. I think it would matter to anyone to have someone he loved and counted on jilt him that way. It might not matter, except to your pride, if you didn't care an awful lot, but if you did—"

"A guy should be able to take it," Kenyon said morosely. "Until then I guess I'd got by all right but after that I didn't care. I missed assignments in maneuvers. I sulked.

When I got tossed in the guardhouse it didn't matter. And you need something else beside physical fitness to be a good soldier. All I was looking forward to was the day I could get out and it came earlier than I expected.

"Just before the war they started to let out all those selectees who were twenty-eight or over." He chuckled grimly. "And I was one of the first. They couldn't get rid of me fast enough. I guess that's why they never called me up again. I didn't have the courage to go back and face Hazel and take the job that was waiting for me. . . ."

He gave Sally a covert glance. She had one end of the pillow under her chin, trying to fit it into the slip. "I didn't mean to cry about it but I guess that gives you an idea."

She kept working on the pillow and finally shook it down. She put it across her knees and began to smooth out the creases.

"Had you ever been away from home before? I mean, aside from school. Had you ever worked anywhere but Gainsburg?"

"No."

"Were you good at sports in college?"

He watched her, trying to figure out what she was driving at, and saw her put the pillow aside.

"No. My father was killed in an accident and I was the only child and I guess it did something to my mother. She wouldn't let me play football or baseball, even in high school. I lived with her and an aunt—"

"And they babied you."

"If they did it's still no excuse."

"Sit over here."

She pointed to a chair and he got up and moved to it, watching her spread the sheet. He forgot what he had been saying until she spoke again.

"I don't think you ever were a bum. I think you had an inferiority complex for one thing. You were never knocked around like other men. I can imagine how it would be, being coddled by two women. I don't think you ever had a real chance until you went in the army."

She tucked in the sheet and shook out the blanket. "And you admit you did all right until that other thing happened and then you were terribly hurt and you hadn't anything much to fall back on and help you over that hurt. The only way you've been a bum is in your own mind, Tony, and that's because you've been afraid. . . . There."

She stepped back, smiling faintly and pointing to the bed she'd made. "It will probably be too short for you, but I hope you can make it do." She started away and Kenyon, on his feet now, still could think of nothing to say. At the little hall she smiled. "I'll use the bathroom first," she said, "and get out of your way."

Kenyon sat down again, automatically, as though all this was happening in a dream. He was still sitting there when the hall door opened and her smile appeared in the crack.

"All right," she said. "Good night, Tony."

He said good night, but later, when the light was out and he settled himself under the blanket, he was still thinking, trying to figure out why she had told him all those things, wondering how it was possible for anyone to be so young and desirable and possess such understanding.

Kenyon awakened at dawn but it was so quiet that he fell asleep again. When he woke the second time the smell of coffee filled the room and dishes were rattling in the kitchen.

He turned over. He could see the breakfast nook and part of the kitchen and for a few seconds he lay there and watched. Sally wore a simple gray dress and a red-checked gingham apron. Sometimes her back was toward him and when it wasn't, when she passed the doorway, he played possum—until she caught him at it.

"All right," she said, shaking a fork. "You've got five

minutes."

Kenyon grinned and said good morning. He sat up, wrapped himself in the blanket, and went into the bath, carrying his clothes under his arm. Stripping, he bathed quickly and rinsed his mouth and peered gloomily at his sprouting beard. He did the best he could with his soiled shirt and took especial pains with his tie. When he got back, crisp bacon was drying on brown paper and two eggs sizzled in the pan.

"You can pull that toaster down," she said.

He did so, watching the two pieces of bread disappear, and with each passing minute his incredulity mounted. He still could not quite believe this could be true. He said so.

"I don't believe it," he said.

"What?"

"That this can be happening to me. Maybe if you pinched me real hard—"

"On such short acquaintance? Perhaps this will convince you." She put the bacon and the eggs in front of him.

"Hey. What about you?"

"I never eat them in the morning."

"But—"

"Eat," commanded Sally. "And you can pull the plug out of the percolator too."

Kenyon did so, and then the toast popped up and he was busy buttering it. He drank his orange juice and got to work on the bacon and eggs and there wasn't much talking until he had finished. The glow in his chest was constant and stimulating and for a while he forgot everything else and reveled in the mere fact of being here, of sitting across the table from her and hearing her voice.

But it could not last. Smoking a cigarette, he began to think again, remembering why he was here and what had happened last night. He recalled in detail the things he had told her and the memory of his confession brought a twinge of shame.

He took these thoughts to the sink with him when they washed and dried the dishes, and though they talked of many things of no importance, his mind was busy reviewing the arguments she had given him. She had said he'd never had a chance or been knocked around when he was younger. What she meant was that he had never learned to fight back and he saw that this was so.

Well, it was different now. Something had happened. He had no hope of escaping Nash for long, but somehow he wasn't so worried any more, somehow he felt that he could find an answer, that in the end he could do what Comstock had asked of him.

It was, he thought wryly, a little late to be waking up, but so long as he had his freedom, so long as Sally was on his side, there was a chance. . . . He began to think back, starting with the time he had arrived at the house and taking each sequence in order. He was still thinking hard when they went back into the living-room, and always his mind came back to the same question. He waited until Sally had folded the sheet and blanket on the sofa before he asked her about it.

"We still don't know what the murderer was looking for, do we? And why he searched my room, and Nora's—after he killed her?"

Sally gave him a startled look. She sat down on the sofa, holding the blanket on her knees.

"No."

Kenyon came over and sat down beside her.

"Think," he said. "Are you sure Comstock didn't say anything to you? He didn't give you anything at all that day?"

"No." She shook her head slowly. "The only thing I brought here was my attaché case. He went to the study to get it for me that evening. There was some copying—"

She broke off, watching Kenyon. He sat up, eyes half

closed and lips tight. He remembered now, how Comstock had said he would get Sally's case, and remembering thought, *If he wanted to get something out of the house without anyone knowing —*

He reached out and grabbed her hand. "Did you do it, that copying?"

"Why—no. I couldn't, somehow. I thought of it once and that reminded me of Andy and—"

"Get it!"

Her lashes lifted at his tone and for a second she searched his face with troubled eyes. She put the blanket aside and stood up. Kenyon rose with her, impatience riding him as he watched her go to the hall closet and take out the tan attaché case.

He put it on the table, opened it, seeing the handkerchief, the book of matches, the pack of cigarettes, half empty, the sheaf of yellow ruled paper with penciled longhand. Underneath this was a manila folder containing plain white paper, another folder with carbons. When he lifted this he saw the envelope. So did Sally, and reached for it first.

It was just a plain white envelope, the ordinary business size, sealed, and with something written across the face.

"What's that?"

"I—I don't know," she said, her voice hushed.

She twisted it to see what was written on it and Kenyon read the message over her shoulder. All it said was: *Sally— hold this for me.*

Kenyon cursed under his breath and grabbed for it but Sally was already tearing it open with trembling fingers. What she took out was a thin, paper-covered notebook, about the size of a small bankbook and no thicker. And right then, with the tension clamping down on him, he knew the answer. Not what the book meant, for when Sally snapped the pages open all he could see was a meaningless jumble of figures, but how it got there.

Given a start like this it was easy to think back, to re-member his chase of that first prowler and how, when he and Morley came back to the drawing-room and told what had happened, Comstock's hand had whipped up to his chest. Kenyon could see the startled gesture now and knew that this book had been in the man's inside pocket, that his hand had moved involuntarily to reassure him that it was safe.

He told Sally this now. "He had the book on him, but he knew that there might be another attempt and his best bet was to get it out of the house."

"But—he could have told me."

"Sure. He could have told us what was in it too. But he didn't. It was something he didn't want to talk about. He was going to turn it over to Fleming. If he had told you what he was doing he would have told you by inference that the book was dangerous. He probably didn't want to frighten you and this way was just as good. You wouldn't find it until the next day—"

"Yes," Sally said, "I see," and then they had their heads together, going through the book.

It meant nothing at all to Kenyon. Just a lot of figures and words, tightly written on each page. He could see that each one was different from any other, and he noticed then that each was numbered in red ink at the top.

He was halfway through it when Sally's head jerked up and he felt her stiffen beside him; then someone pounded on the door and he spun about, hearing her gasp, feeling her hand on his arm.

"Open up!" The voice struck at them through the door and it was Leon Morley's voice, "Come on, kids. I know you're there."

Sally was tugging at Kenyon's arm and he realized she was saying, "Hurry. The back way."

He shook his head and grinned at her. There might have been a time when he would have run for it, just on general principles. But no more. Not ever. There was going to be no more running.

"To hell with it," he said softly, and put the attaché case on the floor and kicked it under the sofa. "Go ahead. Let him in."

Chapter Twenty

THE UNINVITED GUEST

LEON MORLEY WAS IMMACULATE in his dark suit and gray topcoat. His rugged face looked as though he had just come from the barber and smelled that way. He came in slowly, amber eyes darting to all corners of the room, and suddenly he grinned.

"I should have known it," he said, closing the door. "I must be slipping. I couldn't figure where all those high-minded scruples came from that first day." The grin broadened as he looked at Sally. "It was the chick, here, all the time, wasn't it?"

Kenyon studied him a moment and was amazed to find that he felt pretty good. It made a lot of difference, once you'd made up your mind about a thing, and that's how it had been with him ever since he woke up. Never again would Morley worry him. He didn't know what the other's plans were, or whether he intended to turn him in to Nash, but whatever happened now he could take. He gave Sally a sidewise glance and a smile.

"Yes," he said, "it was the chick."

Even Sally smiled at that. It didn't last and she did not look very happy, but she didn't say anything; she just watched Morley and waited.

"How's Nash?" Kenyon asked.

"Steaming. But you got one break. There's nothing in the papers. According to them the police of six states are looking for Missing Finger, and that's okay. But Nash wanted no publicity about you and your run-out and the Shermans agreed. . . . Look, can we sit down?"

Sally took a chair and Kenyon and Morley sat on the sofa, the detective crossing his legs and balancing his hat on one knee while he hauled out a stick of gum.

"How do you stand?" Kenyon said.

"Not too bad—now."

"But Nash must know—"

"Sure Nash knows. But that isn't doing him much good. Our offense—which didn't come off because no money was paid—was against the Shermans, the way things stand. And they're okay now—because I got to them quick and made a deal."

"That I can understand."

Morley gave him a sidelong glance, half grin.

"What is that, sarcasm?"

"Whose story about how I got here did you tell the Shermans?"

"Yours. The right one." He grunted softly and began to work on the gum folder. "I did a lot of talking. Yes, sir, Morley did an awful lot of talking—fast, loud, and long. I was very frank. I practically threw myself at their mercy but I also convinced them that no harm had been done and that it wasn't my fault young Comstock had got killed, and that I'd worked hard enough to earn the ten grand anyway and besides what was the beef? Now they were splitting the estate right off, where if it hadn't been for me they'd have been held up while they traced young Comstock and got proof of death and one thing or another. Oh, I cooled them off after a while."

"Don't tell us you talked them out of the bonus."

Once again the grin went away. Morley looked at Sally and then squinted at Kenyon.

"What is it with you this morning? Am I screwy or are you the same guy I picked up—"

"No," Sally Hayden said. "He's not the same one at all."

"I don't get it." Morley was still squinting. "Now that you're one jump ahead of a prison cell and pretty fair murder rap you're not scared at all. Before that you went around like—"

"What about the bonus?"

"Oh, that? Well, it's like this. The Shermans don't pay off, and they sign no complaints—not even against you. You're clear, except for this murder business, and I think I've got them convinced that you had nothing to do with it. Of course, Nash is a cop. I can't do anything there unless—"

He stopped and sat up. "It's like this. I can still get ten thousand bucks if I turn in the killer."

"Oh," Sally said. "They offered a reward?"

"Not exactly, and not they. Paul wouldn't go for it and it's not exactly a reward. It's a sort of a deal. Carl Sherman wants the guy that killed Nora and if I can deliver I can collect from him."

Kenyon thought it over, and knowing how Carl felt about Nora, it made sense. That Morley had suggested the proposition—and that he had as good a chance as any of succeeding—also made sense when he considered the detective's regard for money.

"Are you going to turn me in?" he asked.

Morley looked insulted. "Hell, no. That is, unless I should get hold of some proof that you might be the killer. No. I came to see if there wasn't something you could think of that might give me a lead. I don't have to turn in this Missing Finger, or whoever he's working for, single-handed. But I've got to be in on it, and the farther in, the better."

Kenyon glanced at Sally and found her watching him. He had an idea what she was thinking and knew she was leaving it to him. It didn't take him long to make up his mind. He had no great liking for Morley personally, but he did have respect for his ability. The detective was shrewd, tough, and tenacious. With money as an incentive he'd go all out to produce, and Kenyon believed the things he had just said.

He got down on his knees and fished out the attaché

case. He opened it and handed Morley the notebook, seeing the interest kindle quickly in the other's eyes as he
reached for it.

"What the hell is this?"

"We don't know yet," Kenyon said. "What do you
think?"

"Why"—Morley flipped pages, studying them intently
—"it's a code book of some sort. Where'd you get it?"

Kenyon told him the whole story.

"How do you like it?" the detective said, exasperation
riding his words. "Here all the time and—" He broke off,
brow furrowing. "Look," he said, and got up, moving to
the table and spreading the book so Sally and Kenyon
could see. "These pages are all different. And see those
red numbers at the top? They run up to thirty-one. Thirty-
one pages of code. Why? What is thirty-one?"

"Some months have thirty-one days," Sally said. "Could
it be—"

"The days of the month," Morley finished. "Why not.
Sure." He looked at Sally with new respect. "Say, you're
all right."

He stopped, frowning again. No one said anything.
Kenyon stared at the opposite wall, searching for the next
clue. Morley walked round the table and came back to
the book.

"If we're right, it wouldn't make any difference if there
were thirty-one days in a month or not. Thirty-day months
they'd probably just forget the last page. . . . What happens
every day in the month—every month?"

"A newspaper comes out every day—if it has a Sunday
edition," Kenyon said, and the moment he heard his voice
he was way ahead of them, his thoughts flicking back to
his talk with Marion Sherman and the things she had told
him about Paul and Spence Arden. He did not mention
this now, but sat down and waited.

Sally was troubled. Her brows were twisted and there

was apprehension and bewilderment in the look she gave
Kenyon.

"But how? I don't see—"

"We don't have to know now," Morley said, "but I
can think of one way. Look. I don't know about newspapers but you do, Kenyon. Suppose a guy had the chance
to write pieces every day, maybe editorials or something.
Suppose he was an enemy agent. Why couldn't he send
out information every day?"

"He could," Kenyon said, "if someone didn't edit his
copy. That would spoil—"

"But suppose nobody did? Suppose he was fairly high
up? Hell, yes. Stuff could be sent in to him by other
guys in his bureau and he could write it out. Those papers
might be mailed to every important agent in the East."

"I—I don't believe it," Sally said, but she wasn't very
convincing.

"Because you don't want to believe it," Morley said.
"Because you're friends with Sherman and that Arden
guy." He closed the book. "It doesn't have to be them, but
I'll lay you that it's somebody on the paper. Otherwise
how would the old man know? He must have found this
book and figured what it was. He didn't say anything
because he wasn't sure, one way or another, but he phoned
the FBI just the same. . . . Listen, suppose I take this
along—"

"Where?" Kenyon asked.

"Where do you think? To Fleming."

"And how'll you tell him where you got it?"

Morley looked at him and quick craftiness touched the
angles of his eyes.

"I can tell him, all right, but there's something else.
What's the date? The eighteenth? Okay, where's a piece of
paper? . . . Maybe this is better," he said when he sat down
and began to copy page 18 in the book. "Nobody's going to
freeze me out of this now. Let Fleming figure this page

out and then we'll see. If he's satisfied to work with me I'll tell him where I got this and where the book is."

He signaled for silence when Kenyon started to interrupt. "Keep it," he said to Sally. "That's the way to do it. Keep it and sit tight. If Fleming'll play ball like I think he will we'll be back—"

"But what about Tony?" Sally asked.

"Don't worry. Before we come I'll phone you. That'll give you plenty of time to shove him under the bed"—he grinned—"or in a closet or some place. Fleming's not going to be poking around. He's going to want this book and you can tell him I came over this morning and questioned you and you remembered the case and looked inside. Tell him the way it happened, only leave Tony out of it. . . . There isn't any hat or coat or anything to give him away, is there? Then quit worrying."

He got up, folding the paper and returning the book. "Boy, you two did a good morning's work—and so did Morley. This'll probably save your neck, chum, and as for me—hah! Just relax till you hear from me, kids."

He was gone then, and Kenyon stood staring at the closed door until he felt Sally touch his arm. She examined his face anxiously and her voice was low.

"Did we do the right thing, Tony?"

"What else could we do?"

"But, I mean, can we trust him?"

Kenyon thought it over. "I think we can. He's after that ten thousand and I don't think he would turn me in—unless he had some proof that I actually was the murderer. I'm pretty sure he doesn't think that."

He reached down and took the book from her hand. "Let's have a look at it, shall we? You don't have to go to work, do you?"

She shook her head. "I generally go down to the paper at nine when I'm not at the house. I can phone and tell them I'll be down later."

She went to the telephone and while she made her call he moved chairs up to the breakfast-nook table and got more paper and a pencil. He had no great hope of learning anything from the book, but it was something to do while they waited.

She sat down beside him and they put their heads together and after that Kenyon wasn't much good. Her nearness, the faint fragrance of her hair got in his blood and it was all he could do to keep his eyes on the page. The figures and words became blurred and meaningless. From time to time he would hear her suggestions and write them down and answer her questions. They spoke in whispers, like conspirators, and for a while she was all eagerness and enthusiasm.

Finally, he did not know how much later, she sat back and gave a long sigh of resignation. "No," she said. "I'm through. I'm going mad. Who started this, anyway?"

She pushed the paper away from her and put the book on top of it. She wrinkled her nose at him and stretched so hard that when she relaxed it was practically a collapse. He smiled back at her and folded the paper and put it in his pocket. He had just picked up the notebook when he heard a faint and unfamiliar sound and glanced at Sally to see if she had made it.

She was staring at something beyond him, sitting erect, a puzzled frown upon her face. She said, "Look," with her lips and pointed.

Kenyon turned. From where he was sitting he could see the front half of the living-room. She was pointing at the door and then, with a start, he saw why.

The knob was turning and even as he watched, it stopped and began to move back. When it finally came to rest there was a moment of silence, and then a knock.

Kenyon turned to the girl, holding up his hand to keep her from answering. He did not know what this was but his nerves were suddenly taut and an odd vibration ran along them. Why should anyone try the door before he knocked? Why, indeed?

Without realizing it, he found himself on his feet. He signaled Sally to come with him and held a finger to his lips. Just then a scratching sound came from the door and as he watched he saw the key tilt out and fall to the floor; after that he moved swiftly, not really knowing what he intended to do until he did it.

He was in the center of the room now and, remembering the notebook, he stepped to the Governor Winthrop desk, opened the stop, and stuffed it in a pigeonhole. Already a key was scratching in the lock and he wheeled, taking Sally's arm and pulling her toward the closet in the hall.

"The closet," he said, and turned back, looking for something he could use as a weapon.

There were a pair of candlesticks on the gate-leg table by the wall but he didn't dare take the time to get them. The only other thing was a copy of a woman's monthly magazine, and he snatched this up, aware that, rolled tightly, it would be nearly as good as a club.

Sally was already in the closet and he was glad that it was spacious. He motioned her farther back, pushed some hangers aside, and stepped in, pulling the door behind him until only a two-inch crack remained.

"I don't know what this is," he said, his lips to her ear. "Maybe I'm nuts, but this'll be a good place to watch from."

He heard the lock click back as he finished. He heard the door open, though he could not see it. He could feel Sally's hand fasten around his elbow as she waited and then he was holding his breath and peering out into that segment of the room the crack revealed.

The door closed. Something moved into his range of vision—part of a man's leg and coat. For a second it stopped. Then it turned slightly, moved on, and stopped again.

Kenyon could not see the face but he could see the thick, broad torso, the massive shoulders. He could see, also, the automatic pistol in the right hand. The left, as the man turned, was empty and where the third finger should have been there was a stump.

Chapter Twenty-One

SURPRISES FOR FOUR

WHEN KENYON RECOVERED from the first shock of seeing this man the police had sought for the past three days, he remembered the magazine and began to roll it. He made it good and tight and it had a solid, comforting feel in his hand.

The man had gone on now and Sally moved beside him, her hair brushing his cheek. "Who is it?" she said, not whispering but making words slowly and with her lips.

"The guy we've been waiting for," Kenyon told her just as quietly.

"The one with—"

"Yes. Don't talk any more."

"But—what are you going to do?"

Kenyon did not answer her. He didn't want to take any unnecessary chances of being overheard, and besides, he didn't know. Even without the gun the man would be a formidable adversary, and remembering his futile struggle that other night, he doubted if he would be any match for the fellow in a fair fight.

There was, he saw, a chance of taking him from behind —if he could pick the exact moment to step out, and if he could swing before the fellow turned. But there was still another way that surprise might help him. If any search of the apartment was made, Missing Finger would probably open this door, and that would be the time. A good belt in the face with the magazine might give Kenyon all the edge he needed. . . .

The man moved past his range of vision again and Kenyon stopped thinking. Then he had disappeared and presently there came another sound, like that of a window

being raised. Ten seconds ticked by before it was closed
again and there was no other sound until, from the direction of the kitchen, he heard a door close. That told him
why the window had been raised. Missing Finger had signaled to someone out on the street and that someone had
come up the back way.

Like that the odds had doubled against him and Kenyon felt a growing vacuum in his stomach. He was more
than ever conscious of Sally and wondered if she could
remain undiscovered in case he had to come out. He held
his breath, listening, and all he could hear was the thump-
ing of his pulse and, at his ear, the sound of Sally's breathing.

Suddenly that silence was shattered. A voice he had
never heard said something and then a second voice
replied, a crisp, brusque voice that had a peculiar cadence
he thought he recognized. Even as he heard it, Sally gasped
and he turned quickly, clamping his hand across her
mouth. When he glanced out the crack again he knew the
reason for the gasp; for that voice belonged to Spencer
Arden.

He spoke again as Kenyon watched. "Did you look the
place over, Rudy?"

"No one is here," Rudy said. "The door was locked."

Still holding to Sally's mouth, Kenyon pulled her face
close. "Yes," he said. "Arden. It's all right. Don't make
a sound."

He could feel her tremble in that instant before he
released her, and then he tried to think, to cover all possibilities. It would not matter so much now if Arden found
the notebook, for Morley—and Fleming—had a sample
page and from that the others might be figured. In any
case Arden would be picked up immediately, providing
they were not discovered.

But if they were, what then? What would Arden do?
There was no doubt now that he was working for the Axis

and as Comstock had told him, that made this a bigger thing than murder. Once Arden and Rudy were caught, the authorities might uncover the whole system; to prevent that, Arden would not be fussy about his methods.

Kenyon's face was hot and damp. He tried to think, to find some precaution that might be taken, and in his mental search he remembered the pencil and paper in his pocket. After that it did not take long. He tore the paper in squares and in the blackness wrote a different set of words on each. *Watch Arden,* he wrote. *Follow Arden. Search Arden. Arden and Missing Finger.*

He had written perhaps a half dozen of these when it happened. He never knew whether it was his fault or whether Sally in moving, had somehow hit the metal coat hanger. However it happened, he felt something glance from his sleeve. There was a sudden clatter at his feet that, in the little closet, was deafening in its volume; then everything was still again.

In that first instant, Kenyon froze, every muscle rigid. He heard a faint, gasping sob from Sally and then, with the silence clamping down again, he thrust the pencil and paper in his pocket and turned to face the door.

For what seemed an hour there wasn't a sound from outside, and, no longer daring to keep his eye at the crack, he could only wait, feeling the sweat trickle down his spine, hoping that the noise had not been heard outside. Presently a curt, thin voice with a snap in it said:

"Come on out and have them up!"

The stiffness went out of Kenyon like air out of a toy balloon and his strength came flowing back.

"Okay," he said, and in that same moment caught Sally close and put his cheek against hers so she alone could hear him. "Get back as far as you can and stay there! If I can get away with it, phone for Morley and Fleming after we go."

Then he had turned and was pushing the door with his

foot, his hands shoulder high and not realizing until then that he still clung to his tightly rolled magazine.

Spencer Arden stood ten feet away and to the right. Rudy, the gun in his hand, was a like distance to the left. Kenyon closed the door part way with a nudge of his shoulder and waited, seeing the look of utter surprise on Arden's handsome blond face and then the quick freezing of his pale eyes as they stabbed at Rudy.

"So," he said, his voice tight. "No one is here. You fool!"

"I did not think—"

"You are not supposed to think. You are supposed to be sure." He looked back at Kenyon and some of the angry stiffness went out of his face. "You, eh?" he said. "Alone, I presume?"

"Certainly," Kenyon said, as though none of this mattered greatly. "That's why I didn't answer the door when your pal knocked."

Arden smiled at him. It was an attractive smile until you remembered it didn't mean a thing.

"All right," he said, "come over here by the table. That's better. Watch him, Rudy!"

The big man merely shifted the gun. Kenyon tried to look blank but when he saw Arden take out a small, flat automatic he knew it wasn't going to make any difference. He watched the fellow step toward the closet and was glad he'd thought to write a few notes while he had the chance.

Arden kicked the door open, the gun steady in his hand. He peered inside, kicked the door wider; then he grinned.

"Oh, hello," he said pleasantly. "Come on out and join us."

Sally Hayden walked out with her chin up and her shoulders back. She might have been frightened but she didn't show it and after she had looked Arden and Rudy over she continued to the sofa. Arden told Kenyon to go over with her and then twisted a chair and sat down.

"I'm sorry about this. It makes it rather awkward. I

thought you'd be working, Sal; I guess I should have phoned down and made sure. . . . Well, what's done is done."

"What do you want?" Kenyon said.

"I'm looking for a little notebook."

"And you think we have it?"

Arden did not seem to hear. He had been looking through the attaché case and now his head had come up and he was inspecting the room, his gaze stopping finally on the breakfast-nook table. There were two or three sheets of paper here and Arden moved over and picked them up.

Kenyon knew there was no writing on them because he had only used one piece, yet he watched curiously while Arden lifted the top sheet and, holding it flat, tipped it from side to side, as though he wanted the light to strike it from various angles. Then Kenyon knew what he was looking for and held his breath. That top sheet had been a cushion for the one he had written on while trying to solve the code, and if the pressure of the pencil had been great enough— When he saw the other's flat, bright smile he was prepared for what was to come.

"Could it be," Arden was saying, "that you have been experimenting? Could it be that the book *is* here?" His narrowed glance moved from Kenyon to Sally. "I don't suppose you'd want to turn it over and save a little time? . . . I was afraid you wouldn't. Well, all right. Come here, Sal."

The girl hesitated, looking at Kenyon. Rudy moved up close. Sally rose and walked to Arden.

"I'm afraid we'll have to do some searching," he said. "First you, Sal. Then Tony. After that we'll have to try the room—with your help. Do you want to take your dress off or shall I?"

Sally stared at him, her face chalky. Kenyon got his feet under him, one eye on Rudy's gun. He saw Arden reach out and spin the girl toward him, catching her about the waist, her back to him, and reach for the zipper that ran down the side of the dress. Then, Kenyon forgot everything else in a rush of blind fury.

He jumped up, seeing Rudy cock his wrist but not much caring, and stepped in, slugging with his right. The big man's gun missed his head and the knees buckled with the punch, but Rudy kept his feet and Kenyon's following left landed high. Rudy grunted and swung. Kenyon tried to pivot but the blow caught him on the side of the head. He went down, shaken but unhurt, and then, still unmindful of the odds, with one knee under him and about to dive in low, something clicked in his brain, warning him of a detail he had forgotten. The thought staggered him more than Rudy's punch. He caught a breath and got up slowly, hands at his sides, knowing what he had to do.

"All right," he said. "I'll tell you."

Arden, holding tightly to the girl, had not moved. Now a gleam of satisfaction showed through his smile.

"Tony!" Sally cried.

She jerked free and faced him, eyes shocked.

"No! Do you hear? Do you think I care what he does to me?"

"Well," Arden said, "at least we're making progress. What about it, old boy?"

Sally took a step toward him. "You can't, Tony!"

"I'm afraid I'll have to," Kenyon said, "sooner or later." He took a breath, seeing the quick scorn in the girl's gaze, knowing what she was thinking. "It's in the desk."

"Oh!" Sally shuddered and her voice was thick with contempt. "Can't you see what you're doing? Oh, I should have known you wouldn't—"

"Which part?" Arden asked.

"Top."

Kenyon watched the girl turn and sit down. He wanted to explain, to shout at her and make her listen, but there wasn't anything he could do. She did not know about the notes he had written, or that they were in his pocket. He could not tell her that when they had searched her and found nothing they would search him. She did not realize that Arden could not just walk out and leave them here after he had found the notebook. She had forgotten that Arden had committed, or was involved in, murder. When he left here, they would go with him, of that Kenyon was sure. What would happen then he did not like to think about.

"In one of those pigeonholes," he said, and put his hand in his pocket, seeing Rudy's suspicious glance and pulling out a pack of cigarettes to reassure him.

After that it was fairly simple to keep his hand in his pocket and fold, surreptitiously, the bits of paper bearing his message. From where he sat he could reach the end table and he picked up the ash tray very casually and put it in his lap. He had already palmed one of the slips and presently, when he put the ash tray back, that slip was underneath it.

He heard Arden's low cry of exultation as he found the notebook and by that time Kenyon's hand was again in his pocket. When he took it out it held another slip. He began to talk, to waste time.

"Comstock had it that day when he left the office, didn't he? And the lieutenant was right?"

"Right?" Arden said absently, still examining the notebook. "About what?"

"He said the hit and run you arranged did not look like a clean-cut murder job. All you needed was an accident, wasn't it? You knew Comstock had the book—"

"I knew it, all right." Arden gave him that cold smile. "He found it in a filing cabinet where I'd slipped it in a hurry, but both Paul and I used the office so it wasn't anything he could pin on me definitely. He asked me about it. Of course, I'd never seen it before. Had no idea how it got there—unless Paul had put it there."

"And so you phoned Rudy," Kenyon said, and straightened a pillow beside him, one of his slips now underneath
it. "You planned to follow Comstock out when he left.
Rudy would clip him. You'd be the first to come to his
aid. Whether you killed him or not was beside the point.
All you needed was for him to be unconscious. It would be
a cinch to lift the book while you examined his injuries,
and that would be that.'

Arden was still smiling. "You've got it all figured,
haven't you?"

"When you missed you came back that night. You're
the one that socked me in Comstock's bedroom. But you
hadn't much time to search because you'd only left the
house a few minutes before. So you—or Rudy—came back.
. . . Well, you were pretty damn lucky at that."

"Yes," Arden said. "And slightly stupid." He glanced at
Sally. "You fooled me, Sal. The other night when I was
pumping you for information you convinced me that you
knew nothing about it. I believed you. That's why I didn't
come here sooner."

"She didn't know anything about it," Kenyon said, and
explained how Comstock had hidden the envelope in the
attaché case; this gave him another idea and he palmed
a third slip as Arden continued.

"So that was it? Well, it's lucky I came, isn't it? When
I couldn't find it at the house I decided the police might
have it, but last night I found out they hadn't. . . . Well,
I've got to get back to the office."

He glanced at his strap watch and moved over to the
windows, a straight, lithe figure, slim-hipped and com-
petent-looking. When he turned, his blond brows were
warped in thought and he ran his tongue around the
inside of his mouth as he glanced from Kenyon to Sally.
Suddenly the frown went away and he was smiling again.

"Shall we get started? Get your coat, Sal. And a hat if you

want one."

Until then Sally Hayden had remained pointedly silent, her eyes avoiding Kenyon. Now she sat up and looked at Arden, quick alarm lifting her lashes.

"Wh—what are you going to do?"

"What do you think?" Arden said, very pleasantly, and sounding as though they were discussing a place to go for cocktails. "I couldn't very well leave you, could I? And have you phone the police the minute you were alone?"

"But—"

"What do you think would happen to me—and Rudy?"

"I won't go," Sally said.

"Nonsense," Arden said. "Let's not make it any more difficult than we have to. It's nothing that can be helped now."

"No."

Arden looked at Rudy and shrugged. He looked at Kenyon. "You'd better tell her how it is. She's going, one way or another. I shouldn't like to have to knock her out and have Rudy carry her."

Kenyon rose, knowing that resistance would do no possible good now. Sally would be hurt if she persisted, and nothing would be gained. He stepped to the table. "I think we'd better, Sally. There doesn't seem to be any choice."

He thought she was going to be stubborn. She set her jaw and her cheekbones got white, and then she gave him a scathing glance and stood up.

"I suppose you're right," she said, her voice acid. "I couldn't do much alone, could I? It was silly of me, wasn't it, expecting anything from you?"

She went to the closet, Arden moving with her. She put on her coat and thrust her hands in the pockets; then waited, legs spread solidly, defiance in every line of her young body.

"We'll go the back way," Arden said. "We've a car

around the corner."

He took his gun out, inspected it, and put it in his side pocket. Kenyon took that moment to drop the third slip of paper in the attaché case and then he moved past the table, Rudy following.

"You go with her, Rudy," Arden said, "and do what you have to do. . . . All right, Tony. Let's go. You first."

Chapter Twenty-Two

NOT A QUITTER

SPENCE ARDEN STOOD GUARD and supervised the arrangements while Rudy tied Kenyon to a chair, deftly fastening each ankle to a separate upright and then bringing his arms round the chair back and securing his wrists. Sally, hands still in her coat pockets, sat on a couch next to the wall and when Rudy had finished with Kenyon, Arden told her to lie down.

"It will be eight or nine tonight before I can get back," he said, "and I think you'll be a lot more comfortable here than in a chair."

He arranged the two soiled pillows and moved the square, unpainted table a little closer. There was an oil lamp on it, and an ash tray, and Arden put cigarettes and matches beside it.

"I think we can leave her arms free, Rudy," he said. "So long as she behaves. Can you rig up something that will keep her here and still not make her uncomfortable?"

Rudy went into the kitchen and came back tearing strips of cloth. He had a length of rope under his arm and Sally just looked at him sullenly, not moving until Arden asked her whether she wanted to lie down of her own accord or be held down. She swung her feet and leaned back, propping herself up with her elbows.

Rudy was clever with a rope. He wrapped his strips of cloth about her ankles so the rope would not chafe them and then by some rather complicated device of his own made them fast to the standards at the foot of the couch, so that while she had a few inches of freedom for each leg, she could not roll from the coach or stand up. Arden, meanwhile, had found two magazines of the true-detective type on another table and tossed them down beside her.

"I'm sorry there isn't anything else to read," he said.
"These are about the only kind that Rudy seems to enjoy.
. . . Well, I guess you'll be all right now." He looked at
the big man and his voice thinned out. "You know what to
do. I think you also know what will happen if they are
not here when I return."

"They will be here," Rudy said.

"Good."

"And what about me?" Kenyon said. "Don't I get a
chance to smoke?"

"Certainly. Rudy'll release your hands whenever you
like. And if you get hungry just speak to him. He'll find
something." He smiled at Kenyon, took a final look at
Sally, and went out.

Rudy went to the window when the car started up. He
watched until the sound of it had all but vanished, then
moved a chair up to the table in the center of the room,
put his gun on it, and sat down, folding his arms. Without
his hat his head was round and close-cropped. His brows
were bushy and his lips were thick, and though he did not
look very bright, he looked exceedingly powerful with
those massive shoulders and bulging thighs.

Kenyon took his time studying the man, then glanced
at Sally. She had leaned back, hands clasped behind her
neck. Not once had she spoken to him since they left the
apartment and thinking about how she had stared out
the car window during the ride from town made Kenyon's
mood a little blacker. The fact that no attempt had been
made to prevent them from knowing where they were
being taken told him that Arden had no intention of
releasing them, nor any fear that they would talk.

They had driven north from the city and then, perhaps
four miles out, had turned right along a narrow dirt road.
This place, hardly more than a shack and made of shingles
and insulating board, was on the edge of the river. At one

time it might have been used as a summer cottage but now weeds and high grass choked the yard and from the outside it had a look of complete abandonment. From his brief glimpse of the river bank, Kenyon had seen no other house on either side and he had an idea a person could stay here a long time without discovery; he also had an idea that the river itself would make a good place to put things you didn't want found.

He hauled his thoughts back to the moment when he heard a match strike, and saw that Sally was lighting a cigarette. He looked over at Rudy.

"I'd like one too."

Rudy got up. He looked at his gun, as though considering the best place for it, and left it on the table. He walked behind Kenyon and released his wrists. He made no move when Kenyon put his hand in his pocket; in fact, he made no move at all, but stood two feet behind the chair and waited until the cigarette was so short Kenyon had to throw it away. Then he tied the wrists again, went back to his chair, and sat down.

"Sally." She was leafing through one of the magazines now and glanced up briefly as Kenyon spoke. "It probably wasn't anything in the paper at all. The code messages, I mean. It was probably the radio program."

She continued her inspection of the magazine and Kenyon went on doggedly. "He writes his own program and it would be a cinch to broadcast coded messages every evening if he had to. That's a lot better than a paper. It's quicker, and every enemy agent in this part of the country could listen in. Wasn't that it, Rudy?" he said, when he saw she wasn't going to answer him. "Arden has been using the radio program, hasn't he?"

Rudy just grunted and Kenyon fell silent. He wished he could tell Sally what he hoped would happen. He knew she thought he was a quitter, and though he could not blame her, it did not help the ache in his chest. He wanted to tell her why he had given in so easily; he wanted to tell her that if Morley came back and found one of those slips of paper in her apartment they might have a chance, and if he had been searched they would have had none. He wanted so badly to tell her these things and make her understand that he even considered doing so in front of Rudy. What stopped him was the thought that Rudy might tie them more securely and leave to tip off Arden. He, Kenyon, had no way of telling when Morley would get back to the apartment, and if Arden should get there first it would be all over.

Even in the beginning he had not kidded himself about Arden's plan. The man had too much at stake to take any chances. With his own failure a whole network might collapse, and therefore he was not going to fail. When he came back, when it was dark and there was no chance of discovery, he would have a plan of taking care of them. It would not be a question of murder, it would be a question of murder handled in such a way that no suspicion could fall on him.

Kenyon sat for an hour or more thinking about these things. He knew that, some way, he had to outsmart Rudy. Considered sensibly it seemed hopeless, yet there had to be a way and, still not knowing how, he did realize that his best chance lay in establishing in the big man's mind a false sense of security. . . . He asked for another cigarette.

"What's the matter, Rudy?" he scoffed when the other again waited behind him. "Do you think I'm going to run?"

"No."

"Well, you're right there. It's you that's going to do the running—back and forth untying and tying my hands."

Rudy said nothing. When the cigarette was finished he tied Kenyon's hands and sat down. Kenyon looked at Sally and found her engrossed in her magazine. He gave Rudy twenty minutes and asked for another cigarette. Rudy got up. They went all through the routine again and fifteen minutes later Kenyon wanted another smoke. This time Rudy shook his head.

"No," he said. "You just had one."

"You heard what Arden said," Kenyon reminded him. "You're to release my hands whenever I like. . . . Well, come on!"

Rudy thought it over, but he got up because he was trained to obey and he remembered the order. This time Kenyon talked as he smoked.

"Maybe before the day is out you'll get it through your thick head that it'll save you a lot of trouble if you'll let my hands loose. Then I can smoke when I like without bothering you." He chuckled. "That is, unless you're still afraid of me. Of course I'm tied to the chair, even when my hands are free, and you probably outweigh me by sixty pounds, not counting the gun."

He hesitated, aware that Rudy had moved round to one side and was glaring at him. He glanced over at Sally and found her watching him over the top of the magazine, her brow furrowed and a look in her eyes that said, *What are you trying to promote now?* Kenyon cocked an eye at Rudy and laughed at him.

"With one hand behind your back, Rudy, you and I might make a fight of it—that is, if my feet were loose and you'd promise not to use the gun. You didn't need it the other night when you jumped me. Oh, by the way, did you snitch the bottle of whisky I had? Yes, I thought so. . . . What's the matter, do you think I'm going to take the gun away from you? Or maybe you just like to hold it."

"You talk too much," Rudy said, but the goading had nettled him and he stepped behind the chair and snapped the rope. With one quick motion he passed it under Kenyon's arms and drew it tight. When he moved away the upper part of Kenyon's body was tied to the chair—

but his arms were free. Rudy went back and sat down.

"Go ahead," he said. "Smoke. Just the same, I watch."

"Okay, Rudy, you watch," Kenyon said, and thought, *That's the first step. Now what?*

The outlook wasn't very encouraging because what he had told Rudy had been the truth. Man to man, and all even, he would not stand much chance with Rudy; still, there could be other ways. He glanced about, taking stock and trying to find one.

The room was squarish and not very large. There were windows on three sides and a small porch in front. At the rear, a doorway led to two smaller rooms, probably a kitchen and bedroom, and to get to them one would have to pass quite close to the couch. Kenyon considered this a long time, estimating the distance between his chair and the couch and the doorway. Maybe six feet to the couch, another five to the doorway.

Dusk was creeping through the windows before he realized how much time had been lost and when he glanced at his strap watch he saw that it was nearly six. Sally had put the magazines away and was watching him now and then, worry streaking her face and her eyes anxious. Rudy was merely a big hulk sitting motionless in the chair. Once his head nodded and Sally saw it and tried to sit up on the couch and reach for her ankles, but a spring creaked and Rudy's head jerked up. Since then he had been constantly alert.

Now, Kenyon knew he must have Sally's help. He had a vague plan but he would have to give her some idea of what he wanted her to do; that was why, a little later, he said to Rudy:

"How about some food?"

Rudy stood up. "There isn't much," he said.

"Never mind," Kenyon said. "Get it!"

Rudy picked up the gun and put it in his belt. He started for the kitchen, passing between Kenyon and the couch.

When he heard the stove lids rattle Kenyon began to talk.

He was never sure what he said, but he kept it chatty and confident for Rudy's benefit and pretended to be reassuring her that everything was going to be all right. But as he talked he pointed to the lamp until Sally understood what he meant. He nodded and said, "Could you use it if you had to?"

Rudy came in and looked at them. It was almost dark and he went over to light the lamp on the center table. When he came to Sally's she looked at Kenyon and he shook his head violently.

"Never mind, Rudy," she said quickly. "I'm not going to read yet. I'll light it if I want it."

Rudy went out and Kenyon began to work his chair closer to the couch. "Could you, Sally?" he asked. When she said she thought she could he grinned at her and winked. "Good girl," he said, and in pantomime pretended to be slugging someone on the head. "If we get the chance I'll yell," he whispered. "It's got a good stout base. Just be sure and bear down when you swing it."

Rudy came in again, eyeing them suspiciously. Kenyon had moved the chair so little that he did not notice it and went back to the kitchen. Kenyon kept at it, but it was slow work to move at all, much less move silently, and when Rudy finally appeared with food the distance to the couch had been narrowed hardly more than two feet.

"There's no cream," Rudy said, putting a plate of ham and potatoes on Sally's table and adding a cup of coffee and a piece of bread.

"A fine thing," Kenyon said.

Rudy served him on a small tray which he balanced on his lap, but when Rudy went back to the kitchen he did not pass between Kenyon and the couch, but detoured behind him. Kenyon swallowed his disappointment along with his food and waited.

His chance did not come until he had almost given up hope of getting it at all and it was Sally who was responsible. Rudy ate at his table, watching them. He cleared the things away a few at a time, always passing behind Kenyon as he went to the kitchen. Now, as he sat down and prepared to continue his watching, the girl called to him, her voice edged with strain.

"Will you show me how to light this, Rudy, please?" she asked, her eyes signaling Kenyon that this was all she could think of. "I'm not sure I know how."

Rudy rose with a sigh, and perhaps because his patience was worn thin by his constant waiting on them, walked directly toward her, the gun in his left hand, away from Kenyon. He passed through the alleyway between the chair and the couch and as he went by Kenyon took off from his toes, getting what spring he could, hurling himself and the chair at the fellow's legs and reaching out with both arms.

He yelled to Sally, not knowing what he said, but merely yelling, felt his head hit Rudy's legs and then his arms clamped tight about the man's powerful knees, pinioning them. Rudy toppled. He struggled to free his knees, to take a step and get his balance, but Kenyon held on grimly and Rudy went down, throwing out his hands to break the fall.

Kenyon felt the jar as the other hit the floor. He heard Rudy grunt, and yelled again, knowing there was no time left.

Rudy twisted and kicked with his legs. Then Kenyon heard the solid, sickening thud against a background of smashing glass and suddenly the smell of kerosene was in the air and the legs he clung to so desperately went limp.

He pushed back, found the gun under Rudy's hand and dragged it to him through shattered glass and oil. He tipped himself and the chair over, swinging the trigger guard on one finger, and clawed himself along the floor away from the prostrate figure. When he saw it stir, he turned on his side.

"Your feet," he said to Sally, but she was already sitting up struggling with the knots.

He watched her as he got his finger on the trigger. Still on his side, he saw Rudy push up on his hands and shake his head, blood and kerosene flying as from a dripping dog's back. Rudy got his knees under him. When he finally turned his head he was looking smack into the muzzle of his gun.

"Stay there!"

Rudy stayed there. Sally slid off the end of the couch and ran to Kenyon, dropping to her knees and attacking the knots around his ankles.

Rudy got up, one joint at a time, and only once after that did he rebel. That was when Kenyon ordered him to sit down, when Rudy looked at the ropes and knew what was coming. He shook his head. He did not say anything, he just took a slow forward step and then another, ignoring the command to stop.

Kenyon fired at his feet and a furrow slashed the floor inches from the shoe.

"Sit down!"

Rudy sat down, his face paler than Kenyon had ever seen it.

"Okay," Kenyon said. "But next time you get it. Don't move. Not an eyelash."

He walked behind the man, fashioning a slip knot. He dropped the noose over Rudy's head and shoulders and jerked it tight to the back of the chair. After that it was easy, and he concentrated on his task until Sally spoke. What she said surprised him and he glanced up, wondering if he had heard correctly.

"What did you say?"

Sally was undoing a knot on the last piece of rope.

"I said, 'And I thought you were a quitter.' "

"What else could you think?" Kenyon said, and went on to explain why he had acted as he had. "If I had been searched it would have been too bad. Now it doesn't matter whether Morley comes or not." There were a lot of other things he wanted to say but he did not dare to look at her, nor take the time now. Instead, he said, "Let's go. It can't be more than a third of a mile back to the highway. Once there we'll be all right."

He took her arm, gave Rudy and the room a final glance, and opened the door. They stepped out on the porch and went down two steps and he had nearly reached the corner of the house when he stiffened and pulled Sally back.

"What is it?" she said, instinct warning her something was wrong.

Kenyon was staring straight ahead and what he saw made his scalp crawl. For he was watching the shadows among the trees at the edge of the lot where no shadows should be. Moving shadows, growing blacker as he watched, because some distant light was striking them and getting stronger. It wasn't until then that he could hear, faintly, the sound of the car.

Sally heard it too. "He's coming back," she said. "Oh, Tony."

Kenyon made up his mind on the instant, knowing now that if the road had approached from the front they would already be trapped. Ahead was the river; on either side, underbrush and a scattering of pines and scrub oaks. Alone he could run for it, but with Sally—He thought of a better way. "Come on," he said, and pulled her up the steps and across the porch.

Sally Hayden did not argue nor ask him what he was going to do. It was as if she realized that she must trust his judgment now and do exactly as he said, and Kenyon sensed this as he hauled Rudy and the chair to the front corner of the room where he would not be visible from the windows overlooking the porch.

"Get on the couch," he told Sally. "There's a chance he may glance through the windows as he comes in. I don't think he'll stop to look for ropes; he may not even look at all."

He sat down on the chair as Sally stretched out on the couch. He put his hands behind his back, facing the door. The sound of the car was close now and he thought of one more thing and spoke of it.

"When you hear him at the door jump off the couch and get into the bedroom. You can slip out a window. It's not far to the ground and if this doesn't come off you'll have a start."

He wanted to say more but the motor stopped suddenly and he did not dare. He looked at Rudy. "If you open your mouth you get it," he whispered, and then he was bracing his feet and tightening his hold on the gun.

He heard a car door open. Outside the windows the lights went off, and he thought he heard hurried steps on the ground. It was a job to sit still then, but he held himself motionless by sheer will power, waiting for the sound of someone on the steps. The sound came almost at once and he stiffened, still waiting, hearing the steps on the porch now; direct, unhesitating steps that came straight to the door. When the knob turned he jumped up and strode forward, his gun level. He saw Sally slide from the couch and then Spence Arden came in, taking a full step before he saw the gun.

"Okay," Kenyon said. "Watch yourself!"

Arden jerked to a stop. For an instant surprise and incredulity struck at him, then, inch by inch, his blond, good-looking face froze into a white hard mask.

"Shut the door!"

Seconds ticked by in absolute silence. Arden reached behind him. Very slowly, he closed the door. He took two steps toward Kenyon, eyes darting about the room and blazing fiercely when they fell on Rudy. Kenyon told him to turn round.

"And get those hands up," he said. "Now!"

Arden obeyed and Kenyon moved up and put the gun hard against his spine. That was when it happened. From behind and to one side there was a sudden crashing of glass and then a new voice, thin and raspy, filled the room.

"Drop it, mister!"

Kenyon very nearly did, the unexpectedness of it, the shocking sound of the glass and that voice paralyzing him momentarily. He saw Arden start to lower his hands. He pushed with the gun, half expecting a bullet in the back, but saying, "Hold still!" and seeing the other stiffen again.

"You heard me," the voice behind him said.

"Yeah." Kenyon's nerves were strung wires, taut and sharply sensitive and suddenly he realized that he was not whipped yet. "I heard you," he said, not glancing round, "so what happens next?"

"I think I'll put one right between your shoulders."

"You shoot me and I shoot Arden, is that it?"

"You catch on," the voice said, "but first I plug the dame. *Stand still, sister!*"

Kenyon had not seen Sally come, and seeing her now in his slanting glance, he felt his insides turn to liquid and all resistance went out of him. She was standing just inside the doorway, her mouth white and a frightened wideness in her hazel eyes. She was not looking at Kenyon, but at something behind him.

He turned his head. A thin, pale face watched him from the broken window and a heavy automatic was pointed right at Sally. Kenyon let his arm down slowly and would have dropped the gun had not Arden spun and snatched it from limp fingers.

Chapter Twenty-Three

MURDERS THREE AND FOUR

KENYON WAS STILL STARING at the thin, pinched face in the window. When he could speak again his voice was wooden, addressing Arden.

"The night Rudy chloroformed me there was another man in the room. I thought it was you."

"No," Arden said. "That was Clarence. Clarence has been a big help to me, especially tonight. It's nice that I decided to bring him. . . . Come in, Clarence, I'll watch them."

Kenyon turned. Sally had not moved. Her lips were tight to keep them from trembling and now she tried to smile, to reassure him, to show him it was all right and she was not afraid. Something tore at Kenyon's chest and his throat got hard and thick.

"You didn't run," he said huskily.

"I couldn't," she said, trying to explain with her eyes. "Not alone. I—I guess I was afraid."

He had to look away. He couldn't stand seeing those things happen to her face. He couldn't find any words to comfort her, or even think of any lies that would help; all he could do was to say, over and over, silently, prayerfully, *I've got to get her out.* If only I can find a way I'll do anything she asks. . . .

Clarence came in and Arden said, "Watch them!" and stepped over to Rudy, his face working with suppressed fury. "You fool! You stupid, brainless imbecile!"

Rudy lowered his eyes, saying nothing, and then Arden hit him, slapping the barrel of the gun hard against the man's jaw. Rudy flinched but made no sound. A white welt jumped out on the side of his face and presently it began to darken with blood at one end.

"I think I shall probably kill you," Arden said quietly, and there was something in his voice that made Kenyon's blood congeal.

The other stepped back, the gun hanging at his side. He looked at Kenyon with narrow-lidded speculation. He looked at Sally and seemed to be making up his mind about something. Whatever that something was remained a secret; for just then there was a sharp, cracking sound and glass shattered, and a cold flat voice said:

"Get 'em up! Fast!"

For the briefest of instants there was a complete and deadly silence. No one moved and for a long time after that Kenyon did not even think. He was watching Arden. He saw him turn, gun in hand. Then the man was staggering and a shot had exploded in the room, and Kenyon's glance jerked toward the sound and he caught sight of Morley just as the gun in his hand hammered again.

The detective was standing in the window Clarence had used and in the one next to it was Fleming. He had his gun aimed at Clarence and he yelled something, and Clarence, too surprised to use his own gun, dropped it as if it were hot.

"Go ahead," Morley said. "I'll cover him."

Something else thudded to the floor and Kenyon saw it was the gun in Arden's hand. The man was still standing. His mouth was sagging and the look of utter surprise in his eyes turned suddenly to a vacant stare as his knees started to buckle. He grabbed for the edge of the table, missed, and then went down limply, falling on his face.

Fleming came in on the run. "You two all right?" he asked, and without waiting for an answer grabbed Clarence, gave him a swift and expert searching, and spun him to one side. He collected the two guns on the floor and bent over Arden, feeling for a pulse, muttering something under his breath as he dropped the lifeless hand.

"Damn it all!" he said as Morley came in. "Why didn't

you cut the legs out from under him?"

Morley took stock of things and put away his short-barreled revolver.

"He had a gun in his hand, didn't he? You saw him turn. I should take chances with a guy like that." He grunted. "Maybe I should have tried to shoot it out of his hand. Maybe if I was an expert I would have—but I doubt it."

He walked around the body, watching Fleming open Arden's coat and search the inside pocket. "I was a cop long enough to know it's pretty silly to take chances with a killer. If he had dropped the gun he'd've been okay, but he didn't. I don't think he wanted to—and I guess I'm glad he didn't." His voice was morose, his stare sultry, and he seemed to be speaking more to himself than anyone else.

"Maybe you'd forgotten what happened to Comstock, but I hadn't. He was a client and when something happens to a client you're supposed to be protecting, you're supposed to do something about it. And there's something else. A pretty decent sort of woman named Nora, who was smothered face down in her bed and murdered in cold blood. Either by him or that gorilla in the chair.... That's it, ain't it?" he said, looking over Fleming's shoulder at the notebook the agent had taken from Arden's pocket.

"That's it," Fleming said, and he was obviously more interested in what he had found than in anything Morley had said.

"We found your notes," Morley told Kenyon. "We tailed him up to where the dirt road cuts off and then we had to douse the lights. We parked and ran the last couple hundred yards so they wouldn't hear us."

He started toward Rudy and Kenyon heard a sigh and jumped toward Sally as her eyelids fluttered and she started to sag. He got both arms about her and she leaned against him and it was all he could do to stand and hold her.

As though at a great distance he heard Morley and
Fleming talking to Rudy and Clarence. He did not know
what they said. He himself said nothing at all, nor did
he move until the shudders stopped and his own knees
ceased to tremble. When he felt her stir in his arms, he
looked for a place to sit down and was grateful that the
couch was so near. He took her hand as she sank down on
it, and then he sat down beside her and wondered if he
could get out cigarettes without dropping them.

Paul Sherman was pacing up and down the floor of
the Comstock drawing-room, head down and hands winding and unwinding behind his back.

"I never dreamed he was a Nazi," he said. "Never had
the faintest idea."

"Nor I," Marion Sherman said, "though I must say it
seems obvious enough now. He was the one who informed
the Gestapo about some of your other friends. He actually
did represent a London paper and that's how he could
talk to you as he did, pretending to be so bitter about the
whole thing and all the time working behind your backs."

"I thought I was smuggling him out of the country," Paul
said. "I thought his life was in danger. I'd told him I was
coming back here eventually to work for Andy and he
knew I'd help him get a job." He looked at Kenyon. "No
wonder he offered to do the radio program for nothing."

"Well, no one blames you." Marion was standing with
her back to the fireplace, the long cigarette holder in one
hand, a Scotch and soda in the other. She wore a plain
black dress that made her slim figure even straighter and
accentuated the pale angularity of her face. "We're all just
lucky that it ended as it did."

Kenyon heard the doorbell and presently Hilton glided
down the hall. Carl Sherman went over to the table and
made a fresh drink. He hadn't said but a half dozen words
in the time Kenyon and Sally had been there and now he

went back to his chair, his round face tired-looking and colorless.

Lieutenant Nash and Morley came in and Marion said hello and to fix themselves a drink. Morley said he would and Nash said, "Thanks, I could use one."

Sally Hayden was sitting next to Kenyon, her shoulder touching his. She was looking straight ahead and he studied her profile fondly, speculating on the softness of her cheek and tracing the lovely line of her throat.

"Would you like to go home?"

"Not yet, Tony. I—I want to find out what happened first. I mean, about those other men. Rudy and that other one."

"Where's what's-his-name—the federal man?" Marion asked.

"Still busy," Nash said. "He found some names and addresses in Arden's apartment and he thinks they might be something. He thinks they might make a real roundup if we can keep this out of the papers for a couple of days. I told him I thought we could."

"He was acting like a clearinghouse for information," Morley said. "Arden, I mean. Agents from all over the East sent him stuff in care of the paper and he put it on the air every night."

Here Kenyon felt Nash's keen inspection and finally met it. "Still sore?" he asked.

"No." Nash shook his head and looked into his glass. "Not any more. If it's all right with Mr. Sherman it's all right with me. Only if I could've got my hands on you last night— You were in Miss Hayden's apartment all the time, huh?" A slow grin came as he heard Kenyon's explanation and he eyed Sally with new respect. "Well, I guess I can't blame Hafey for not finding you," he said finally. "And maybe it's just as well. If you hadn't been there this morning, if you hadn't left those notes around for Morley—"

"Did Spence kill them both?" Marion asked.

"We don't know," Nash said. "I'm not sure we'll ever know whether he did them both himself or ordered them done. Rudy's not going to talk and if he does he's going to say Arden did them. So is the other little rat, that Clarence. Anyway, it doesn't matter much. We can put Rudy away for twenty years on the kidnaping rap and Clarence will be out of circulation for quite a while as an accessory and one thing or another."

"Did this Rudy talk at all?" Carl Sherman asked.

"A little. At the beginning. He admitted Arden told him to run down Mr. Comstock but when we got around to murder he shut up and stayed shut. . . . Of course, we haven't proof but I'm pretty sure it was Arden who killed the woman. It was someone she knew, and she'd seen Arden around the house and knew who he was. Whoever killed her came into her room through the door or window and if it had been Rudy she would have screamed; somebody would have heard her. The guy would be enough to scare anybody, especially at night."

He took some more of his drink and sucked his lips. "What probably happened is that she learned something about the first murder—something she saw or heard or suspected. Maybe that first night and maybe not. Maybe she didn't even know what she had. But whether she did or not, somehow Arden got wind of it and knew he had to get rid of her. If he came down the hall and knocked she'd probably let him in long enough to find out what he wanted."

"But if she knew something," Carl Sherman said, "why didn't she say so?"

"We don't know," Nash said. "It seems funny that she should hold out if she knew something, but let me tell you, Mr. Sherman, that is one thing that makes murders tough to crack—some murders, that is. People just don't always tell what they know. Personal feelings often influence their judgment and then they never seem to realize that their own necks may be in danger. They can't get it through their heads that there is no additional penalty for a second or third or fourth murder. And anyway, I'm not sure that it's it. The room was ransacked, either because he thought there was a chance the book would be there, or to cover up something else. . . . But what I came for was to ask about the paper. Fleming is seeing the *Standard* and I said I'd speak to you. If we can kill this story for—"

"Certainly." Paul Sherman removed his glasses and rubbed his eyes. "Anything you say."

"I'm glad you killed him."

Kenyon did not recognize the voice at first. He had to glance round to see that it came from Carl Sherman. He was looking at Morley, and he was not the same man Kenyon had first met. He did not look neat and well-groomed any more. He needed a shave and his shirt was open at the throat and his black hair was not sleek, but tousled, and in his eyes burned something hot and bright.

"I only wish I could have done it myself. I wish I could have seen him die."

There was a lot of silence all of a sudden. It was an uncomfortable silence until Marion broke it with a rather bad attempt at changing the mood. "Don't be grim, Carl," she said. "It's much better the way it was."

"I didn't have much choice," Morley said to Carl.

"I'm glad you didn't. I'm glad he didn't put his hands up. . . . Oh, I suppose you'd like a check?"

"If you think I earned it."

Carl rose and left the room. Kenyon went over to the table and put whisky and soda in his glass and Nash gave Morley a sardonic stare.

"If I could only be a private dick and work for rewards," he said.

"You're jealous," Morley said, and grinned.

Carl came back with a check.

"You earned it," he said. "It's the best money I ever spent."

Morley glanced at the check and thanked him. Carl went back to his chair.

"What about mine?" Kenyon said.

Morley gave him a deadpan look. "Your what?"

"My five hundred. That was what we agreed on, wasn't it?"

"But this is different."

"It isn't my fault it's different. I did what I was supposed to do."

He could see many things battle it out in the detective's square face. The others were watching him and Morley knew it, and that may have made a difference, for suddenly his grin came back.

"Okay," he said, "chiseler." He pulled out his wallet. He folded the check, took out the bills he had and gave most of them to Kenyon, four hundreds and two fiftys.

"Thanks." Kenyon counted the new bills and put them in his pocket.

"Satisfied?"

"Not quite. About the money, yes. Very much so. But there's something else I've never been able to figure out and maybe you can tell me about it."

"Shoot."

"Remember the night Comstock was killed and you came down the hall and said you were going to get a drink and did I want one?"

Morley's eyes got flat and suspicious and something moved in his face. Something moved in Kenyon's body too, tension, winding up tight. It took Morley five seconds to reply.

"Sure, I remember. What about it?"

"I guess I know about Nora," Kenyon said, speaking slowly and making each word distinct, "and I know *why*

Comstock was killed but I've never been able to figure out whether you killed him before you came down the hall or afterward—just before you fired the shot."

For a second or two the room was deathly still, then someone gasped. Someone else started a laugh, an almost hysterical sound suddenly cut short. Muscle ridged the line of Morley's jaw and one lid twitched. That was all.

"Are you nuts?"

"Not about this, I'm not."

"Okay. But I hope you know what you're doing."

"Wait a minute!" Lieutenant Nash spoke up sharply. "Can I get in on this? Are you trying to say Morley killed Comstock?"

Kenyon answered but kept his eyes on Morley. "I am saying it."

Morley's thin lips twisted. "And slugged myself on the back of the head."

"That's right. Even the doctor said it was a superficial gash. On the *back* of the head, remember? They tell me the skull is thickest there. Anyone could swing that statuette with its sharp base hard enough to make a cut like that, but I doubt if anyone could swing hard enough to knock himself out; not in that spot, Morley. . . . Well, when did you do the killing, before or after you came down the hall?"

Morley's grin came back, flat and nasty. His voice was taunting.

"You're telling it. Go ahead. And while you're at it, don't forget the motive. I'm always sort of partial to motives. I guess the lieutenant is too."

Kenyon took a sip of his drink to wet his throat. "You killed Comstock because *he found I wasn't his son and he told you so that night.* You killed him because you couldn't stand losing that ten thousand dollars. It took me a long time to figure things out, Morley, an awfully long time, but once you get an idea you're right, things you never thought of before fall into place fast."

He went on, speaking rapidly, succinctly. "The real Joe Comstock had a birthmark on his left shoulder. The old man probably didn't mention it to you because he figured you could identify the boy without undressing him. But the night he was killed he stopped in my room to say good night. I was standing at the chest, my back to him. My shirt was off. I saw him in the mirror. He was saying something and he stopped suddenly and I saw him stare. It didn't mean anything then and by the time I turned he was gone. He didn't say anything about it to me. Maybe he was too stunned just then when he saw my shoulder bore no birthmark.

"So he came back to the study. I can imagine what he said and I can imagine how you felt when you saw that ten thousand slipping away. How you killed him is unimportant, though if I had to guess I'd say you followed him into the bedroom, still arguing, probably. Maybe he threatened to have your license taken away. Anyway, you saw the letter opener there and used it while he was standing by the bed. And then you knew what you had to do and came down the hall to let me know you were out of the study. You came back and rapped yourself on the back of the head and fell across the threshold, firing your gun to bring me in quickly—I had the end room in the wing—and discover you unconscious."

"Are you guessing," Nash cut in, "or are you—"

"Certainly I'm guessing. I say it probably happened that way but I wouldn't put the other way past Morley. With him it could have been premeditated, because with him there could be no stronger motive than money. If you knew him as I do you'd know what a dollar meant. You'd know how he crabbed when he spent one, how he was driven by his crazy desire to get that ten thousand. Why else would he figure out his scheme to get that bonus? And right when he practically had it in his hand his plan blew up because of something he could not know about.

"That's why I say murder would not stop him. If he did not kill before he came down the hall, he *planned* it before. Perhaps Comstock told him off and went to bed and Morley sat out in the study, brooding, seeing the money slipping away, knowing that nothing but murder could prevent it. He could plan it all right—going down the hall and calling to me and then walking in while Comstock was in bed and using the paper cutter he knew was there, knowing that with the man dead and me under suspicion I would not dare tell the truth."

He took his gaze from Morley long enough to explain about the knife and handkerchief that were planted in his traveling-bag.

Nash cursed softly, eyeing Morley narrowly. "You never said anything about that one."

"Of course he didn't," Kenyon said, "and I was too scared to wonder much about it. He sent me for more whisky while he phoned you from the study. He knew I'd be gone three or four minutes and all he had to do was step out the study window, walk twenty-five feet, and step into mine. Then, later, he asked me if I had the credentials. I went to get them and if I hadn't he would have insisted—to be sure I found the knife."

Kenyon paused. "At that he nearly missed. If your sergeant had come in three minutes earlier I'd have been caught cold, and that was something Morley did not want. He wanted me right where I was, under suspicion so he would have that hold on me, but not too much under suspicion. He hadn't forgotten there had been an attempt on Comstock's life by Rudy, nor that I had found a prowler earlier, in the bedroom. The chloroforming the next night made it even better. What ruined things was me finding Nora and putting myself under even more suspicion."

Morley waited, lip still curled, nothing changing in his face.

"Oh, yeah," he said. "That brings us to Nora, doesn't it. Well, guess about that."

"I've been doing a lot of talking," Kenyon said. "I hope I'm not boring you."

"I can stand it if the others can."

"All right," Kenyon said. "And if you want to know why you killed Nora I'll tell you. You killed her because she told you she wouldn't play ball any longer. She had fallen for Carl and she was going to tell him the truth— and that again was my fault."

"Maybe we could have some details," Morley said nastily.

"The afternoon before she was killed I talked to her. Until then she had thought I was going to play along and be Comstock's son and inherit half the estate and she was going to get a phony divorce and a settlement."

"I don't believe it," Carl Sherman said, his voice so hoarse Kenyon did not recognize it.

"It's the truth," he said, and stopped to explain some of the things Nora had told him. "But that was before she figured out the other. She liked you. She said she did, and she thought you liked her. She thought she could marry you and it was all so sudden that she hadn't got around to thinking what would happen if I walked out. I can still see how she looked when I asked her if it hadn't occurred to her that I might do just that. That told her where she stood and it told Morley where he stood when I repeated that conversation to him a few minutes later.

"He could figure just as well as Nora. He knew if I walked out he got nothing, and she knew that if I walked out—or told the truth—she'd look like a cheap little chiseler to you, Carl. I scared her, because she really fell for you. She was smart enough to see that if there was any telling to be done, she should do it. That way you'd think her pretty decent and forgive her original impulses because she voluntarily righted the wrong and doubled your inheritance; and she would marry you and everything would be all right."

He stopped, realizing his hand was cold and stiff from holding his glass. He shifted it to his right hand.

"But Morley also saw what might happen. When I left the house to meet him that evening Nora was talking on the telephone. She sounded impatient, a bit annoyed, but she was agreeing to something. I never stopped to ask myself who she could be talking to—she was a stranger here and knew no one. I didn't think at all. But I know now."

"She was talking to me, huh?" Morley said.

"And you were getting her to promise not to tell Carl the truth until you had seen her. You made a date, didn't you? To see her at the house. She got in fairly early and went to her room right after I arrived, saying she wanted to talk to me before I went to bed. If only I had gone in with her then—"

Kenyon broke off. Weariness and strain were riding him now and he had to concentrate to keep talking.

"But I didn't. What I did do was gum things up for you again, Morley. You wanted me to get drunk in your room. It would have been a cinch to slip something in my drink and keep me there. I'd never know the difference in the morning and I wouldn't be under suspicion. You weren't worrying about yourself because there was always Arden and Rudy, but you worried about me. And I got stubborn and came here, and I got caught by Carl after you'd found out she was going to tell the truth; after you'd clipped her on the chin to silence her—so she wouldn't struggle—and smothered her on the bed. It must have been a shock, coming back and finding me in the spot I was in. You'd killed twice and still you weren't getting that ten thousand. You knew the police would check, and that when they found I was a phony—"

"Look," Morley said. "I'm getting a little tired. If I

didn't know better I'd say you'd been hitting the weed.
It makes a swell story but"—he broke off, turning his
crooked grin on Nash—"it doesn't amount to a damn. If
you don't think so, ask the lieutenant. Ask him if he thinks
he could get an indictment on it."

Nash glanced from Morley to Kenyon. When he finally
spoke his voice was thready and remote.

"With a little proof I could try."

"Go ahead," Morley said, "give him the proof."

"I will," Kenyon said, and that was when he saw something change in the squarish face, something flicker in the
amber eyes before they steadied.

He took a last look around. Nash was standing near by,
his hands on his hips. Paul Sherman, beside his wife,
peered owlishly through his glasses, and Carl leaned forward in his chair, a tenseness in his body and his eyes
bright and dangerous. Kenyon took a breath and plunged
ahead, knowing he must crack the man or quit.

"You had a swell plan, and the nerve and ruthlessness to
carry it out—even to shooting Arden before he could talk.
But the same thing that drove you to murder—that greed
of yours, the lust for money—is going to hang you. Comstock had a drawer safe in his desk. That first afternoon
he gave me five hundred-dollar bills. And he had a little
book and checked off the numbers—"

"He always did," someone said.

"And that evening Nora, not knowing what the score
was, asked for money and I gave her the five bills. She
had no chance to spend them. She wasn't out of the house
except with Carl. *And yet a few minutes ago you gave me
four of those same bills.* The numbers will check and you
know it. Because after you killed her you searched the
room to make the pattern right and you found those bills
in her purse and—"

That did it. This was proof. The odds had finally caught
up with Morley and he knew it. Kenyon knew it too, and

he had been waiting a long time and now, when it happened, he was ready. He had known, somehow, that Morley would never submit without a struggle, and though the detective moved with uncanny swiftness, Kenyon moved with him, flinging the rest of his drink right at the savage, twisted face.

Morley had stepped back, reaching for his gun. The gun came out as the whisky and ice splashed into his eyes and he had to shake his head to clear them. That was time enough for Kenyon. He stepped in and swung at the gun, hitting hard with his fist and knocking it spinning across the floor. Then Morley hooked him on the side of the head and he went up against the table and stumbled to his knee.

Morley must have realized the gun was too far away now, and with no weapon he had no choice but flight. Nash yelled and grabbed for him and Morley slugged once and went past, heading for the French doors and the terrace.

Nash did not go down. From one knee Kenyon saw him reach for his gun. He saw it whip out finally and heard his command to stop; then a woman screamed and Kenyon turned. Carl Sherman stood braced, one hand outstretched. In the hand was Morley's gun and as the French doors opened Sherman shot the detective three times in the back from a distance of twenty-five feet.

Morley staggered, half pulling himself through the opening, and took one more faltering step. Then he pitched forward into the darkness of the terrace.

The room got still. Carl Sherman looked at the gun, turned it over. He walked up to the table and put it down carefully. He picked up a glass, held it at eye level, as though he wanted to be sure he got just the right amount, and poured a drink.

Chapter Twenty-Four

CANCELING ALL DEBTS

IT WAS A LONG TIME before the various representatives of law-and-order left the Comstock home, and when Hilton finally closed the door behind the last of them and quiet descended again, the Shermans and Sally and Kenyon came back to the drawing-room.

"Just look," Marion said as they sat down. She waved a hand to indicate the room at large, which now reeked with stale tobacco smoke, and was cluttered with glasses and empty coffee cups, and ash trays overflowing with cigar and cigarette butts. "A three-night stand, and every night policemen. I'm dead," she said. "I really am. I've got to go to bed—if I have the strength to get there—but there's one more thing I have to know."

It was a long speech for Marion and she rested. Sally moved a little closer to Kenyon and linked an arm with his. Next to her, Paul Sherman took off his glasses and stretched his long legs straight out, and Marion tipped her head on the back of the divan and stared at the ceiling. Over in his chair, Carl was folding and unfolding the check that Nash had returned to him.

"I can understand how all the details dropped into place once you made up your mind it was Morley," Marion continued presently, "but how did you know? What made you start to think about him?"

"Yes," Paul Sherman said. "You didn't know he had those bills on him."

"No," Kenyon said. "I hoped he had. If he hadn't given them to me I think I could have persuaded Nash to make a search for them. I was pretty sure Morley had them— either on him or in his room. Because if you knew him you'd know he had too much miser in him to pass up five hundred dollars, especially when he figured he could get away with it. It was like a disease with him, and when he found those bills he had to take them."

"You knew they were gone?" Paul said.

"Yes. When I found Nora I saw the room had been searched. I saw her pocketbook on the floor with its contents dumped out. There was no five hundred dollars and the police didn't find it later. But then it meant nothing. We all thought Missing Finger had done the job and I certainly took it for granted that he had taken the five hundred. After all, why shouldn't he? But then—"

"Yes," Marion said. "Now we come to what I asked about. And, Paul, please don't interrupt. I want to know what made you think of Morley. When did you find out?"

"Not until tonight. There were things to be put together —his love of money, the planting of the knife, the birthmark I didn't have and Comstock seeing me with my shirt off, the knowledge that Nora could ruin his plan—but I didn't even think about them until after Morley had shot Arden."

He felt Sally tug at his arm and looked down at her. "Why, Tony?" she asked. "How did that—"

"It wasn't his shooting Arden," Kenyon said. "Of course he shot him to keep him from talking and furnish an acceptable solution. He was pretty desperate by that time. He'd lost his original bonus but he'd talked Carl out of a reward and then he got lucky when he came to Sally's place and found us with the notebook."

"It wasn't luck he found those notes you'd left," Paul Sherman said. "If you hadn't done that—"

"Well," Kenyon said, finding he could still grin, "I was pretty desperate too and it's a damn good thing Morley—"

"Oh, now really!" Marion cut in. "Can't you answer my one little question so I can go to bed?"

"Sorry," Kenyon said, still grinning. "I got the idea

from something he said. He'd shot Arden and Fleming was a bit miffed and Morley began to talk. About how he was taking no chances with a killer, and how he had to even up for his client Arden had murdered. Then he said, 'And there's something else. A pretty decent sort of woman named Nora, who was smothered face down on her bed and murdered in cold blood.' "

Kenyon paused, looking from one to the other. They were still waiting and finally Marion said:

"Well?"

"Did any of you know she was smothered *face down?*"

More silence.

"Was she?" Paul Sherman said finally.

"She was."

"You never said so," Sally said.

"No, I didn't. I pulled her from the bed and that's how Carl found me. The doctor asked me if there was a pillow on her face and I said there wasn't. I didn't even bother to explain how she had been lying. I was too whipped to say much of anything. He never asked me exactly how I'd found her and so I never told him. But just the same she was face down. Morley hit her and picked her up and put her on the bed and smothered her by holding her face in the pillow and pressing down·so hard on the back of her head she could not breathe."

"Oh," Marion said.

"So who besides me would know she had been left face down?"

"The one who killed her," Paul said.

Marion sighed and Sally shivered. Marion said, "A little thing like that."

"So little I didn't begin to wonder until a few minutes later. Morley made his argument to Fleming too convincing, that's all. He knew he'd left her face down and he assumed the fact was known to the others—or perhaps he didn't think about it at all."

For another five seconds the room was quiet; then Marion sighed again. "Thank you," she said. "Now I understand."

"You did all right," Paul said, "once you got started."

Carl Sherman cleared his throat. "If I made out another check like this would you accept it?"

The offer came so simply and unexpectedly that for a moment Kenyon could only stare. Then, suddenly, he knew how Carl felt. He shook his head.

"Thanks, Carl, but it wouldn't be right, would it? Whatever I did was largely luck and I've already been paid."

"Yeah," Carl said, rising and tearing the check. "Well, it was just a thought. . . . I think I'll go on up. I think I'll be able to sleep tonight."

He went out. When they heard his footsteps on the stairs, Paul Sherman pulled his legs in and sat up. He put his glasses on and looked at Kenyon.

"I've been thinking," he said. "If you like it around here—" He stopped to look at Sally and there was a gleam of understanding in his glance at he brought it back to Kenyon. "I mean, we'll be needing somebody down at the paper, and you've had experience. We could use you if you'd like to come."

It took a while for Kenyon to answer. His blue eyes were bloodshot, his lean face deeply lined with fatigue and dirty with its two-day beard. He could not think as fast as he wanted to and it took time for him to realize just how much had happened in the past week.

Something had happened to him too. He wasn't quite the same man who had taken Morley's easy job, nor the one who had appeared here four days ago intent only on collecting five hundred dollars as a hired deceiver bent on fraud. Even the shame of that deception had somehow passed and underneath his weariness there was something cleaner and more solid. This, he knew, was an older man, and wiser; and sitting here now, listening to Sherman, feeling the soft touch of Sally's shoulder, he knew he was finding something he had lost a long time ago—a little thing called self-respect. He'd forgotten how much difference it made, and its possession warmed him strangely.

"I would," he said. "I'd like it very much. The thing is, I couldn't start for a while."

"Oh."

"I don't suppose you'd want to hold it open?"

Paul Sherman glanced at Sally and shrugged. "Why not? We'll find a place. Only I thought—"

"It's like this," Kenyon said. "There's another job I once started and never finished. I never wanted to. But now I guess I'd better, so that when I come back I'll have all debts canceled."

"Oh," a still small voice at his shoulder said. "You're going back in the army."

"If they'll take me," Kenyon said. "And this time I think they will."

"Yes," Sherman said. "Well—if you feel you should—" He let it go at that.

They all stood up and Marion yawned. "You know you're staying here," she said to Sally. "Come up when you're ready." She nodded to Kenyon, said, "Come on, darling, before you have to carry me," and took her husband's arm.

Kenyon and Sally moved slowly into the hall. He stepped back to turn off the room lights and then came to her and for a moment some new embarrassment seemed to seize them both. She watched the front of his coat and finally he reached down and took her hands.

"You're tired," he said.

She looked up at him, her eyes tender as they searched his face, and what he saw in their hazel depths told him it was going to be all right.

"But I have to do this," he said, and bent and kissed her mouth, not hard, but firmly and without haste. "You didn't like the first one. Is that better?"

He let go of her hands and she stepped back, her smile curving softly and her glance shining.

"Much better." She put her hand on the newel post and started up the stairs. At the landing she glanced back. "I think," she said, "it might be even nicer without the beard."

Kenyon rubbed his chin and watched her go, a wide grin on his face, another in his heart. He took them both to his room and the one on his face was still there when sleep caught up with him.

Dell Proudly Presents

C E L E S T E
the Gold Coast Virgin
By ROSAMOND MARSHALL

The author of *Kitty* and *Duchess Hotspur* has shifted her scene from the gay doings of eighteenth-century London to colorful California in the early nineteen hundreds. Rich oil strikes and feverish gambling, high living and unmentioned pasts complicate this romantic love story of a golden-haired virgin in lusty Los Angeles at the turn of the century.

Bart Strang, wealthy young New Yorker, is negotiating with the impoverished, ancient Marquesa de Telada for oil rights to the fabulously rich Rancho Los Cerros grounds, when he meets the innocent and lovely Celeste. The course of young love runs smooth—until Bart discovers that Celeste's mother, Dolly Wills, is an ex-Barbary Coast queen who runs a swanky gambling establishment with suites of exotically furnished *chambres séparées* on the side. Celeste is broken-hearted when Bart seeks solace in the inviting arms of pretty Josie Farnley, singer of naughty ditties and high-kicking can-can dancer of the Apollo Theatre troupe.

Bart and his partner, fast-living Sir Harry Trevor, discover that the salty old marquesa is a gambling fool. She has mortgaged Los Cerros to the hilt at Dolly's roulette table. Tough Jim Stagg, unscrupulous rival oil man, has offered to stake the marquesa to gambling money and to raise the mortgage on the rancho.

Haunted by Celeste's golden beauty, and driven mad by the paradox of her seeming innocence and sordid background, Bart resolves to have her on his own terms. In a violent love scene, Celeste is bruised and shaken by the force of Bart's passion. From this point the story develops in a crescendo of action that includes a thrilling chariot race at the Tournament of Roses, and a brutal bare-fisted battle, to a triumphant romantic climax.

On Sale March Third
Wherever DELL BOOKS are sold

WISTERIA COTTAGE

A DELL BOOK
By Robert M. Coates

The story of a man who wants to be father, husband, and brother to three women.

If you were a young woman and met Richard Baurie at a cocktail party, you might accept his invitation to dinner. If you were a suburban husband or wife, you might well ask him out for a week-end. Gay enough and sensitive enough to be good company, Richard would give no reason to suspect that he has a split personality, and that he is a potential murderer.

Richard is invited by the Hackett family, in all innocence, to spend his summer week-ends in their cottage on the shore of Long Island Sound. The family consists of a pleasant widow and her two very attractive daughters, and Richard loves them, especially Elinor, the younger daughter. They do not guess that he hates them too, for they typify something he desperately wants but which is beyond him. To his harassed mind, befogged by a nightmare of fear, anguish, and apprehension, the cottage houses forces of evil which he must destroy.

This is a terrifying story, a story that takes you deep into the mind of an abnormal personality and lets you follow, step by engrossing step, down the path to explosive violence. Yet the essence of the terror is in its apparent normality. This is the sort of thing that might happen to you or to the people in the next block. That is why *Wisteria Cottage* will hold you in its grip from the first page to the last a book that throws considerable light on the times in which we live.

⋯⋯⋯⋯⋯ Wherever DELL BOOKS Are Sold ⋯⋯⋯⋯⋯